SIGN OF THE THRONE

Book One in the Solas Beir Trilogy

Melissa Eskue Ousley

Renton, Washington

Castle Garden Publications
A Division of Gazebo Gardens Publishing
www.GazeboGardensPublishing.com

Edited by
Laura Meehan, S. C. Moore, and C. E. Moore
Cover Art by Aaron Cheney

This is a work of fiction. All of the characters, names, incidents, organizations, and dialogue in this book are either products of the author's imagination or are used fictitiously.

Printed in the United States of America.
Copyright 2013

www.MelissaEskueOusley.com

978-1-938281-32-7 (hardcover)
978-1-938281-33-4 (paperback)
978-1-938281-28-0 (e-book)

Library of Congress Control Number: 2013935542

For my Father, for whom nothing is impossible,
For Chris, Aiden, and Elliot, the loves of my life,
And for my dad, the first writer I ever met.

Acknowledgments:

Thank you to Shelley and Caitlyn Moore and Gazebo Gardens Publishing for taking a chance on a first-time author. Shelley and Caitlyn, your guidance, editing, and openness to exchanging ideas have been invaluable, and I'm thrilled I've gotten to work with you.

My appreciation to Jessica Glenn and MindBuck Media for finding a publishing home for *The Solas Beir Trilogy*, and for your wonderful guidance promoting the series.

Thank you to Laura Meehan and the crew at Indigo Editing and Publishing for editing the manuscript. Laura, I appreciate your friendship, advice, and encouragement, and that you tell me what I need to hear to strengthen my writing.

My thanks to Aaron Cheney for your incredible work on the book cover and the Cai Terenmare map.

My gratitude to Jessica Morrell for your amazing writing advice and mentoring at Summer in Words.

I have been so blessed with love and encouragement from my wonderful family and friends. There are too many of you to mention by name, but please know that you are in my thoughts and have my gratitude. I must list a few people who have been unceasing in their support, cheering me on through each step of this journey.

Thank you to my sweet husband, Chris, and to the coolest boys on the planet, Aiden and Elliot, for the sacrifices you made in giving me the opportunity to write. Thank you to my parents, Rick and Beverly, for your unconditional love and support. Thanks to my brothers Michael, Nathan, and Roman, and to my sisters-in-law Lisa and Tanya, for your encouragement from the very beginning. My appreciation to Sandy, my fabulous mother-in-law, for being a strong woman I admire and one of my most vocal supporters. And last, but not least, thanks to the beautiful, amazing friends who have encouraged me and indulged me as I've chatted about the folks living in my head: Deb ("The Force of Nature"), Jessie, Djay, Z, Justin, Pefy, Jen, and Kristina.

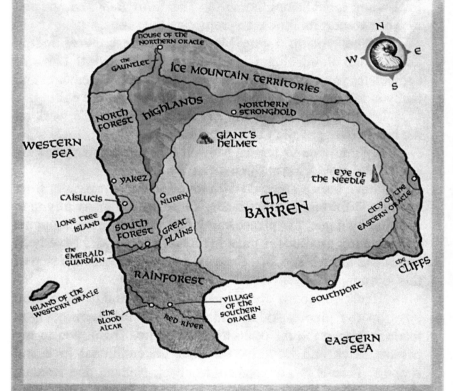

PROLOGUE: STOLEN

The woman in the hooded cloak fled down the cavernous passage, a small bundle clutched in her arms. The shouts and armored footsteps of the soldiers reverberated with deafening echoes off the stone walls; there was precious little time left.

Looking behind her, she could see menacing shadows growing larger by the second, and then the harsh glare of torches and the glint of cold, deadly weapons. Pressing the cloth-bound bundle closer to her chest with one arm, she blindly stretched her other arm out into the darkness ahead, frantically searching for the hidden door leading to the portal.

At last her fingers closed around the perfect circle of carved stone in the wall. She pushed the stone inward as hard as she could, and for one panicked second, heard nothing. Even the advancing guards seemed to fall silent as she waited breathlessly. Then, a small metallic click, and the silence was broken. She could hear the grind of stone on stone as the small door opened. A roar of sound rushed back to her ears as she returned her focus to the clanging of armor in the corridor behind her. The soldiers were close—a few more seconds and her neck would become intimately acquainted with the edge of a sword. She fell to her knees, pushed the tiny package through first, and then crawled in quickly.

Once inside, she immediately rose and pressed a corresponding round stone that closed the door just as torchlight flooded the secret passage. Without hesitation, she scooped up the bundle and ran down a long, narrow room toward a tall, gilded mirror. As she stepped fluidly through the glass, she remembered the first time she had crossed through a portal, the way the membrane between worlds had sucked at her skin, her clothes, her long hair. It wasn't a painful sensation, but it had taken a great deal of effort to squeeze through, to free herself from the portal's sticky embrace.

She'd had a lot of practice traversing worlds since then, and now she effortlessly stepped into a dimly lit, wood-paneled hall full of mirrors. A framed dome of glass dominated the ceiling, and as the full moon emerged from behind a cloud, silver shafts of moonlight illuminated the room, infinitely reflecting her image in the mirrors. She could see the silver glow of her pale blond hair when she pushed back her hood.

She was well aware she was beautiful, but she wasn't interested in gazing upon her own reflection. Instead, wasting no time, she snatched a heavy candelabrum from the marble pillar nearest the gilded mirror she had passed through. She raised it above her head and threw it at the glass. Her reflection shattered into a thousand shards. The fragments rang out as they struck the polished wooden floor. Shielding herself and her bundle with her cloak, she turned and ran toward the door at the end of the room. A low rumble filled the hall and the building began to shake.

One by one, the other mirrors in the hall exploded in a storm of glass. Bursting through a set of carved wooden doors, the woman fled the quaking ruin of the mansion into an overgrown garden. She gasped at the cutting winter air as the wind whipped her cloak around her. She could smell the sea and she knew she was close. Her task would be finished soon.

ຂວຕຽຂວຕຽຂວຕຽ

From the shadows, the creature watched the old woman. She couldn't see him—he was well hidden within the hedge of white oleanders lining the garden's rock wall. He had taken care to camouflage his dark, feline silhouette among the inky shadows cast by the bushes' leaves, far beyond the reach of the light from the buzzing electric fixture suspended over the back stoop. Performing the moonlit ritual that had been followed by her family for generations, the woman dripped honey into warm milk, stirring in the sweetness, releasing a pleasant aroma.

It was ironic, he thought grimly, that the woman thought of the ritual as superstition and didn't believe in the existence of the creature mere steps from her door—she was simply honoring a tradition from her childhood. The ritual made her feel connected to family who had long since passed on. And the creature didn't care what she believed, so long as he was paid tribute.

His long, prehensile tail twitched in anticipation, but he waited—he wasn't invisible, and it was best to remain unseen. Had he revealed his true face, he could have made her an instant convert to believe in the old ways, but he didn't want to drive her to madness just yet. Whatever she believed, the woman remained faithful to the deed. She reverently set the bowl on the steps and went back inside, pulling the door shut behind her.

While the creature waited for the porch light to be extinguished, a stray dog entered the yard. It was ragged and mangy, although with care, it would be a handsome animal. Narrowing its large, glowing red eyes, the creature watched as the starving canine, drawn by the sweet smell of the offering, dared to partake in *his* meal. Porch light or no porch light, this was not acceptable. Teeth barred, the creature crept forward, growling menacingly. Surprised by the creature's presence, the dog yelped and ran, retreating with its tail between its legs.

The creature laughed, a low chuckle that was often mistaken for the purr of a cat. He lapped up the sweet milk, savoring the taste. There was plenty of time. He would hunt down the dog later. It would be good to feed on something with a pulse.

ಹಾಡಾಹಾಡಾಹಾಡಾ

The knight stood outside the queen's chambers, his fingers on his temples, trying to rub away the unrelenting pounding in his head. The headaches had become more frequent in recent months. He thought perhaps they had begun with the poisoning of the *Solas Beir,* the king. That was the day Cael realized he had underestimated Tynan Tierney.

It was no secret the murderous lord had coveted the throne, and a coup had long been feared. Cael was charged with the protection of the kingdom, and mistakes were not acceptable. Underestimating Tierney was the worst mistake of his military career. Cael could not dismiss the feeling that he had missed a critical clue, that the assassination of the Solas Beir could have been prevented. And tonight only served to confirm that. He should have known.

At least the *Kruor um Beir* had been captured after the assassination, before his armies had the chance to cripple the kingdom's forces. Now the man who called himself King of Blood and Shadows was locked in the Wasteland, condemned to sit under a cobalt sky on fiery orange sand, with no hope of escape. There would be no respite—no rain, no nourishment, not even a sip of water to cool Tierney's wicked tongue. He would be mercilessly compelled to count scarlet grains of sand over and over. Forever. But now—now Cael had the unpleasant task of telling the queen he had failed her. He knocked on her door and entered.

🙰🙰🙰

Queen Eulalia was crumpled against her child's cradle, hunched and sobbing, allowing her black hair to cascade around her like a canopy of waves. Hearing the knight's hesitant steps, she fell silent and still. She raised her head and turned to him, feeling hope in spite of her dread.

"My queen…" Cael began. He hesitated, absently running his hand through his dark hair. He was clenching his strong jaw, and his ruggedly handsome face looked strained.

The queen suspected this was partly due to finding her in such a vulnerable state. "Did you find him?" she asked, knowing the answer, but not wanting to hear it—the finality of it. Her baby was all she had left of Ardal, her fierce bear of a king. He was the only heir. He was her only child. Little Artan. Much too little for this.

"No, Your Majesty. We were moments too late. She crossed to the other world and destroyed the portal."

And there it was—the other reason why Cael looked so stressed—he was the bearer of terrible news.

"No. This cannot be." The queen shook her head. "I cannot believe Lucia would do this. She is my sister. She would not betray me—or her nephew." She remembered the way Lucia had looked at Artan on the night of his birth, the way she held him as if he were her own. Lucia would never put her nephew in danger. She would die for the child.

"Eulalia…" Cael crossed the room to enfold the queen in his arms. "I am so sorry. But you must know that we have reason to believe she was involved from the beginning."

Eulalia pulled away from his embrace. In other circumstances, his familiar touch would have been a comfort, but not tonight. She could not afford comfort, not when Artan was missing. "What do you mean?" she asked.

"Lucia's handmaiden came to me this evening," Cael said. "She told me that Lucia would often vanish from her bed in the middle of the night, only to reappear before dawn, smiling, and was always pleasant to her servants. She never said anything because she thought your sister had a secret love and she did not wish to betray her mistress. But after Tierney was banished, Lucia's demeanor changed. She became irritable and treated her servants cruelly. It was only tonight, when Lucia and the prince went missing, that the handmaiden realized the truth. The secret meetings were with Tierney."

"Be careful, Cael," Eulalia warned. "You accuse my sister of treason—on the word of her maid."

"I do accuse her, Your Majesty, but with what I believe is just cause. There is more: we know the labyrinth fire was no accident. The flames were blue, which means someone used magic to start it. There are only a handful of people in this kingdom with that kind of power, and one of them is imprisoned in the Wasteland. But Lucia has magic, and I believe the fire was a diversion. Lucia took your son while our attention was on the blaze. The last person to see Lucia tonight was her handmaid. She saw her mistress enter this chamber, and then she was called away with the other servants to help put out the fire. That was right before you found Artan missing."

"Lucia often enters my room to check on Artan," Eulalia said. "She is a great help to me. The suggestion that she would do something so wicked is entirely offensive."

"Then I must risk further offense with a more grievous accusation," Cael said. "I believe that it was Lucia who poisoned the king."

Eulalia gasped, feeling as though her heart had stopped. "I will *not* believe that," she said, glaring at him. "I know Lucia was angry about my marriage, and I heard rumors she objected to Ardal's policies, but Lucia would never murder anyone. Never. Please Cael, tell me you have not spent these last hours listening to idle gossip rather than searching for my son."

Cael flinched.

Eulalia stared at him as he rubbed his forehead and temples. She could see how the events of this night had taken a physical toll on him. His was not an easy job, especially since the assassination. Cael had lost more than a king; Ardal had been his friend, too. Eulalia felt a pang of guilt about the power she held over him—not just because she was queen, but because Cael had meant something to her once, long ago, before Ardal chose her as his wife. She could tell that her words stung him. If anyone else spoke to Cael like that, he would have taken the tongue lashing without any show of emotion. He prided himself on never showing weakness. But he had always been vulnerable with her, and his love for her had only brought him pain.

"Eulalia," Cael said, "my only concern this evening has been for your son. He may not be my child, but I love him too."

"Do you?" Eulalia asked. "Do you love him?" Perhaps her anger at him was misdirected—perhaps he was right and the woman she should be angry with had vanished.

Cael pulled Eulalia into his arms. This time she allowed his embrace.

"Of course I do. He is yours. My love, please hear me— time grows short and we cannot spend it at odds with one another. Before today, I never would have accused your sister of such treachery. Lucia was a trusted advisor with full access to this castle—no one would have suspected her of siding with Tierney. But if she is guilty, I fear the worst for the prince."

Eulalia looked into his dark brown eyes. "Then please, help me. We must find him."

"Yes, but how? We know where she crossed, but she destroyed the portal. My troops cannot find a way through," Cael insisted.

"There is another portal," Eulalia replied.

"Then I will organize a hunting party—too much time has already passed. She must be captured as soon as possible and forced to hand over the child."

"No," Eulalia said. "I will go. Alone." Cael opened his mouth to argue and she silenced him with a look. "Do not protest—she is my sister and she will listen to me. I cannot make an appeal for compassion if I am surrounded by soldiers."

"And if she harms you? You know I could not bear that," he said.

"I know, Cael. But I cannot live without my child."

⁗⁗⁗

Lucia stood in the shadows just outside the home's wrought iron gate. It was almost midnight, but the electric lights in the massive old Tudor style revival were still on, and she could see two figures silhouetted through the sheer curtains. She cautiously opened the gate and walked up a flagstone path to the large front door with its oversized brass door knocker, intricately engraved with the letter C. Placing the bundle on the stone steps in front of the door, she knocked and slipped behind the trunk of the ancient oak that filled the front garden. A sandy-haired man in his early thirties opened the door and, seeing no one, was about to close it, when he spied the bundle. He pushed up the long sleeves of his sweater and hunkered down to inspect the package.

"Who is it?" a young woman called out.

"It's...a baby," the man said, as he pulled back the silken blankets protecting the child from the cold. "There's a note wrapped in his blanket. It says, 'Please take care of this child. His mother is no more.'"

"What? You've got to be joking."

From her hiding place, Lucia could hear the woman's excited footsteps as she hurried to the door.

Margaret Corbin took the sleeping baby from her husband, gasping in wonder as he woke, stretched, opened his eyes, and smiling, looked straight into hers. The child had a full head of dark, curly hair, and round cheeks.

Although he appeared to be only a few months old, there was an ancient wisdom in his pale blue eyes. "Oh my goodness. Philip, look at him. He's so beautiful."

Philip was preoccupied, still puzzling over the note. "His mother is no more. What does that mean? She died?" Looking up, he peered out into the dark street for whoever had left the baby.

Margaret held the child close, staring into those startling blue eyes that seemed much too aware for an infant. There was something about this child, how he held her gaze. She knew nothing about him, but she loved him. She couldn't help herself. She loved him.

Logic would say it was because she wanted a child so badly. After several miscarriages and a diagnosis guaranteeing she would never have a child of her own, she was heartbroken. If she were honest with herself, she would have admitted that it wasn't just her heart—*she* was broken. All the things that used to matter to her—her husband, her home, her affluent lifestyle—all that had faded into the background and become white noise against the constant, beating thought that she wanted, no, *needed* a child.

She looked up at her husband, squinting again at the mysterious note. She had considered adoption, but Philip was hesitant. He insisted that they hadn't yet exhausted their options to have a biological child—that there had to be more medical tests, in spite of their doctor's conclusive diagnosis. His refusal to accept that they were out of options made her tired. She knew she could never carry a baby to term, and she knew that frightened Philip.

He was a man used to having control. Young as he was, he ran his business with a tight rein, and he was very, very good at it. Their house, built in 1935, was one of the largest in all of Newcastle Beach and on prime real estate no less, with a magnificent view of the Pacific Ocean. It was much too big for the two of them, but it had been a wedding gift for her. Philip joked that nothing was too good for his bride, but she knew that he bought the old house less for his bride and more for his pride—not that she would have brought that to his attention. He supervised its restoration himself, in his usual hands-on way, dealing with the architect and construction crew with the same presence and energy he brought to building his firm.

His ability to have a child of his own was the one thing he could not control, and yet the idea of caring for an adopted child came with so many unknowns, it terrified him. She suspected his pride played a part in that as well. They had fought about it, and the strain that put on their marriage only made the house seem bigger…and emptier.

Now, looking into this child's eyes, Margaret Corbin knew this was what she had been waiting for. This child made all that heartache worthwhile. It had only taken a second, but in that second, she was unconditionally connected to him. She knew Philip wasn't going to like what she was about to say, but she didn't care. "It doesn't matter where he came from or how he got here—I've been praying and praying for a baby, and this is the answer I've been waiting for. This is fate."

"Meggy…" Philip began. "You know we should call the police and go through the proper channels. We should make sure the boy wasn't taken from someone, or that something terrible hasn't happened to the mother." He was looking at her in that condescending way of his. She thought of it as his, "Do I really have to explain this, little girl?" look. She hated that look. She wasn't stupid—*obviously* something terrible had happened to the mother. As a rule, babies didn't appear on doorsteps because something good had happened.

But if *she* were a mother and something awful happened to her, wouldn't she want someone to care for her child? Someone who would love the child as if he were her own? And she *could* take care of him, more than take care of him. She'd always felt a bit guilty about having money—maybe that was because her family had been nouveau riche and still held to working class ideals, a fact her old-money neighbors were all too happy to help her remember. But she also had a fear that tragedy followed money—like you could only be blessed so much before you had to pay your dues.

She looked at the child's face and then her husband's. Philip could say what he wanted, but this time she would not bend. "I'm keeping this baby—he's ours now."

Philip sighed. "All right then. He'll stay with us tonight. We'll have to watch the morning news and see if we hear anything about a missing child. I'll call my attorney tomorrow and find out what needs to be done." He folded the note, looked at the baby, and grinned. "I will concede that he's awfully cute. Seems like a smart little guy, too."

"He's got an old soul," Margaret cooed. "My little wunderkind."

Cael could hear the swish of the queen's silken gown as she rushed down the stone hallway to the door of the second portal. She was so desperate to find her son, she hadn't bothered to change from the delicate white gown she wore to a court banquet earlier in the evening into something better suited for travel. She seemed convinced that if she hurried, she might be able to reason with her sister.

Cael had begged her to let him go in her stead, but she wouldn't hear of it. Eulalia said Lucia would be more receptive to an appeal made by her sister, and that Cael's presence as a soldier would compromise Eulalia's negotiations for the return of her son. She said that in the absence of the king and the queen, a strong hand would be needed to keep her people safe from Tierney's army, and there was no one she trusted more than Cael.

Before leaving her chamber, Eulalia had quickly written a letter to the court council, leaving the kingdom in Cael's hands. He had accepted the letter and the queen's charge with a heavy heart. If Lucia had been so bold as to assassinate her king and kidnap her nephew, what would stop her from harming the queen? But Cael's arguments were to no avail—the queen would not, *could not* hear him.

He insisted on escorting her to the hidden portal, begging her to change her mind all the while. Once he realized there was no chance of this, he simply asked for a promise that she would be careful and return. Eulalia assured him that she would, but Cael feared it was a promise she would not be able to keep.

Cael noted the second portal, like the first, was hidden behind a secret stone door. But instead of housing a tall mirror, the narrow passage ended in a shallow pool that emitted a glow, as if it were lit from below.

For the second time that evening, he found himself surprised by castle secrets and wondered what other information Ardal and Eulalia had kept from him. Cael was charged with castle security, and how could he protect the royal family if he were not privy to knowledge about hidden passages and portals? As Cael followed the queen to the pool's edge, he could see stone steps disappearing into dark water that sparkled when disturbed, as though it held a thousand stars.

Gathering the folds of her gown around her, Eulalia entered the pool. As she descended, tiny bursts of light illuminated the fabric of the dress and the pale skin of her neckline and face, and trickled like diamonds through her dark tresses. "I will return soon," she promised, and disappeared below the surface.

Cael felt his breath catch; he knew he might never see her again. He felt a familiar sense of loss, a dull ache in his chest that had begun long ago when he learned of her betrothal to Ardal. It was a pain that had never gone away but now, as always, he forced the feeling out of his mind, trying to focus his thoughts elsewhere. Unfortunately, in this secret chamber, no tasks required his attention; nothing distracted him from his heartache. All he could do was wait for her return. The throbbing in his head increased.

Kneeling, Cael dipped his hands in the water, cupping the liquid. He sighed heavily, and let it pour through his fingers into the pool, watching sparkling crystal droplets create expanding ripples of light in the water. Then he sat down to wait.

ℬℭℬℭℬℭ

Lucia remained hidden until she saw that the baby was inside and Philip Corbin had closed the door. She smiled, satisfied the child would not be found. Then she slipped away. "Almost done," she whispered to herself. Avoiding the street lamps, she hurried eastward to a three-story Victorian home. She had been here before, and she knew the old woman would be alone, sleeping in the bedroom on the ground floor.

As she crossed under a frostbitten, wisteria-covered arch and through the small flower garden framing the front porch, she heard a car passing, and ducked into the shadows. Entering the back garden, she allowed her form to become darker, almost transparent like smoke, except for her eyes, which glowed bloody scarlet, allowing her to see as well as she could in daylight. She approached the back door and, instead of turning the knob, passed straight through the wood. Ghost-like, she glided down the hallway through the door of the bedroom.

Inside the dark room, Lucia heard soft, contented snoring. The woman looked peaceful, buried under a warm mound of quilts. Her long white hair was splayed across the pillow, and Lucia saw that she was dreaming, noting the movement of her eyes under the lids. Stretching out her arms, Lucia rose from the floor and floated from the foot of the bed to the head, descending horizontally until her face was an inch above the old woman's. She breathed out steadily, and smoke encircled the dreamer's head like a dark halo. Immediately, the woman's breathing became irregular, and she began wheezing, her chest rising and falling painfully as she struggled to breathe.

Her death didn't take long. With one fitful last effort to expel the smoke filling her lungs, the woman coughed violently. Her last breath was sucked from her as the smoke changed course and rose from her lips, dispersing into the air around her ashen face. The rhythm of her heartbeat wound to a stop. She was gone.

Lucia opened her eyes and found herself lying on her back staring at the ceiling in the complete silence of the empty room. There was no sound at all—not even the ticking of a clock. Every timepiece in the house had stopped when the old woman died, and they would never work again. Lucia brushed coarse, stringy white hair from her face and sat up. She threw the covers off the bed and, fighting the stiffness in her legs, went to inspect herself in the bureau mirror. Except for the eyes, which had grown so dark the irises were one with the pupils, the transformation was perfect.

☙℃℘☙℃℘☙℃℘

As Eulalia held her breath and swam forward through a narrow stone corridor, a worrisome thought occurred to her: *What if the second portal was destroyed as well?* Surely Lucia had not been privy to all the king's secrets. But still, what if there was no way to get through? How could she turn around in such a tight space on so little air? Once through the portal, she would be all but immortal, but here, in a claustrophobic underwater passage linking two worlds, she was vulnerable. This tunnel could well become her tomb.

Eulalia tried to banish her worries, to think only about her son and how much he needed her. With tiny explosions of light distorting her vision, it was impossible to see more than a few inches in front of her face. Lungs aching, she squeezed her eyes shut to block out the brilliance of the light, and reached out for the portal. And then she found it.

The portal was solid but viscous, and she found she could pass through it with some effort. The gelatinous substance felt thick and sticky, and tingled against her skin like the sting of a sea anemone, pulling at her hair, her gown. She pushed herself upward and kicked hard with her legs, the weight of the dress pulling her back. At last she broke the surface of the water and gulped icy air that burned painfully in her throat.

But before she could regain her strength, something pulled her back below the surface. She gasped in surprise as dank water flooded her nose and mouth. She swallowed and opened her eyes wide in the murky liquid, trying to understand what had grabbed her. In the light from the other side of the portal, she saw it. To her disbelief, the portal was shrinking, and the train of her dress was caught fast, pulling her back under to be trapped between worlds. She grabbed the waterlogged material and jerked on it. Nothing happened.

Lungs on fire, she planted her feet on either side of the portal and tugged again. This time the fabric ripped, launching her to the surface. She reached out to grasp the marble lip of the reflecting pool and dragged herself from the muck. She filled her lungs with delicious air, lying on her back on the icy stone surface of the edging that framed the rectangular pool, her dirty, sopping dress spread out like a ragged fish tail.

After a short rest, Eulalia sat up and looked around at the world she had entered. The pool lay just outside a glass conservatory, which was attached to a mansion. Something bad had happened here—she could feel it on the wind and see it in the cracks of the building's plaster walls. Beyond the mansion's front door, she could hear the sound of something heavy falling. She stood up and walked past the Spanish colonial facade just in time to see an entire wing collapse, a remnant of the damage that must have been set into motion when the portal was destroyed. She listened for signs that the mansion was inhabited, but heard nothing. At least Lucia had not harmed anyone in her flight from Cai Terenmare. Perhaps that was a sign that she had not harmed Artan either.

Eulalia knew one thing for certain: she had underestimated Lucia's knowledge about the portals. Not only did Lucia know how to use them, she had rigged the portal to close if triggered from the other side. Cael had been wrong about trying to capture her—his army never could have passed through the water portal.

While Eulalia regretted her own impetuousness, she also knew that she was fortunate to have escaped the trap. What if the portal had closed when she was halfway through? She didn't want to think about that. But with the first portal destroyed and the second diminished to a sliver, how could she return? She needed to send a message to Cael to find the Sign of the Throne, a magical pendant, and pass it through what was left of the tiny portal. Her son was to be the next Solas Beir, and she was a *cai aislingstraid,* "a dreamer who sees." Between the two of them, they would be able use the Sign of the Throne to reopen the portal. Artan would have to be older to make the journey, but as long as he was safe, they could wait here.

She knew there wasn't much time—Artan would age more quickly in this world, like a human. He would become mortal and lose the light within. But once he returned to the other side, that would change. On the other side, he would be strong. Ardal, his father, had been strong—the Great Bear King, he had been called, and so he had been. When he transformed into his warrior form, the white spirit bear, he was nearly invincible; he kept the armies of the Kruor um Beir at bay for hundreds of years.

If Cael was right about Lucia's betrayal, it was only the treachery of a woman and a meal laced with poison silver powder that had brought Ardal down at last. But as long as Eulalia and her son made it back to Cai Terenmare before Artan's twenty-third birthday, all would be well. Tierney, that ruthless wyrm, would remain imprisoned, and Artan would ascend his father's throne, vanquishing the darkness that had gathered in the king's absence. And if they didn't make it back in time…Artan's birthright would be forfeited and Tierney would claim the throne. That simply could not happen.

Eulalia walked toward the large, iron gate, which was dusted with a light frost. She was wet and cold, but she could worry about that later. Once she had her son.

She reached out to open the gate, and as she grasped the handle, a new chill swept through her, a deep cold that enveloped her heart and spread throughout her body. To her horror, her left hand, still touching the handle, began to wither. She snatched her hand away, but not soon enough. The withering spell, hidden in the enchanted metal, spread up her arm, past her shoulder and neck, and up her cheek. She shrieked in pain as her left eye was overcome with blindness.

Her beautiful raven hair turned white, and she was left disfigured and alone, in a world not her own.

She was trapped. Now that the gate and wall surrounding the mansion were cursed, crossing them would mean death. She could neither return to her world to heal, nor escape the boundaries of the ruined estate.

Cael was right. Lucia *had* been jealous when Eulalia had married Ardal and become queen, and Lucia had also opposed the king's policies against the *Kruorumbrae*, likely because of her alignment with Tierney. Then she had killed Ardal for her love of that monster. *Curse Lucia—curse her for her betrayal and her cruelty.* Eulalia wept. This was too much—to be so close and to lose so much—first her husband, and then her child, her health, and any chance to change fate.

℠℟℠℟℠℟

Under the sapphire sky of his prison, Tynan Tierney sat on a desert floor, his hands cupping the scarlet sand. Head bowed, he was intent on his task, mumbling the numbers to himself—counting, counting, counting. Suddenly, he stopped, raised his head, and smiled. Somewhere a queen was weeping—and soon, all of Cai Terenmare would be his.

℠℟℠℟℠℟

The queen sat by the reflecting pool for hours. She cradled her withered arm and sobbed, too devastated and overwhelmed to move. Eventually she fell silent and gazed with her remaining good eye into the black nothingness of the water. She stared at the reflection of her face, which had been twisted into the mask of something ancient and terrible. The moon set in the west and the night grew dark, too dark even to see her ruined reflection. She had no sense of time passing. She was numb from the cold, her mind drifting in a fog of hopelessness.

Somewhere in the stillness of the night, she heard a small, insignificant chirp. A little frog had crept to her side, unnoticed until it began croaking softly. The creature was miniscule, small as a coin, with velvety smooth skin the rich emerald color of forest moss and wide black pupils set in circles of gold. *How strange*, thought Eulalia, *that this creature would be here, resistant to winter's sleep.*

The tiny frog blinked intelligently at the queen, and then shuddered, as if from the cold. Its amphibian form fell from it, vanishing like fading ash, and standing in front of the queen was a small, green faery with webbed fingers and toes.

"I am Fergal the Valorous," he croaked, bowing formally. "I hope Your Majesty will not be angry with me, but the knight Cael asked me to follow you, in case you might need my assistance. He was worried when you did not return, my queen."

Eulalia had wept so much, she thought she had run out of tears, but somehow the presence of this brave sentry brought forth new tears. "My dear friend," she said, "I am not at all angry with you."

Fergal nodded, silent and waiting.

A chance for hope, however slight, was better than none at all. Composing herself, the queen wiped her face on the sleeve of her good arm. "You found the portal? You were able to make it through the tiny opening?"

"Yes, Your Majesty," Fergal replied. "And I am prepared to return for help."

"Thank you, loyal and courageous one. My fate now rests with you. You must tell Cael what has happened here. He must leave the kingdom in the hands of the council and make haste to the Northern Oracle to find the Sign of the Throne. When he finds it, you must bring it to me. Only then can the portal be restored. I will walk with him in his journey, if only in his dreams."

Fergal nodded, and resumed his amphibian form. With the slightest of splashes, he vanished.

ORDINARY
Twenty-Two Years Later

There was nothing remarkable about eighteen-year-old Abigail Brown's life. She came from an average, middle-class household and lived in a modest three-bedroom home with her father, Frank, an accountant, her mother, Bethany, a middle-school teacher, and her ten-year-old brother, Matthew, who was a pain in the butt more often than not, but only because he looked up to his older sister and liked to mess with her things. Even her last name was ordinary. *What kind of name is "Brown"?* she thought. *Average. Boring. That's what kind.*

Neither skinny nor heavy, Abby was simply a teenage girl of average height and average build, with light brown hair that fell in soft curls just past her shoulders. Her most striking feature was her bright blue eyes; they might have caught more attention had she not been such a wallflower.

It wasn't that people didn't like Abby, but she was introverted and had only a few friends she considered close. She could pass as pretty, but with limited finances and little knowledge about fashion, she kept her makeup minimal and her wardrobe simple. The usual Abby Brown uniform consisted of jeans, sneakers, and a T-shirt from one of several favorite underground bands with odd monikers, such as the *Well-Meaning Sociopaths* and *Epic Pickle Chuck*. She had banished the T-shirt identifying her as a "Pickle Chucker" to the back of her closet after a barbaric incident in the cafeteria involving a pickle slice projectile. Thankfully, the condiment had sailed over Abby's head, but hearing its juicy smack against the wall was enough to convince her that the shirt was a social hazard. Funny how nobody ever chucked things at her when she identified herself as a "sociopath."

Now that she was a senior in high school, Abby planned to attend college and studied hard, but she ranked only slightly above average, according to her report card. She was intelligent and clever, but did not stand out among her peers, who held starring roles in academic competitions. The word *brilliant* was something she associated with other people, the kind of people who earned scholarships and had college recruiters knocking on their doors. No one came knocking at the Brown residence, and Abby knew her last year in high school would mean the end of her career painting sets for the theater club's musicals and working more hours to save for college the next fall.

It was the overwhelming normality of her life that drew Abby out of her own boring neighborhood and into the attractive historic district of Newcastle Beach. Here was a place in the universe where nothing was simply average. In Newcastle Beach, stunning, successful people drove gorgeous cars and lived in beautiful, sprawling homes with impeccably manicured lawns. Even the paint on the Newcastle Beach houses was a little bit brighter than in the rest of the world. The exclusive community had been built next to the beach on the western edge of the city of Santa Linda.

Bounded by a wall of smooth round stones, a circle surrounded the entire neighborhood. Large iron gates marked the eastern and western entrances, and the cobblestone paving of the Newcastle Beach streets was in stark contrast to the potholed asphalt roads of Santa Linda. Parallel to the shore was one of the oldest buildings in the neighborhood: the Newcastle Beach Inn.

Although it remained a working hotel, and at times entertained guests of great wealth and fame, the inn was more of a country club for the residents of the community. The children born in the neighborhood learned to swim in the resort pool, wandered the many gardens during the annual Easter egg hunt, practiced their tennis skills on courts with a view of the sea, and, as they grew older, attended more formal functions in the grand ballroom.

With its clean, whitewashed plaster and tiled fountains, the Spanish colonial architecture of the inn stood in contrast to most of the other buildings in the town. It was larger and grander, with an old-world presence. The only building that came close to matching its greatness was an old mansion across the street, but its grandeur had faded after it was damaged by an earthquake decades before.

With cracked plaster, broken windows, and a ruined reflecting pool filled with water the color and consistency of sludge, the mansion was shrouded in an overgrowth of trees and brush, surrounded by a tall, imposing wall. Children in the neighborhood avoided it as a rule. Only the bravest among them dared to peer through the large, wrought-iron gate, returning to scare their young friends with ghost stories of a mad lady in white, a witch who lurked in her dark lair, waiting to steal and eat snooping children.

On nights when there was no wind, strange noises could be heard emanating from the bowels of the intimidating, lightless building. Ravens seemed to be drawn to the trees surrounding the estate. The large, black creatures called out mockingly to would-be trespassers, unnerving anyone who came too close.

Abby was fascinated by the ravens. She was also fond of Edgar Allan Poe, whose works she had studied in a literature class sophomore year. She could imagine her Newcastle Beach ravens in a more Gothic setting, with a chorus or two of "Nevermore." They seemed even more magical than the rest of the historic district. On the days when she walked to her job at the inn, Abby preferred the north side of Ocean Avenue just so she could watch the ravens before crossing the street to the resort.

With dark, gold-rimmed eyes, the birds cocked their heads as she passed by, and she sensed their otherworldly intelligence as they stared back at her, unafraid. She had always loved animals, and as a child had attracted many a stray, much to her mother's chagrin. She remembered an elementary school field trip to the Ocean Research Institute at the University of Santa Linda, during which she had gotten separated from her class because she lingered at the dolphin tank, not even realizing her teacher and classmates had moved on to the next exhibit.

From the viewing area below the main exhibit floor, she was watching the dolphins intently, pressing her small hands and forehead to the cool glass, when one of the dolphins broke from the pod and floated at eye level in front of her. Mesmerized, she dared not move or break eye contact, until she heard her teacher worriedly calling her name, chastising her for leaving the group.

It was the same feeling with the ravens—a strong connection that felt both familiar and foreign, like meeting an old friend she had not seen for a very long time. The ravens made her love the tree-lined neighborhood even more, with its intricately decorated Victorians and sprawling Tudors, homes with shaded windows like half-lidded eyes, coyly keeping secrets.

ഇൟ

Abby began working at the inn the summer before her senior year. The job was not prestigious, but she got to spend time with her best friend, so it wasn't all bad.

Her relationship with Jonathon Reyes had quite literally begun the day they were born—their mothers bonded in the maternity ward, and gave birth within hours of each other. Soon after, Jon's father decided he wasn't ready for a kid. He walked out of the ward and never came back. Suddenly on her own, with her closest relatives back in Mexico, Blanca Reyes and her infant son had moved into the rental next door to the Brown's, just outside of Newcastle Beach.

Abby and Jon had been inseparable since they could crawl, sharing birthday parties, friends, classmates, their first kiss, and a tree house they had built together at the age of ten. Jon had the good looks of a mischievous but charming boy intent on having a good time and getting into a little trouble, but nothing too serious. It didn't help that he was whip-smart, witty, and had his mother completely wrapped around his little finger. He could have done better in school—academics came easily enough—but so did boredom, and that was the problem.

They'd tried dating once, and Abby had the sneaking suspicion that Jon wouldn't mind trying a romantic relationship again, but that's where things got complicated. She loved Jon—it was easy to be with him, and she felt like she could tell him anything. It was a matter of chemistry—Jon was charismatic, but he could be a little too wild.

The only reason Jon had never gotten in real trouble was because he'd never been caught. Once, when their neighbor Mr. Burke was on vacation, Jon dared Abby to jump the fence and take a dip in Mr. Burke's pool. Abby took the dare, and she almost got caught when Mr. Burke's adult daughter stopped by to check on his house. That was too much of a close call for Abby.

The next spring, when Mr. Burke put his house up for sale and moved out, Jon suggested that they trespass again. Abby stayed home that time, and she ended up glad. It turned out that some of the friends Jon recruited for the dare had gone skinny-dipping in the pool. Mrs. Johnston, the elderly woman who lived across the fence from Mr. Burke, called the cops when she heard the ruckus coming from his backyard. It was a miracle Jon wasn't arrested—and Abby was grateful she missed her friends' moonlit swim anyway. It would have made for a really awkward Monday morning at school.

Jon's unbridled enthusiasm for pushing limits overwhelmed Abby. She wasn't sure she could keep up with his energy, and she thought there were romantic boundaries he was willing to push that she wasn't ready to test. She had heard about some of his exploits from a mutual friend he had dated. Not that Abby believed the story. She'd known Janie long enough to know the girl was fond of exaggeration. But still, given her own knowledge of Jon, Abby suspected he was more experienced than she was, and she was too chicken to ask Jon how much of Janie's story was true. So she relegated him to best friend/soul mate and kept him at arm's length.

𝔦𝔨𝔦𝔨𝔦𝔨

While Abby held the glamorous post of pool hospitality, making sure hotel guests had luxuriously plush white towels and picking up used towels, trash, and empty cocktail glasses, Jon was something of a minor celebrity, working as a lifeguard. His job description involved four tasks: making sure no one drowned, improving his already perfect tan, accepting adoration by awkwardly proportioned preteen girls, and being ignored by the beautiful girls he admired. There were three in particular who held his interest: Michal, Monroe, and Marisol—M^3 for short.

Michal Sloane was a classic California beach beauty— statuesque, shapely, tan, and blond. She was the self-appointed leader of the trio and seemed to take sadistic pleasure in flirting with Jon and then dashing his hopes, bluntly reminding him that her station in life was well above his. Michal verbally bullied Abby when Jon wasn't around, and although Abby tried to dismiss the snide comments directed at her, she couldn't ignore mistreatment of her best friend. *That* she could not forgive. She hated Michal for it, but was at a loss for what to do about it. If she retaliated, she knew it would cost her the job, and she needed the money—college wasn't going to pay for itself.

Monroe Banagher was no less beautiful, with dark skin and eyes, and curly hair that fell to her shoulders, framing perfect cheekbones. Abby towered over Monroe by several inches, but she had a feeling the girl could hold her own in a fistfight. Considering how intimidating Monroe could be, it was easy to forget that she was tiny. She wasn't quite as mean as Michal, but she usually went along with whatever Michal wanted, an accessory to cruelty.

Marisol Cassidy was kinder, and Abby thought she might actually like Jon, even if she weren't brave enough to say something in his defense. She had inherited captivating green eyes from her father, a wealthy businessman from Dublin. Her gorgeous body and the dark hair that fell to her waist in soft curls came from her mother, Esperanza Garcia, a world-renowned model turned artist from Mexico City. During more than one episode of teasing, Abby had noticed her smiling shyly at Jon, as if she were silently apologizing for her friends' rudeness.

For his part, Jon seemed impervious to rejection, and was not at all deterred by a lack of success. "They want me, you know," Jon said, helping Abby fold towels.

"Who?" Abby asked. Of course she knew who he was talking about. It was a topic on the verge of becoming an obsession with him. She didn't have the heart to tell him how awful Michal was behind his back, and she was annoyed at herself for that. And annoyed that he couldn't let it go. Was he really so oblivious that he couldn't see the truth?

"M^3. Michal and entourage. *She* wants me for sure."

"Which is why she always leaves you hanging, pool boy? I think you're suffering from delusions of grandeur. Or maybe too much sun," Abby teased, playfully elbowing his arm.

Apparently he *was* that oblivious—still, it was better to play along. She rationalized that saving his feelings was better than crushing him.

"No, seriously. Every rich little daddy's girl has a fantasy about a 'pool boy.' It is a well-documented fact," he insisted.

"Really? Interesting," Abby said. "But tell me this—do you hear voices? Maybe see things that aren't really there? I ask only because I'm concerned about your mental health—love you like I do."

"Mental health?" asked a petite woman approaching the guest services cabana. She looked to be in her late thirties, with auburn hair and a puckish sparkle in her hazel eyes. Behind her trailed two small boys and a girl. "I hope, Jonathon, that you are discussing your finished psychology paper?"

"Oh absolutely," Jon replied. "I was just explaining Maslow's hierarchy of needs, in fact."

"Is that so?" The pixie of a woman smiled mischievously, amused at Jon's creative attempt to cover the glaring fact that he'd been engaged in a far more interesting topic than psychology theories. "Excellent. Because I'm *really* looking forward to reading your paper—it sounds fascinating. So, are you going to recruit your friend to my class?"

"Class?" Abby asked.

"Yes," said the woman. "Jon is getting a head start on college. He's enrolled in my evening class at the university."

"Wow," Abby said. "Why didn't you tell me, Jon? That's great."

Jon shrugged. "Eh, you know me—gotta keep people guessing. Anyway, Miss Abigail Brown, allow me to introduce you to the ever brilliant Dr. Cassandra Buchan, Professor of Psychology and Statistics at the University of Santa Linda."

Cassandra Buchan smiled. "Kissing up won't help you on that paper, Mr. Reyes." She turned to Abby. "I'm pleased to meet you, Abigail, and there's no need for formalities—just Cassandra is fine. And this is the Buchan brood: Ciaran is five, and my twins, Siobhan and Rowan, are two."

"It's nice to meet you all," Abby said, waving at the children. "And I just go by Abby. I'm not much for formalities either."

Ciaran, a towhead with his mother's eyes, waved back shyly. Siobhan, a miniature of Cassandra, and Rowan, a sturdy toddler with dark hair, were indifferent, more interested in watching a sparrow hopping near the pool's edge.

"Don't let Jon fool you," Cassandra said. "I know he has this reputation of being a slacker, but he's actually one of my best students."

"Hey, I've worked very hard on that reputation," Jon said.

"Well *that* is definitely true," Abby grinned.

Cassandra laughed. "You know, Jon, since I have you captive at the moment, tell me about your paper—your *real* paper, I mean. How's the class going for you so far?"

Abby let them talk, excusing herself and dutifully returning to folding towels.

Suddenly, Abby felt a strange sensation of vertigo. The world around her snapped into focus and she saw the scene unfolding, as if she were viewing it from a distance and in slow motion. Ciaran and Siobhan stood next to their mother, the little girl obediently holding her older brother's hand. But Rowan, clutching a plastic toy triceratops in a chubby fist, was tottering dangerously close to the deep end of the pool, having wandered away unnoticed during the conversation.

In a flash of intuition, Abby knew he was about to fall in. She raced around the service counter, moving faster than she had ever imagined she could, like a bullet speeding toward the child. He was leaning toward the water, his little bare feet perched on the edge. Then he lost his balance. Lightning quick, Abby reached out...and caught him under his arms. Rowan looked up at her with wide blue eyes and let go of his dinosaur. With an audible *plop*, it dropped like a stone, drifting lazily down to settle on the bottom of the pool.

"Cerapops," he said simply.

Abby nodded. "Yeah. Cerapops."

"Way down," he explained, craning his head to peer into the pool.

"Yep, waaaaay down," Abby agreed. She scooped up the boy and turned to see that the conversation had come to an abrupt halt. She brought Rowan over and handed him to his mother.

"Wow. Good save," Jon said.

Cassandra looked from Rowan to Abby and held the toddler close. "Oh my goodness...I didn't even notice he was so close to the edge. If you hadn't been watching...Rowee— didn't Mama say to stay close? You are not allowed to go near the pool without an adult—do you understand?"

Rowan just nuzzled her shoulder with his forehead. "Cerapops?" he asked.

"I'm on it," Jon said, and dove into the pool. Within a few seconds, he bobbed to the surface, flopped up poolside and sauntered back over, plastic dinosaur in hand. "Here ya go, buddy."

Cassandra rubbed her forehead and sighed. "This one will be the death of me. I've developed more grey hair since he was born...honestly. Thank you Abby—I appreciate your quick response."

"It was nothing," Abby said. She felt embarrassed and a little bit impressed with herself at the same time.

"On the contrary—it *was* something. You're good with him. Can I interest you in a babysitting job? Starting this Friday? Good hours, and I'll pay more than they pay here," Cassandra said.

"Well, sure. That would be great," Abby said. "I could use a second job—I haven't saved as much for college as I need to." She had originally hoped to save enough money for college and a car, but after learning that college was going to be more expensive than she'd thought, she'd decided all the money she saved from working had to go toward tuition and books. She couldn't even afford a clunker, not if she didn't want to take out a loan. And it wasn't like her parents could help her out in the vehicle department—not when they were trying to help with college *and* pay all their regular bills. It didn't matter how hard they all worked—somehow it was just never enough.

THE BOY AND THE SHADOWS

That night, Abby had a more vivid dream than she'd had in a long time. She stood in a mirrored hall with a glass-domed ceiling. Sitting on the polished hardwood floor in front of her was a chubby toddler with pale blue eyes set in a round face, framed by jet black curls. The boy was playing with a silver hand mirror, so entranced by its shine that he was oblivious to a pressing darkness gathering around him. The shadows began to undulate like smoke, taking on wraith-like humanoid forms with long arms and reaching fingers.

Abby knew she should be terrified at the looming danger, but those hungry, lusting, blood-red eyes angered her. She made a decision to protect the boy, no matter the cost, and felt no fear. She planted her feet, straightened her shoulders, and prepared to fight for him. She felt a weight in her shoulder blades and realized she had pure white angel wings. She could feel the wings unfolding, stretching, with a muscular tension that made her feel strong and powerful. She heard the soft rustle and snap of the feathers catching the air like a sail as the wings stretched to their full span. Protectively, she stood over the child, the wings shielding them both from the rising darkness. Then she woke.

ଓଔଓଔଓଔ

Abby liked the Buchan family; the children were sweet, imaginative, and well behaved, and it was easy to engage them in activities, especially anything involving animals. The children begged her to draw countless animals from exotic locations—Kenya, Thailand, Tasmania—and would educate her with all of the facts and trivia they knew about their favorite subject. They also had a passion for sticky paste and a shimmering rainbow of glass bottles filled with glitter (*faery dust*, according to Ciaran) and spent a great deal of time improving Abby's drawings with these. Together they explored the great Victorian's maze of rooms and passages, pretending they were on safari in distant lands.

Abby was enamored with Cassandra and romanticized her role as a professor. She admired Cassandra's unconventional approach to the world, and thought she was brilliant, beautiful, witty, and sophisticated. She learned something new with every interaction: theories about abnormal psychology, myths about statistics, insider tips for applying to college, and how to dress for various social gatherings.

She even adored the quirkiness of Cassandra's husband. Riordan Buchan was a self-confessed obsessive admirer of all things Gaelic. He was madly in love with the British Isles, tracing his ancestral roots to Ireland and Scotland. Early in their marriage, he had whisked Cassandra off to stay in a castle turned bed-and-breakfast in the highlands of Scotland. He had written several books pertaining to the history and folklore of the country, and taught evening courses in history at the University of Santa Linda. It was not uncommon to find him wearing a kilt, sitting at a desk avalanched by books, and muttering to himself as he scribbled in a leather-bound journal.

Lying on his desk was a silver-plated, dagger-shaped letter opener that bore the family crest. It was little more than a Scottish novelty item, but the Buchan clan motto was inscribed on the hilt—*Non inferiora secutus*—"not having followed the inferior." It was a philosophy he took to heart as he diligently pursued his interests. Abby could see where the children got their insatiable thirst for knowledge.

The only dark cloud appeared when Riordan introduced Abby to his aunt. Aunt Moira was not terribly gracious about the introduction of a babysitter to the household, and Abby was convinced the woman despised her.

The trouble started one afternoon when Abby and the children were playing in the dining room. Cassandra was teaching at the university, and Riordan was editing his latest book, so he'd sequestered himself in his office. Abby had taken the children downstairs to give him a quiet space to work. She borrowed the quilt from Ciaran's bed and draped it over the dining table, transforming it into a fort. She was inside it with the kids when she heard someone knocking on the top of the table.

Abby crawled out to find Moira standing there, looking none too pleased. She held her arms crossed over her thin frame, and her long, white hair had been pinned up in a tight bun, pulling the skin around her dark eyes tight, making her features seem more harsh than usual. "Is it really necessary that they play down here?" the old woman asked.

"Oh—are we disturbing you?" Abby asked.

"I would say so. They are quite loud," Moira said, narrowing her eyes. "I can hear them from my room."

Abby looked back into the fort. The kids *were* chattering quite a bit, and the youngest two were pushing the chairs across the floor to make the fort bigger. "I'm sorry," Abby said. "We'll play upstairs."

Moira nodded and, without another word, returned to her room. Abby watched her go, shocked at what had just happened. It took her a moment to gather her thoughts.

"All right guys. Let's take the fort to Ciaran's room, okay?" She folded the quilt and returned the chairs to their proper places. Then she scooped up the quilt and the children's toys and carried them upstairs. Ciaran followed with his brother and sister in tow.

A half hour later, the kids were happily playing in the reconstructed fort when Abby heard a knock on the doorframe of Ciaran's room. *Not again,* she thought. She crawled out of the fort, surprised to find Riordan standing in the doorway.

"How's it going?" he asked.

"Good," Abby replied. "We're not bothering you, are we?"

"Oh no," Riordan said. "Sounds like you're having a lot of fun in here."

"How's the book coming?" Abby asked.

"Take a look. I just got an email on the artwork for the cover." Riordan held out a piece of paper he had printed. On it was the title, *Legends of Monsters and Ghosts: Tales from Scotland.* Below that was Riordan's name and an illustration of a castle ruin, shrouded in fog. It looked as though there were glowing eyes in several of the castle's windows.

"That's *really* cool," Abby said. "I didn't know you were into ghost stories. I thought you were more of a history guy."

"I *love* ghost stories!" Riordan exclaimed. "I love history too, of course, but when you start exploring the mythology linked to all these historical sites—it's just fascinating."

Abby smiled. "I'll bet. I'd love to read the book when you're done."

"Thanks—I'd love to hear what you think after you read it. I even included a few legends passed down from my family," Riordan said proudly. He turned his attention to the fort. One corner of the quilt had come out of where Abby had tucked it between Ciaran's dresser and the wall. "I thought I heard you guys making plans to turn the dining table into a fort."

"Oh," Abby said, "well, we did, but I think we got a little too loud. Moira asked us to take it upstairs."

"I see," Riordan said. "She can be kind of abrasive—I hope you don't take anything she says personally."

"Oh no, not at all," Abby said. "It's fine."

Riordan gave Abby a look that said he didn't quite believe her. "Well, if she gives you a hard time, I hope you'll tell me so I can intervene." He laughed to himself. "Not that she's all sunshine and rainbows with me either. She wasn't too happy when we wanted to move in, but this house belonged to both her and my mother, and before she died, my mother made me promise that I'd help care for my aunt, since she doesn't have any children of her own." He frowned. "Moira thought I was motivated by the inheritance. She didn't quite accuse me of wanting to do her in, but things got pretty hairy there for awhile."

"What happened?" Abby asked.

"I worked really hard, doing repairs on the house and cleaning up years of clutter. And Cassandra and I both took over cooking and cleaning to make life easier for Moira, so I guess she finally decided our intentions were pure," Riordan said. "Still—Moira's always been fiercely independent and never shies away from sharing her point of view. But she doesn't really mean to be obstinate. She's got a good heart, and she's given a lot to this community over the years. People respect her. I think it's been tough for her to take a step back because of her health. It's hard for her not to be in the middle of everything—she feels disconnected from people."

Abby tried to imagine what life must be like for Moira, to have been a central figure in Newcastle Beach, and to be forced to slow down when her body could no longer keep up with her spirit. She thought maybe she could understand why Moira was frustrated. Even so, she didn't want to be on the receiving end of the woman's wrath. She decided to keep the kids out of Moira's territory downstairs.

ഒരു ഒരു ഒരു

After several weeks, Abby hit her stride, spending her days at school, some afternoons and occasional evenings at the Buchans', and weekends at the inn. She mastered avoiding Moira and enjoyed her time with the Buchan clan.

But then, strange things started happening in the old Victorian. Abby first noticed it one evening when Cassandra and Riordan went out to dinner. She was bathing the twins with her back to the bathroom door, when the lights flickered. She felt something strike her back and heard it clatter to the floor. She turned, expecting to catch Ciaran giggling in the doorway, but no one was there. A baby lotion bottle, which had been on the sink countertop on the opposite side of the

40

room, lay at her feet. Not wanting to leave the toddlers unattended in the tub, she quickly looked across the hall into Ciaran's room. He was already tucked under his blankets in bed, leafing through a picture book, and there was no sign of anyone in the hallway. Puzzled, Abby returned to her task.

Around the same time, she began dreaming vividly almost every night. Many of the dreams centered around the same figure—a handsome young man with pale blue eyes and curly jet black hair. The first time she dreamed of him, he was standing in a garden in the shade of a large tree. The place felt familiar, as if she had been there before. Their eyes made contact, but he said nothing; his face remained expressionless and impossible to read. She had a very clear sense of his spirit, his intelligence, and she found herself irresistibly drawn to him.

Upon waking, she felt a terrible sense of loss. It was as if she had met her soul mate and lost him in an instant. The sense of grief was almost as deep as she would have felt in losing a member of her own family, but the emotion felt like it originated outside of her, as though she were caught in someone else's nightmare. She tried desperately to fall asleep again, hoping to return to him, but the dream was gone.

In another dream, she found herself at the entrance to a labyrinth of overgrown hedges. A pure white doe stood motionless before her. The doe stared straight into her eyes, unafraid, and then turned and entered the labyrinth. Abby followed her through the maze of towering, twisting emerald walls, trotting to keep the deer in sight. She caught a glimpse of the doe before the animal disappeared around a corner, but when Abby turned down the corridor, the doe was gone. Instead, she saw a beach and waves framed by an evergreen

41

arch. Exiting the labyrinth, Abby saw the young man, looking out to sea, his back to her. He turned, their eyes met, and she woke.

ဆဝာဆဝာဆဝာ

Abby kept her dreams secret, sharing her thoughts only within the journal where she kept sketches, but she found herself thinking about the young man often. The dreams felt real, and they always left her with a sense of longing. She was so drawn to the young man that she began to call out to him in the dreams, but he remained out of reach, and she always woke just as he turned and met her gaze. She was powerless to change the outcome.

Then, everything changed. Amid the tedium of folding pool towels, lost in a daydream, she became aware of a familiar presence. She looked up and saw him—he was walking along the patio at the opposite end of the pool. He moved with the fluid grace of a lion, with powerful but restrained steps, a thin veil disguising strength. He was beautiful.

Although he was dressed casually in a black leather motorcycle jacket covering an understated white T-shirt and jeans, he emanated charisma. Abby was awestruck; a sensation of warm electricity tingled through her veins. Her heart raced and she felt the whole world move in a wash of dizziness. She steadied herself, taking in a long, deep breath. Irresistibly compelled, she left her post and followed the young man as if in a trance, through the garden toward the hotel lobby. She walked out the front entrance, but he was already gone. Disappointed, she returned to the pool, where Jon was waiting for her, leaning against one of the carved wood columns supporting the guest services cabana.

"Where'd you go?" he asked.

"Did you see that guy?" she questioned.

"What guy? I didn't notice a guy," Jon said absently, winking at a couple of bikini-clad teen girls walking by. "Hey, how's it goin'?" he flirted. The girls giggled.

Abby looked from the girls to Jon, annoyed that his attention was elsewhere. "What guy?!? Are you obtuse? Dark curly hair, black leather jacket, impossible *not* to notice?"

Jon winced. He turned back to Abby. "Um, okay Abby, don't go nuts. I was kidding. First of all, just for the record, I tend to notice women, not guys. Second, sure—I think you are talking about David Corbin. Third, and not to say he's out of your league or anything, but he has a reputation for being unattainable."

"Unattainable?"

Jon shrugged. "Yeah—standoffish. Snobby. Kind of a jerk."

"Oh." Abby felt a sinking feeling in her gut, hope deflating like a balloon with a slow leak.

"Sorry—don't be mad," Jon said. "What I mean is, it's him, not you. I'm just trying to protect you—he's *not* worth your time. Besides, it's not like he's sticking around anyway. Rumor has it he just got back from a world tour to find himself and he's off to some fancy exec job in the UK, all courtesy of his daddy. This is according to M³ though, so consider the source. But you know that huge house down the street? The one overlooking the cliff? That's his."

Given Jon's less than stellar opinion of David Corbin, Abby decided it was best to downplay her attraction to him and to keep the dreams to herself. She had dreamed about David *before* she saw him, but it sounded insane. Jon would play along and give her the benefit of the doubt if she told him that, but he probably wouldn't believe it—he would think she had seen David before and just didn't remember. Jon would not have appreciated the idea that you did not forget a guy like David Corbin.

That night, Abby dreamed of David again, and this time she said his name. Still, he seemed indifferent, and she woke up wondering why she couldn't seem to change the outcome of the dreams. She got ready for work with one thought reverberating in her head: *What does it all mean?*

She tried to focus on her job, but when David showed up at the pool again, she knew. She was smitten, and there was no hope for it.

೫೦೫೦೫೦

As David Corbin walked past the pool, he had the funniest feeling someone was watching him. He turned. It was the girl who worked in the cabana. She was standing in the shade so it was hard to know for sure, but he could have sworn that her eyes were locked on him. Then she lowered her head and returned to folding towels. There was something about her though—something familiar. He couldn't put his finger on it.

He continued on to the lobby, where Michal was waiting for him. She was draped across one of the upholstered armchairs, playing with her cell phone. The spaghetti straps of her red bikini top peeked out from the neckline of a short, white sundress, and she had propped her tan legs up on one of the chair's rolled arms. She looked up at him. "You're late."

"Sorry," he said. "Ready to go?"

"I've *been* ready. We need to stop by my house so I can change."

"What's wrong with the dress you're wearing?" David asked.

"This is a swimsuit cover-up," Michal explained. "My mom would freak if she saw me wearing this to your house for dinner."

"It's a casual meal," David said. "You know it's just my parents hosting a barbeque for a few friends, right?"

"It's a *catered* meal," Michal said. "And you know that there is no such thing as casual when it comes to your parents. Everyone will be dressed up. Especially your mother. And anyway, I bought something special to wear to this. I think you'll like it."

"I'm sure you'll look very nice," David said. Staring at her, he spent a moment wondering why it was so important to Michal that he like what she wore. He frowned, thinking it might be a good idea to bring up that his sort-of girlfriend Amelia would be visiting from London soon. "Let's go."

He held the heavy, ornately carved wooden door open for Michal and they exited the lobby.

Michal stopped and stared at the motorcycle parked in front of the inn. "You brought your bike?"

"Something wrong?" David asked, as he descended the tiled steps to the motorcycle. He straddled the bike, scooting forward on the soft leather seat to make room for his passenger.

Michal crossed her arms. "Just trying to figure out how I'm supposed to stay warm."

David looked at her. It was a warm day, warm enough for a bikini. But he supposed it could get chilly riding on the back of a motorcycle if you were wearing a sundress. *If* you were going fast enough, that is. Not that Michal would indulge his need for speed. She always got annoyed when he held down the throttle too much for her taste. Not that he would admit it, but sometimes he accelerated too fast just to get a rise out of her. He didn't think of himself as a passive-aggressive person, but spending time with Michal seemed to bring that out in him. In Michal's defense, however, she at least was willing to ride with him. The last time Amelia visited, she had insisted on taking David's car.

"Here," David said, shrugging off his jacket.

"Much better," Michal said. She slipped on the jacket and pulled her long, blond locks out from under the collar. Then she situated herself on the motorcycle behind David.

He twisted to look at her. "Ready?"

She nodded.

As David turned to kick-start the bike, his eyes wandered to the inn's front door. The girl from the cabana had come out and was standing at the hotel's entrance. Up close, he could see that her eyes were a very pretty shade of blue, the kind of eyes that might change depending on the color she was wearing. At that moment, she was wearing the inn's standard customer service polo, which was a deep blue, almost cerulean, like the Mediterranean Sea. Her eyes reflected the color. She stepped away from the doors, out into the afternoon light, and the sun picked up golden highlights in her light brown hair, making it shine.

David felt Michal wrap her arms around him. He had forgotten she was there.

"Who's that?" he asked, nodding toward the cabana girl.

Michal looked up and scowled. "Nobody important," she said.

David held the girl's gaze. It almost looked as though she was going to say something, but then she turned back toward the doors.

"Come *on*—we're going to be *so* late," Michal said.

"Right." David started the bike and looked behind him as he backed out of the parking space. When he turned back, the girl was gone.

ᏚᏅᏟᏕᏚᏅᏟᏕᏚᏅᏟᏕ

As she heard the roar of the motorcycle engine, Abby felt her face grow red. She was humiliated. She had thought if David Corbin just saw her, he'd recognize her, and maybe…but no. And the look on Michal's face had only added to her embarrassment. *What was I thinking?* She groaned to herself. *I am an idiot.* She felt like crawling under a rock, but instead she walked back to her post.

Jon was hanging out by the cabana again. Abby avoided looking at him and busied herself gathering used towels from lounge chairs around the pool, hoping he wouldn't notice her change in mood. He did.

"You okay?" he asked, as she walked up to the cabana with her arms full.

She dropped the towels into the laundry bin under the counter and sighed. "My life is as black and foul as a steaming cesspool of filth."

"Ah," Jon said. "So, good then."

47

"Fantastic," she said, pulling out freshly laundered towels to fold. "Please, don't say I told you so..." She told him everything—the dreams, the connection she felt, and now, how she felt like a complete fool. "I think I've lost my mind," she concluded.

"Unlikely," Jon consoled. He grabbed a stack of folded towels and set them on the counter for guests.

"And of course, it *had* to be Michal. She is *so* loathsome," Abby said, scrunching up her nose in distaste.

"*Loathsome*? Who says that?" Jon asked.

"*I* do."

He hid a smile. "Since when?"

"Since...it doesn't *matter* since when," Abby said, exasperated. "The point is, I have absolutely no interest in someone who would be attracted to someone like her." She looked at Jon. "Present company exempted, of course. No offense."

"None taken," Jon laughed, hugging her. "You're right though. We both deserve much better. We really do."

“””

Abby was able to push David Corbin out of her mind for a while. Even the dreams about him went away for a few days. There were other things occupying her thoughts, however, and they did not give her confidence in her sanity.

Walking home from the inn on Friday afternoon, she passed by the old mansion. She stopped to say hello to the ravens, and as she peered through the gate, she saw a flash of white that looked hauntingly like the doe from her dream. *Now what?* She thought. *Am I seeing things? Wouldn't* that *be just lovely.*

The next evening, which she spent babysitting for Cassandra and Riordan, did precious little to ease Abby's mind. She put the kids to bed and laid out her homework on the coffee table downstairs. She was immersed in her work when she realized—the house was quiet. Eerily quiet.

She was used to the familiar creaks and groans of the old house, and night ushered in the occasional chirp of a cricket or flutter of moth wings around the antique sconces lighting the room. Tonight she heard nothing—there was only dead silence. She felt a prickle at the back of her neck and realized she was shivering. The room had gone unnaturally cold, and she had the distinct sense that she was not alone.

Out of the corner of her eye, she saw a shadowy presence, someone standing still, watching her. She turned to look, but there was no one there. She felt a terrible unease twisting in her gut. Something was wrong. Horribly wrong.

Responding to her intuition, she got up and climbed the stairs to check on the children. Ciaran was snoring, perfectly at peace. He had wriggled out of his covers in his sleep. Abby tucked him back in.

Leaving his room, she walked down the hall to the twins' room. The nightlight in the hallway began blinking erratically. She entered the room and froze. Perched monkey-like on the corner of Rowan's crib was a shadowed figure the size of a small boy, leaning over the sleeping child. Sensing Abby, it turned its head, blood-red eyes meeting hers.

Abby gasped with horror as the creature leapt with unnatural agility from the crib and crouched like a spider high on the wall, staring down at her. Slowly, it smiled, revealing rows of pointed narrow teeth, sharp as razors.

And then…it pounced.

Abby raised her arms to shield herself, scrunched her eyes shut, and screamed. But there was nothing. She heard a low chuckle behind her and saw the creature near the door. The shadow boy laughed and ran out. The smoky form changed into a large black housecat before disappearing through the hallway wall.

Abby ran to the twins' light switch and turned on the lights. She checked to make sure Rowan and Siobhan were unharmed, and then hurried to Ciaran's room, flicking on lights as she ran. Ciaran was still fast asleep—her scream had not disturbed him at all.

She jerked open his closet door and found his aluminum baseball bat. Then, scooping him and the quilt up from his bed, she ran back to Rowan and Siobhan's room. She shut the door and nestled the five-year-old into a makeshift bed on the floor. Sitting against the dresser next to him, she hummed, trying to reassure herself. Armed with the bat and the adrenaline coursing through her body, she waited.

෨ඏ෨ඏ෨ඏ

David was having dinner with his parents at the Newcastle Beach Inn. Sitting in front of him was a dish of steaming pad Thai.

"David? You're not eating. Are you feeling all right?"

David looked up to find his mother staring at him, and realized he'd been stirring the noodles around the dish for several minutes without taking a bite. "Oh." He stopped pushing the food around with his fork. "Yes, I'm fine. I was just waiting for it to cool."

Margaret smiled, and the lines in the corners of her eyes crinkled slightly. "Oh, good. I was worried you'd lost your appetite for Thai food after eating so much of it on your trip." She tucked a strand of her straight, dark hair behind her ear.

David suddenly noticed his mother had cut her hair since he left. Apparently she was still getting used to wearing it in a shorter style. Before, her signature bob had grazed her shoulders and she never played with it. The new style was youthful and flattered her face, and he realized he'd neglected to compliment her on it. He had been too preoccupied to notice.

He returned her smile. "No, I still like it. Maybe even more than I used to." He speared a bite of chicken and popped it into his mouth as proof.

"I'm sorry they didn't have any chopsticks for you," Margaret said, placing her hand on top of his. "I suppose it's not the same with a fork."

"It's still delicious," David said, grinning.

Margaret nodded and resumed her conversation with David's father.

David tried to pay attention, but found his thoughts wandering. His mind kept going back to the same thing: the cabana girl.

He couldn't stop thinking about her standing in front of the inn, the way the sunlight had looked in her hair, the way her eyes had locked on his. Well, he thought she'd been staring at him—but then again, he'd thought the same thing when he saw her by the pool, and that was the problem—maybe the connection he had felt was all one-sided. It seemed like she had been about to say something, but then she'd gone back inside without a word. He worried that she had overheard Michal's comment. He should have said something in the girl's defense, but his mind had gone blank. And what would he have said? He didn't even know her name.

He had stopped by the pool the next day, thinking maybe he'd say something, introduce himself at least. But she wasn't there. She probably only worked there on certain days, but he wasn't sure how to find out. He was tempted to ask the staff at the front desk, but he didn't want to look creepy. And he sure wasn't going to ask Michal or her friends. Maybe he'd bump into the girl again and he'd know what to say.

ಬುಡಬುಡಬುಡ

"Abby."

Abby's eyes flew open and she gripped the bat. She looked frantically around the room, trying to make her mind focus. *Ciaran. Siobhan. Rowan.* She reached out for Ciaran to make sure he was all right as she scanned the room for the other two children. Siobhan and Rowan were still in their cribs. The kids were all sleeping peacefully, and there was no sign of the shadow thing.

"Abby," the voice repeated.

Fighting her disorientation, Abby was able to recognize the voice and make sense of what was happening. The bedroom door was open and there were two figures approaching her. "Cassandra?" she asked.

"Yes, Abby. It's us," Cassandra said. "What's going on?"

"What time is it?" Abby asked.

"A little after ten thirty," Riordan replied. "You were asleep. What's with the bat and all the lights on in the house? Did something happen?"

Abby shivered, reliving the moment the creature had jumped at her. How could she have fallen asleep after that?

"Here, come downstairs and we'll talk," Cassandra suggested, dimming the lights in the room. "I'll make hot chocolate."

"No, no we can't…you don't understand…we can't leave the kids alone. Not in the dark," Abby insisted. She stared at the spot in the hallway where the creature had disappeared. Her grip on the bat tightened, turning her knuckles white.

Riordan frowned, eyeing the baseball bat. "Why not?"

"Riordan, sweetheart, could you please bring up some hot chocolate? I'll stay here with Abby. Then we'll sort this out," Cassandra suggested, turning the lights back on and walking over to where Abby was sitting against the twins' dresser.

Abby saw Riordan shoot Cassandra a worried look, but Cassandra nodded reassuringly, and he left the room.

Kneeling next to Abby, Cassandra pried the bat from her hands. There was an extra blanket on top of the dresser; Cassandra took it and wrapped it around Abby's shoulders. "It's okay, sweetie," Cassandra whispered as she sat down next to Abby. "Everything's okay."

At that, Abby began crying, and Cassandra wrapped her arm around her. They sat in silence until Riordan returned, carrying a tray with three steaming mugs. Abby mumbled her thanks as she took her mug. The warmth of the cup felt good to her hands, and the sweet drink was comforting.

53

"Okay then. Can you tell us what happened, Abby?" Cassandra asked.

"You *won't* believe me," Abby resisted.

"I promise I'll—we'll both—keep an open mind about whatever you have to say. We'll take it very seriously," Cassandra said.

Abby studied their faces. Cassandra's eyes were kind, and Riordan looked worried but ready to listen. She told them everything—the creature, the weird dreams about the shadows and David, and the white doe. "I don't understand what it all means, but I am so…so scared. Your children are in danger. We might all be. I know that thing wanted to hurt me, and I don't know why it didn't," she said.

Neither Cassandra nor Riordan answered. From the thoughtful looks on their faces, both seemed to be considering the story. Abby hoped they believed her.

"So…what do you think? Have I lost my mind?" she ventured.

"Not necessarily," Riordan said. "When I was doing research for my book, I read about something similar to this. There are stories in Scotland, and in Ireland too, folk stories about faeries and other creatures. In Iceland, they are called the *huldufólk*, 'the hidden folk.' There are lots of legends about magical tricksters who can change their appearance to fool humans, sometimes for their own protection, sometimes to hurt people, and sometimes just for their own amusement. A lot of these old stories were cautionary tales passed orally from generation to generation throughout the villages in the countryside, as a warning to leave faery folk alone. Most of these creatures were considered beneficent, although some were evil. But some people disregarded the warnings—either because they didn't believe in faery tales, or because they saw some reward in pursuing the creatures—rumors of treasure or having a wish granted. Either way, it didn't usually end well. Or so the stories go."

"So, by tricksters, you mean leprechauns?" Abby asked. She felt calm now, her curiosity eclipsing her fear. In spite of the strangeness of the situation and the inherently irrational topic, Riordan's rational approach and unruffled tone of voice were comforting, helping her disassociate from her nightmarish encounter.

"Yes—and no," Riordan answered. "Sure, leprechauns were part of the stories, and certainly are a popular icon in our society, what with St. Paddy's Day, green beer, the pot o' gold, Frosted Lucky Charms, and all that. And they did have a nasty reputation for being tricky. But no, I'm thinking of something else. There is a kind of hobgoblin called a *phooka*, which often appears in Irish folklore and is seen as a trickster—mostly a benevolent one, pulling harmless pranks, or even warning humans of impending danger. It seems to appear in a number of forms—as a shadow, smoke, or a variety of animals, all with black fur: cats, rabbits, goats, bulls...there even seem to be tales of similar shape-shifting creatures in South America that appear as jaguars. In many of the stories, like the ones about the *talasam* in Bulgaria, these creatures seem to prefer making homes in dark places where they are less likely to be disturbed: caves, attics, basements..." He smiled at Abby. "Perhaps they have even been the bogeyman in your closet or the dust bunny under your bed."

Abby found herself smiling back. She took another sip of hot chocolate. Riordan and Cassandra had already finished theirs.

"The creatures definitely seem to have a dark side though, and in some cultures are considered evil spirits." Riordan frowned. "There's *El Cucuy* in Mexico, a monster said to kidnap and eat children who won't go to bed. And in Belgium, there is a cannibalistic shape-shifter that changes from a human form to that of a black dog. It's called *Oude Rode Ogen,* or 'Old Red Eyes.' Kind of scary, considering what you saw."

Abby nodded, remembering those red eyes staring at her. Putting her mug down, she pulled the blanket tighter around her shoulders. Cassandra put down her mug as well and slipped her arm around Abby again.

Riordan studied Abby's face. "Is this *too* scary? Should I continue?"

"I'm okay," Abby said. "Go on."

"Okay," Riordan said. "I almost hate to though, because the myths get even scarier."

Abby smiled weakly. "Bring it on."

Riordan laughed. "All right, but remember, you asked for it. In some of my research, I found tales of predatory behavior toward sleeping people, and some of the attacks seemed almost vampiric in nature. But it's hard to tell where the legends end and fact begins. For example, there is a similar superstition about the aye-aye, a rare black lemur from Madagascar. It has these large, bat-like ears and a ghoulish face, and the middle finger on its hands has a long claw for digging out bugs from trees—kind of a creepy-looking thing. Combine its looks with a total lack of fear of humans, and you can see where people got the idea that the aye-aye creeps into homes at night to pierce human hearts. The unfortunate irony is that it is a harmless creature that is killed on sight, and it is on the verge of extinction just because it looks scary."

"It sucks to be an aye-aye," Abby said. "What did you mean about the attacks being vampiric? As in *actual* vampires?"

Riordan shook his head. "No, not exactly. Have you ever heard the term 'hagging'?"

"No," Abby said.

"Well, you know what a hag is though, right?" Riordan asked.

Abby nodded. "A witch. An ugly old woman witch."

"Yes. The term comes from Newfoundland and refers to a witch, the old hag, but the phenomenon is worldwide, ranging from Canada to south Asia." Riordan's face lit up—he seemed to be in his element now, enjoying the opportunity to converse about folklore, gruesome or not. "There are legends from all over the world talking about attacks on sleeping people, and there are many names for it—the nightmare, the succubus, being ridden by a witch. In Mexico, it is referred to as *subirse el muerto*, or 'the dead climb on top of you.' The attack usually starts with a rustling sound or footsteps, and then the person sees a horrifying shadow being. The victim is unable to move and feels pressure all over their body, but especially on their chest and face, making it difficult to breathe. In some cases, the attack is so intense that the person suffocates and dies, and there is no evidence of the cause— only the fact that the person died in their sleep. Those who survive say they felt like their breath was being sucked away."

Cassandra raised her eyebrows. "Is this related to that old wives' tale about cats sucking away babies' breath?"

Abby studied her. If anyone were going to be skeptical, it would be Cassandra, given her scientific background. Riordan was the one who liked ghost stories.

"Well, that *is* an old wives' tale, but it's possible that it's related. Maybe that story has its root in hagging, if, similar to what Abby observed, these beings can shape-shift into cats," Riordan said. "There has been some documentation regarding hagging—something called sudden unexplained death syndrome that occurred among Hmong refugees in the United States in the 1970s."

"SUDS? The acronym for that is SUDS?" Cassandra interrupted. She was grinning and shaking her head in disbelief.

"I'm serious, Cassandra," Riordan said. "Anyway, Abby, the theory is that the Hmong had certain rituals and offerings to keep such beings at bay. But, during the Vietnam War, when they were displaced from their homes and became refugees, their way of life was disrupted and they were unable to make the traditional offerings for protection and blessing, and that's when the attacks began."

Abby shuddered. "If all that's true, I am never going to sleep again."

"Riordan, didn't you tell me when you were a kid visiting your aunt here, that each evening she used to put out weird 'offerings' of milk and honey for the neighborhood cats?" Cassandra asked.

"Yeah. I do remember that. It's been a long time since I thought about it, and when I was a kid, I thought she was just a crazy old lady. But I think tonight has given me new insight. I should ask her about that. I haven't seen her do it since we've lived here," Riordan said.

"You know what else is weird," Cassandra said. "In class, I was discussing correlation and causation—the idea that one thing may be related to another, but does not necessarily cause it. I was using Newcastle Beach as an example—that this neighborhood has higher rates of students graduating high school and completing a college degree than the rest of Santa Linda, and how this is related to higher family income and housing prices in the community, but doesn't cause them, and vice versa. And one of my students asked me about cats. She's a volunteer at an animal shelter, and she said there were three times more stray cats in Newcastle than in all of Santa Linda."

"That's odd," Abby said.

Cassandra nodded. "Isn't it, though? So I used that as an example. Sometimes there are weird correlations that show a pattern, but have nothing to do with each other—like intellect and shoe size, or an increase in car wrecks and the occurrence of sun spots. But now I'm thinking, what if the stories are true? What if these shadow things, whatever they are, masquerade as stray cats? And what if people put out these offerings in exchange for protection and increased prosperity? I mean, you could certainly say that this community is blessed in a number of ways—even with fertility rates. I'm willing to bet we have a higher than average occurrence of twin births than the rest of Santa Linda, fertility treatments notwithstanding."

"Synchronicity," Riordan said.

"Sorry?" Abby asked.

"Synchronicity," he repeated. "Meaningful coincidences. Fate. Destiny. Everything happens for a reason."

"Sorry, I still don't follow you," Abby said.

"Synchronicity," Cassandra explained, "is the idea that there are meaningful patterns of coincidence that occur in life.

Some people see this as a psychological phenomenon that occurs when you start noticing something. Say, if you were interested in buying a yellow car, you'd start noticing yellow cars everywhere you go. Others see it as a spiritual thing—a sign from God leading you where you should go, revealing the master plan."

"So there are no coincidences? Nothing just happens randomly?" Abby asked.

"Well, randomness is debatable, at least in real life," Cassandra said. "This is why I love teaching statistics. In statistics, we act like life occurs in a vacuum. When we look at probability, we say something is random if each trial is independent and has an equal chance of occurring.

"So, if I'm rolling a die, and I'm trying to figure out my chances of rolling a six, I might roll it a hundred times and then figure out the probability based on the number of trials, the number of sides to the die, and how many times I get a six. But I'm assuming that I'm rolling it the same way each time and that the die is balanced, that it's not weighted on one side or something. And this works in an example like this, but real life is messy.

"If I'm thinking about my chances of running into someone I know in the grocery store or surviving a car wreck or a shark attack, or being hit by lightning, or whatever the example, there are a lot more variables, different things that influence the outcome. My chances of surviving a car wreck depend on a lot of things: the condition of the car, how fast I'm going, whether or not it's a single or multiple car accident, the condition of the road, the weather…you see where I'm going with this?"

Abby nodded, astounded that Cassandra could calmly switch to professor mode after finding her babysitter holding a bat, holed up in a bedroom with her small children. What was more astounding was that it sounded like Cassandra actually believed her, even though she was taking a scientific approach.

"And then there's fate and probability. Are you familiar with the work of Jakob Bernoulli?" Cassandra asked.

Abby shook her head. "Sorry, no."

"That's okay," Cassandra continued. "Bernoulli was a Swiss mathematician who lived in the 1600s. He was famous for a lot of things, such as the application of probability theory to games of chance. He had a lot to say about fate. Basically, if you take the die example, and you want to roll a six, you will eventually roll a six if you keep rolling. It's only a matter of time. So bottom line, once things are set in motion, they tend to eventually occur."

"Ah," Abby said. "I see. So that leaves me with two questions."

"Shoot," Cassandra and Riordan chimed in unison.

"Jinx," Cassandra laughed, affectionately poking Riordan in the rib. "What is question number one, Abby?"

"Well," Abby said. "If synchronicity is real, and I keep having these synchronicities in my dreams, you know, seeing David in the dream and then in real life, and the dream about the white doe…what am I supposed to do with that?"

"I suppose," said Riordan. "Regarding the white doe— I'd take that as a good omen, if you see it as a symbol the way many cultures do. In Scotland, it's considered especially good luck. Regarding David…hmm, I mean, in the time we've known the Corbin family, I've never noticed anything about him that would associate him with a white doe—"

"Regarding David," interrupted Cassandra, "simply take it as a sign that the universe has something in mind—that your paths will intersect, and see what happens. Don't jump to conclusions, but keep an open mind to other synchronicities that might provide insight."

"Okay," Abby said. "That makes sense, I guess."

"Question number two?" asked Cassandra.

"Question number two—how do we protect ourselves against the shadow boy?" Abby asked.

Riordan shot Cassandra a look. "I'll take that one, since I'm better versed in the legends, thank you very much, lady. Not that I don't appreciate the insight into statistics, Professor."

"I'm listening and being very respectful. See?" Cassandra gave him her best, if not terribly convincing, meek-and-mild smile. Abby laughed.

"Okay," Riordan continued, ignoring Cassandra's theatrics. "There are several folkloric theories on protecting oneself. Silver comes up in a few stories. Your necklace, Abby, is that silver?"

"I think so," Abby said.

"Well, perhaps that's why the creature didn't harm you," Riordan said. "Just to be safe, I think you should keep wearing it. It's possible that the cross pendant on the chain, as a religious symbol, fended him off, but it could just be the silver."

"Correlation does not imply causation," Cassandra said.

Riordan nodded. "Exactly. Some stories talk about hanging silver bells from a doorway to block entrance, so we could try that—I think there's some in the box where we store Christmas decorations—and some stories describe the protection salt gives, when you either throw it at whatever is attacking you or enclose yourself in a circle of salt. Still other stories talk about putting salt, sand, or even seeds by your bedside. The thought is the creature becomes engrossed in counting the grains of salt or sand and will leave you alone. One story says that's the way to capture a witch. She becomes so focused on counting, that she'll do it all night, and you can capture her at first morning's light. Of course, the same story says that the reason people have bed hair is that the old hag rides on your head all night long like a hobby horse."

Cassandra snorted, then laughed. "Not to make light of the situation, but yes, let's try all those things, just to be safe, and see what happens. And we'll all make a pact, among the three of us: anything weird that happens—no matter how unlikely or odd—we talk about it together. Consider it an experiment. We need as much data as possible. And Riordan, seriously, I know you love your aunt, but if I encounter that thing, I'm taking the kids to a hotel. I don't want to leave our home, but I'm not staying here if I can't protect my kids. Agreed?"

"*Our* kids," Riordan corrected. "And yes, agreed."

"Deal," Abby said.

FAERY GODMOTHERS

Exhausted from the terror of the previous evening, Abby slept deeply. Given that the shadow creature's evil smile was burned into her memory, she had expected to have nightmares. To her relief, her dream was peaceful.

She found herself walking toward a towering ivory edifice, surrounded by the foliage of a large, primeval forest. The castle reminded her of exotic architecture she'd seen in books—a fortress with a distinctly Moroccan feel.

A woman was approaching her, crossing a bridge leading from the castle's gates. The woman was beautiful. In a sweeping white gown, she walked with such noble grace that she appeared to float toward Abby. Her raven-colored tresses fell to her waist in waves, and her skin was pale, almost the color of cream. Her eyes burned a brilliant blue, and Abby felt intimidated in her presence. To her surprise, the woman smiled at Abby, and her eyes were kind, with a hint of amusement, as though Abby were her conspirator in a private joke. As she passed by, the scene changed.

Now Abby was on a stage in front of an audience of people she didn't know. She shielded her eyes from the spotlight shining on her. She heard a voice: "David Corbin is looking at you, and you're not even going to acknowledge him?" At this, she turned to her left, and near the stage, she saw him. This time he wasn't indifferent; he looked...intrigued. Yes, that was definitely a small, curious smile on his lips. Abby smiled back.

She opened her eyes and looked around her bedroom. The morning light filtered through sheer curtains and eased any fears from the night before. For the first time, she appreciated the sheer normality of her life: no bogeymen in her closet, no nightmares creeping under her bed.

She remembered something Cassandra had said as she was driving Abby home.

"Does it surprise you?" she asked. "Does it surprise you that we'd stay in the house after all you told us?"

Yes, Abby had admitted. If she had been Cassandra and thought her family was in danger, she would have left that very night. But then, Cassandra did not see what Abby saw.

"It's not that I'm not tempted to leave," Cassandra said, "but we did make a promise to care for Moira. Even if we left, she would never leave, and if an old woman is okay with living in that house, I suppose we can tough it out. But it's not just that. I like it there, and I want to stay. And, it's probably a combination of hubris and morbid curiosity, but if something weird is going on, I want to know. Our family has a long history of encounters with the bizarre—you should have heard the ghost stories told by Riordan's relatives when we were in Scotland. I know this sounds silly, and I don't know how to explain it, but I think we'll be okay. I just don't think there is anything to worry about," she insisted.

Abby wasn't so sure, but she'd wait it out. The experience had bonded her with the Buchans, and she considered them a second family. She just didn't want anything bad to happen to them. But as long as she was around, she would make sure nothing did.

It was Sunday, but Abby had the day off from the inn. With a mysterious grin, Cassandra had asked her to stop by that afternoon.

"There's something I want to show you," she hinted as she dropped Abby off.

Abby got dressed and headed down for breakfast with her family. She stared at her parents as they ate their bran cereal and her brother Matt as he feasted on pancakes. *They have no idea,* she thought. And that was a good thing.

⃢⃣⃢⃣⃢⃣

After lunch, she walked down to Newcastle Beach. In the daylight nothing was amiss. Remembering the previous evening's lesson on synchronicity, she did note, however, that there were quite a few stray cats in the neighborhood, lounging on porches, enjoying soft grass and patches of sunlight. How odd that she'd never noticed them before. She knocked on the Buchans' door and Cassandra answered, looking delighted to see her.

"Come in, come in, come in," Cassandra chimed, clearly boiling over with excitement as she grabbed Abby's hand and yanked her inside the house. She closed the door and cocked her head to the side, looking at Abby. "Okay, are you ready?"

"I guess so." Abby had no idea what she was supposed to be ready for, but she thought it was best to humor her mentor.

"All right. I'm going to ask you a question, and I insist that you say yes."

"That sounds dangerous," Abby laughed, "but go ahead. Ask."

"The Autumn Ball at the inn is coming up in a few weeks," Cassandra said. "Riordan and I are going, and we'd like you to join us. What do you think? Remember, you're supposed to say yes."

"Hmmmm…"

Cassandra frowned and put her hands on her hips. "That is not a yes. Perhaps I should clarify. The Autumn Ball—bigger than the holiday party at Christmas—the place to see and *be* seen. And did I mention that you get to wear something gorgeous and dance with handsome young men?"

"Well, I appreciate the invitation, but…dancing is not one of my strong points. Plus, I have nothing to wear—I'd stick out like a sore thumb," Abby objected.

"Au contraire, my dear. First of all, I can coach you on dancing," Cassandra countered. "That's easy." She grabbed Abby's hand and twirled her around, spinning her away and then pulling her back close.

Abby laughed in surprise, partly because she felt silly towering over Cassandra's petite frame and partly because Cassandra wasn't half bad at leading.

"See?" Cassandra said, letting Abby go. "*Easy*. Second, I'm going shopping for my dress this afternoon, and I'd love it if you'd come along and pick something out. Consider it an early birthday gift."

"Well, I'm happy to come along to help *you* pick a dress, but I can't let you buy one for me," Abby said. "You're way too generous—that's too much."

Cassandra nodded. "I knew you'd say that. And so, on to plan B. Vintage."

"Vintage?" Abby asked.

"Come on." Cassandra grabbed Abby's hand again.

This time, she led Abby upstairs to the spare bedroom on the third floor. USL's Professor of Psychology and Statistics was like a chipmunk on a sugar high, and Abby was fairly certain that she was going to explode with manic joy any second. Still, Abby had to smile. Cassandra's excitement was contagious.

With a flourish befitting a carnival magician, the wisp of a woman opened the door of an antique wardrobe. Hanging from a hook above the cabinet's full-length mirror was a stunning peacock blue ball gown. Abby's jaw dropped. The vintage dress had a fitted strapless bodice with diagonal folds of satin flattering all the right places, complemented by antique diamond brooches at the center of the bodice and on the left hip. The full skirt would sweep to the floor. It was a regal dress, more lovely than anything Abby could have imagined.

"Sooo, what do you think?" Cassandra asked.

"I...I don't know what to say. It's beautiful. No, it's perfect," Abby said.

"I'll take that as a yes then?"

Abby nodded. "Yes. Yes, thank you. I'd love to come."

"And it's on loan, so you don't have to fret about anything. It was Riordan's mother's," Cassandra said.

Abby smiled. "I'd be honored to wear it."

"Well then, try it on! Let's see how it looks on you!" Cassandra exclaimed. The manic chipmunk was bubbling to the surface again. She hurried out of the room, closing the door.

Abby took a moment to take in the dress. It *was* perfect, as if it had been designed just for her. But would it fit? She slipped it on and critiqued her image in the mirror. *Not bad,* she thought. She pulled back her hair, piled it on her head, frowned, and let it fall past her shoulders again. She'd figure out what to do with her hair later. She spun around—for now, she would just enjoy the dress.

Cassandra knocked. "May I see?"

"Oh! Yes, come in. I'm ready," Abby said.

Cassandra entered the room. "Oooooh, Abby. You look so beautiful!"

"Thank you." Abby felt a little self-conscious, but didn't really mind being on display.

Cassandra walked a wide circle around her. "I think Riordan's mother was a little more…what's the best way to put it…*curvy* than you, though. She was kind of this tall, voluptuous Amazon woman. Looks like we might need to take it in just a bit. But no worries, we'll stop at the tailor before we look for my dress. Sound good?"

"Sounds good. Cassandra, thank you so much. For everything. I know it's clichéd, but I'm kind of having a Cinderella moment here," Abby added.

Cassandra laughed. "Well, good—things turned out pretty well for her, didn't they?"

Abby nodded. "They did. There's one thing I'm nervous about though."

"What's that?"

"Going alone," Abby said. "I mean, I know you and Riordan will be there—"

"And Moira too," Cassandra said. "Did you know that she's the one who started the tradition of having an Autumn Ball? And she has yet to miss one. She has always been so involved in this community, especially with events that benefit the less fortunate. This year, all the proceeds are going to the Santa Linda Women's Shelter."

"Oh," Abby said. She had not realized Riordan's aunt would be joining them. That would make things a little awkward, but she still wanted to go. "That's great that she's so dedicated."

"She is *definitely* that." Cassandra chuckled, keeping her voice low and eyeing the open door. "She's as tenacious as a bulldog, but it's usually for a good cause."

"Usually?"

"Yes, well, I sure wouldn't want to see her apply that kind of dedication to an evil one." Cassandra shuddered. "Scary."

"Very," Abby laughed. "Anyway, I just wanted to ask, if it's okay with you—could Jon come with me? As a friend," she clarified.

"Oh, of course! We'd love to have him come. He'll make a nice accessory to the dress, I think," Cassandra said.

Abby smiled, relieved. "Yeah, he can be my arm candy."

ଔଔଔଔଔଔ

Abby changed and met Cassandra downstairs with the dress. She tried it on again at Collin's Tailoring, and the tailor was confident he could adjust the dress to Abby's figure.

She went back into the changing room while Cassandra discussed the adjustments with the tailor. As she was dressing, she heard the bell above the shop door ring.

"Meg! How nice to see you," she heard Cassandra say.

"Cassandra Buchan—I keep meaning to call you. We should have lunch again one of these days," a woman replied. "You remember my son, David, don't you?"

Abby froze.

"David," Cassandra said. "Of course. How are you? Congratulations on your graduation. I know your parents are very proud."

"Thank you," David said. His voice was deep, with a strangely familiar roughness to it. Abby thought back to the dreams. Had she ever heard him speak?

"I hear you've been traveling," Cassandra said.

"Yes, I have," David confirmed. "I recently returned from Sydney after a trip to Asia and the South Pacific."

"What an adventure! There is nothing like travel for testing one's character and learning about the world. So Meg, what brings you to the tailor's on this lovely fall day?" Cassandra asked.

"Getting ready for Autumn Ball, of course," Margaret said. "I designed my own dress, and Mr. Collin made it for me. And David needs a few adjustments to his new suit."

Abby internally debated the merits of hiding in the dressing room until they left, and then decided that being a chicken was not the answer. Summoning her courage, she pushed back the curtain and stepped out, avoiding looking in David's direction. She took the dress over to the shop counter.

"Ah, Abby," Cassandra said. "Let me introduce you to my friend, Margaret Corbin. And *this* is David Corbin."

"It's a pleasure to meet you, Mrs. Corbin," Abby said, hoping David hadn't noticed the way Cassandra emphasized his introduction. "And you as well, David," she said, glancing at him and smiling politely.

71

"Nice to meet you, Abby," Margaret replied. She smiled warmly and shook hands with Abby.

The woman was dressed to the nines in heels and a tailored suit jacket and skirt. Abby had never seen anyone dressed so formally for running errands. Her own mother tended to wear jeans and flip-flops when she went out. Then again, Abby's mother had little need to visit a tailor and had never designed her own dress. Talk about living in different worlds.

David stepped forward and Abby found herself staring into his intense blue eyes as he took her hand. He didn't say anything, but he smiled slightly when he shook her hand, and then held on to it a few seconds longer than necessary before releasing his grip. Abby smiled back and then lowered her eyes when she realized she was still staring at him. Thankfully, Cassandra came to her rescue.

"Abby has been watching my children," she said. "She'll be starting at the university next fall. Riordan and I just love her—she and her friend Jonathon Reyes will be our guests at the ball."

"That's wonderful," said Margaret. "Philip's business partner and his wife, and their daughter, Amelia, will be joining us at our table. They always stay at the inn when they visit from London, and this year we get to treat them to the ball. It really *is* the best party of the year, Abby. I'm sure you'll have a fantastic time. Don't you think so, David?"

David seemed absorbed in his own thoughts. Hearing his name, he made eye contact again with Abby. "Yes, I'm sure she will." He smiled again slightly.

"Well, it was nice to see you both," Cassandra said. "We've got to be off. Abby promised to help me find a dress today. David, I'm sure Moira will want to see you—will you stop by some time?"

David turned to look at Cassandra, breaking eye contact with Abby. "Of course," he said. "Please let her know I'll visit her soon."

৪৩৪৩৪৩

As Margaret Corbin chatted with the tailor, David stared out the shop window, watching Abby walk down La Playa Boulevard with Cassandra. It looked like they were headed toward the shopping district located south of Newcastle Beach.

Now he knew her name, and he knew there was a very good chance he would see her again, since she was associated with the Buchan family. He would definitely be stopping by their house soon. Hopefully he'd run into Abby there, but if not, he thought he might be able to tease some information out of Cassandra. And if nothing else, he now knew that she would be attending the Autumn Ball.

He frowned. Cassandra had said that Abby was going with Jonathon Reyes. David didn't know the guy personally, but he had heard plenty about him. Jon was the flirt Michal was always complaining about. It sounded like the guy flirted with a lot of girls at the pool. David wondered if Jon flirted with Abby too. Probably, since she worked at the pool with him. But Cassandra had used the term *friend*, rather than boyfriend. He wondered how much Cassandra knew about Abby and Jon's relationship. Yes, a reconnaissance mission at the Buchan house was definitely in order.

৪৩৪৩৪৩

Cassandra and Abby were browsing the boutiques in Santa Linda's premier shopping district along Calle de Oro, otherwise known as the Street of Gold. On the west side of the street were a series of hotels perched on the cliff overlooking the Pacific Ocean. While Cassandra was thumbing through a rack of formal dresses, Abby was staring out the boutique window, watching a hotel valet accept the keys to an impressive red convertible. She had a feeling that people who could afford a room in one of those hotels would have an amazing view of Newcastle Beach. Of course, people with that kind of money probably lived in a community like Newcastle Beach anyway.

"Well that was…different," Cassandra said.

Abby turned to look at her. "What do you mean?" Wide-eyed, Abby thought back to her conversation at the tailor's. Had she said anything embarrassing in front of David and his mom?

"David," Cassandra said, seemingly oblivious to Abby's inner angst. "He's never been the most talkative person, but he was really quiet today. I think he took an interest in you though."

"Really?" Abby asked, a little too enthusiastically. She toned it down. "What makes you think that?"

"I'm not sure," Cassandra admitted. "A gut feeling. And the fact that he barely made eye contact with me the whole time. He seemed entirely focused on you."

"I thought he just felt uncomfortable," Abby said. "I mean, we kind of stood there, awkwardly staring at each other—"

Cassandra laughed. "Oh, I wouldn't say he was staring at you awkwardly. I think he was rather fascinated by you."

Now Abby laughed. "Oh, I doubt that."

"No really, Abby. I think he was intrigued. It looked to me like he didn't know what to make of you and was trying to figure you out," Cassandra said. She stopped browsing and turned to look at Abby. "You have to understand that his world is pretty different from yours, Abby. The kind of girls he's known growing up..."

"I know," Abby sighed, resigned.

"No, I don't think you do," Cassandra said.

Abby looked at her. "Sorry?"

"You have *no* idea how attractive you are, do you?" Cassandra asked. She put her hands on her hips and studied Abby's face.

Abby looked away. "Attractive? I think that's stretching it a bit," she said, laughing nervously.

"No, really," Cassandra said. "Sure, the girls in Newcastle tend to be very pretty. They've got good genes working in their favor. It's no secret that wealthy people tend to end up with attractive spouses, so it stands to reason that they have good-looking children. But the girls I've met are also rather self-absorbed. They've had things handed to them—they've never had to struggle to get what they want."

Abby frowned. "Yeah, well, Jon says David has had everything handed to him too."

Cassandra crossed her arms. "That's because our friend Mr. Reyes has a serious crush on you, and he's not going to let you go without a fight. He won't be giving any points to David, I can promise you that," Cassandra said. "Jon is smart, but he's not objective, at least not when it comes to you. But I've known David longer than Jon has, and I can tell you that he may have come from a wealthy family, but he's not spoiled.

Meg and Philip did a good job with him. I'm serious though, Abby, you have no idea how other people see you. Not only are you beautiful, but you know who you are and what you want. You've been tested and tried, and you insist on living on your own terms, no matter the cost. Inner strength like that is very attractive to a boy like David."

"I guess so," Abby said. "I mean, I hear what you're saying, but I don't know—"

"No, trust me on this—that's what first attracted Riordan to me," Cassandra said. She took a dress from the rack and studied it.

Abby smiled. "Now, the way *I* heard it, was that Riordan saw you walking across the university commons and thought you were the most enchanting woman he had ever seen," Abby said. "I believe he quoted, actually *quoted,* Keats's 'La Belle Dame Sans Merci.' I suspect it had something to do with the color of your hair and his weakness for a girl with a Scottish heritage."

Cassandra laughed. "Well *that* goes without saying. I am quite a vision. But seriously, looks only go so far. Trust me, and don't write David off just yet."

Abby shrugged. "I guess we'll see."

"I guess we will," Cassandra said, returning the dress to its place on the rack. "All right. No luck finding something for me to wear in this store. Onward." She and Abby left the boutique and walked down to Cassandra's favorite shop in the Gold District.

Abby had no idea what to make of Cassandra's analysis of David or her continued dreams about him. *Okay, universe, what are you trying to tell me?* she thought. She had started to think she must be wrong about David and the dreams, and had tried so hard to forget about the whole thing. And yet, here she was again, thinking about him, torturing herself over something that could mean everything, or nothing at all. Maybe it was all just a coincidence. And maybe none of it mattered anyway if David was really leaving the country.

She focused instead on being in the moment with Cassandra, enjoying vicarious shopping and trying to be helpful in offering her opinion of the dresses Cassandra selected to try on.

Cassandra had two main concerns when it came to finding a dress. She was petite, so it was hard to find one that didn't leave her swimming in fabric. And her auburn hair, though gorgeous, tended to clash with certain colors.

Upon trying her tenth dress, Cassandra announced, "I feel like an eggplant."

"No, violet's good on you," Abby assured her. "It's a pretty contrast with your hair."

"Is it? I swear I look like a giant grape." Cassandra moved in close to the full-length mirror and studied her face, pulling the crow's feet near her eyes taut. "Or maybe a raisin. Either way, I should *not* spend this much time in front of a mirror. One more dress and I'm done for today." Cassandra looked in the mirror one more time, scowled at the dress, and ducked back into the dressing room.

"How about the green one?" Abby called after her.

A few minutes later, Cassandra reappeared in the doorway of the dressing room. "This one?" she asked.

Abby stared at her. "Wow. Stunning!"

Cassandra grinned and struck an over-the-top pose, with one hand on her hip and the other in her hair. "Think so?"

Abby laughed, nodding with approval. "Most definitely! It looks fantastic!"

The dress looked great and she could tell Cassandra knew it. The one-shouldered, form-fitting gown was a peridot jewel tone that complemented Cassandra's hazel eyes. A line of embroidered flowers accented in tiny crystals cascaded diagonally from the shoulder across the dress to her waist.

"Oh, you're an angel," Cassandra said. "Thank you—I like it too. I do believe I have found *the* dress."

"It *is* the dress. It's perfect." Abby smiled. The gown was just so Cassandra. It was like someone had taken her flitting pixie personality and embodied it into the very fabric of the dress.

"You, my dear, have impeccable taste, you know that?" Cassandra said. "If not for you, I'd have given up and gone as a purple people eater."

ಬಗಬಗಬಗ

That night, Abby had a nightmare. The scene before her was so vivid that she thought she was awake. Her closet door was open, and in the darkness within, she saw a black presence coming toward her. She couldn't make out details, but the form was humanoid and devoid of light, much blacker than the surrounding darkness of her bedroom.

Suddenly, she heard something pecking at her window, followed by the frantic beating of feathered wings against the glass. Something was trying to get in.

Abby startled awake, momentarily frozen with fear when she heard tapping against the glass. The shadow had remained in the dream, but something was at the window.

She got out of bed and walked over to the window, jumping back when a small pebble hit the glass in front of her face. "Jon," she whispered, annoyed. She wrenched up the second story window and looked down. He grinned up at her and put a finger to his lips, gesturing toward the tree house. *Jerk,* she mouthed, smiling. *Be right down.*

ಬಯ಩ಬಯ಩ಬಯ಩

Jon watched as a pajama-clad Abby quietly closed the back door behind her and crept down the porch steps to where he was waiting.

"Hi," she whispered, grinning.

"Hi." He had an afghan draped over his arm, and wrapped it around her shoulders. "Come sit with me." He turned and climbed the ladder to the tree house.

Now that he had reached his full height, the inside of the tree house was much too small for him to squeeze into. But the roof was flat, and since the autumn leaves were thinning in the canopy overhead, it was a great place to stargaze. He climbed up onto the tiny porch and then side-stepped over to a thick branch, which he used to boost himself up onto the roof.

Once he was settled, Abby climbed up the ladder and tossed him the afghan. Then, carefully, in her pajamas and slippers, she navigated the branches beside the tree house to reach the roof. Jon reached out his hand to assist her and pulled her up beside him.

"Thanks," she said, smiling at him. She took back the afghan and nestled in next to him on the roof. She looked him over. "Hey—how come I'm wearing pajamas and you're not?"

79

Jon chuckled, looking down at his worn-out sweat pants and faded T-shirt. "These *are* my pajamas."

"Oh," she said. "Very stylish."

"Not nearly as stylish as yours," Jon teased, tugging on her shirtsleeve. She was wearing a red and white striped button-down top with white piping around the cuffs of the sleeves and along the neckline and hem of the shirt. Her pants matched the top. He looked at her feet and laughed. "Even your slippers are color-coordinated. Are you trying to impress me?"

She laughed and wiggled her red velvet slippers around. "If I was trying to impress you, I'd have done my hair."

He studied her hair. It was pulled back into a French braid. It was a little mussed up, but he liked it. She was pretty cute with bed hair. "I thought you did."

She giggled and patted down a few strands that had come loose. "Oh, you're *smooth*, Jonathon."

"That I am," he smiled. "I missed you today. I had pool duty all by my lonesome."

"I know," Abby said. She leaned her head against his shoulder. "I missed you too. But I did have a good day off."

He looked down at her, surprised that she was being affectionate after he had just hit on her. Usually she pushed him away if he said something halfway flirtatious. Cautiously, he put his arm around her. "Oh yeah?"

"Yeah. Cassandra invited me to the Autumn Ball at the inn, and I get to wear this amazing dress," Abby explained, snuggling up against him. She looked up at him. "And, assuming you're not doing anything that night, I would be most appreciative if you'd join me."

Jon smiled. "*Most* appreciative, huh? Are you asking me out on a date, Abigail?"

He felt her face grow warm against his chest like she was blushing. He looked down at her, but she looked away and it was too dark to tell if her cheeks were red.

"Sort of, but not exactly," Abby said, staring at her slippers as she shifted her feet. "Not a *date* date, you know, but more of an I-want-to-go-but-I'm-terrified-to-go-alone-and-I-need-my-best-friend kind of date."

"Hmmmm," Jon feigned disappointment. "Well, when you put it that way, it's just soooo appealing. I guess I'll have to check my calendar and see if I have any prior engagements..."

She looked up at him. "*Jon.*"

Truth be told, he *was* a little disappointed—he wouldn't have minded a real date, but he hid his feelings with a grin. "Kidding. I'd be honored to escort you m'lady. What do I have to wear?"

"It's black tie, so you'd have to rent a tux," Abby said. "I'd be happy to pay for it though, since I'm the one asking you to come."

"Eh—no worries. I think I can cover it," Jon said. "My job pays *really* well."

Abby laughed. There was a hole in the hem of his T-shirt. She stuck her finger through the hole and tugged on the fabric. "Oh yes, you are just rolling in dough, aren't you?"

Jon shoved her hand away. "Hey—no messing with my shirt. It's vintage."

"That's one way to describe it," Abby teased. "Anyway, Cassandra said they're hiring a car and will come pick us up. It's not that far away, but in heels...oh, and also they needed to rent a nicer car because Aunt Moira is coming. Apparently Riordan's car isn't quite up to her standards."

"What a *lovely* woman," Jon said. "How do you feel about her coming?"

Abby shrugged. "Awkward, but we don't see each other too much. I think she's moved from hating me to pretending I don't exist."

Jon frowned. "I don't get it—what's her problem?"

"I have no idea," Abby said. "I thought I was a pretty charming person. Even more so, considering how her face twists up with disgust every time she sees me."

"Obviously the fault lies with her—you are nothing if not charming," Jon said, taking Abby's hand.

"Thanks," she said, squeezing his hand.

Jon smiled. "I say we turn the tables and ignore *her*. We'll have a good time just to spite her."

Abby nodded in agreement.

Jon looked at Abby. It bothered him that Moira was rude to her. He hadn't met the woman, but he hoped she would be nice to Abby at the Autumn Ball. Abby was a sweet girl, and she deserved to have fun. Jon was going to have to set Moira straight if the woman had anything rude to say when he was around.

He was glad Abby had asked him to go, and not just because he wanted to protect her from a cranky old lady. He looked forward to what promised to be an amazing night with his best friend, even if it wasn't a real date. But there was another reason he was excited to attend the ball. It was the reason he'd woken Abby up and asked her to sneak out with him. But now that she was sitting beside him, he was a little unsure about how to approach the topic. What if he hurt her feelings? He sat beside her in silence for a few minutes. She was looking up at the night sky, watching the stars. Finally he decided to go for it.

"Abby?" Jon asked.

"Yeah?" She turned to look at him.

"Do you think Marisol will be at the Autumn Ball?"

Abby stared at Jon. "Probably. Why do you ask?"

"Oh, just...something interesting happened today," he said.

Abby raised her eyebrows and let go of his hand. "Define *interesting*."

"Well, you were gone, and I don't know where Michal and Monroe were, but my shift was over and I was getting ready to leave, and..."

"And?" Abby asked impatiently.

Jon grinned mischievously. He could tell by Abby's tone of voice that the suspense was killing her. "And Marisol came up and we just started talking," Jon said. "It was nice. She's kind of different when her friends aren't around."

Abby smiled. "I thought maybe she liked you. So, what did you talk about?"

"Oh, I don't know," Jon said, relieved that Abby seemed okay with his interest in Marisol. "School, college next year. She's really smart. She's thinking about law school eventually. She's funny, too—it was easy to talk with her. Kind of like how it is with us, but you know, a little more..."

Abby nodded. "Yeah, I can see that. So what are you going to do? Are you going to ask her out?"

"I don't know. I want to, but it scares me a little, too."

Abby gasped in mock amazement. "You? Scared to make the first move? I thought you were immune to rejection. Fearless."

"Oh, I *am*," he laughed. "But this time, it's different. For the first time, no offense to you, it feels serious. I don't want to screw up."

"You won't," Abby said, taking his hand again. "Just be yourself, I think she already likes you for that."

"You're right. Thanks, Abby." He gave her hand a little squeeze.

"Hey, as long as she treats you well, she has my blessing," she said.

"So, what about you? Any more crazy dreams?" Jon asked.

"Ha—you have no idea."

"What happened?" he asked, concerned.

"Long story," Abby said, and told him what had happened at the Buchan house with the shadow boy.

⬚◕⬚◕⬚◕

Several days later, after school, Abby decided to take a walk through Newcastle Beach. She told herself she needed to clear her head, and thought walking along the beach might be a good remedy. But the truth was she was hoping to run into David again. No matter how much she tried to convince herself otherwise, she was more drawn to him than ever.

Halfway between the old mansion and the beach, she noticed a commotion. Several large alley cats were harassing a raven. The bird was putting up a good fight, but was outnumbered and being overpowered.

"Hey!" Abby shouted. She ran toward the feline predators, waving her arms wildly. An oversized, bob-tailed black cat bared its teeth and hissed at her. She kicked at it and it got the message, slinking away. *Is it my imagination,* Abby thought, *or are housecats bigger than they used to be? That black cat had to have been the size of a cocker spaniel.*

Gently, Abby scooped up the raven, inspecting him for wounds. Nothing looked broken, but when she ran her fingertip along the edge of one wing, the bird trembled and pecked at her hand as a warning. "All right," she said. "No more touching that spot. Let's get you home." Cradling the raven in her arms, she slipped through the mansion's gate.

Once inside, the bird wriggled free from her grasp and took flight, gliding low over a tangle of green bushes that looked oddly familiar to Abby. *I've been here before,* she thought. *In my dream.*

Out of the corner of her eye, she saw a flash of white. *The doe?* Noticing an opening in the knotted snarl of green, she entered an overgrown maze, dark with branches crossed overhead. Trying to remember the pattern of the labyrinth from her dream, she stepped further into the darkness, her arms stretched out to guide her. She turned corner after corner and came to a circular clearing in the center of the emerald maze, with passages leading in three directions.

Which way now? As if in answer to her unspoken question, she heard a rustle above her. Looking up, she saw two golden eyes staring down. Her raven friend cocked his head and then dived into the labyrinth, flying low in front of her. He landed in front of the middle passage a few feet away and hopped impatiently, waiting for her to catch up. "Right behind you," Abby said. "Show me."

She followed the raven through a twisting passage, which was becoming increasingly familiar. Soon, she knew, she would reach the opening to the beach. Would David be waiting for her, like in the dream?

As she turned the last corner, she held her breath in anticipation, fully expecting to see him. Instead, the labyrinth halted abruptly in a solid green dead end.

Then, Abby gasped in horror. A haunting figure appeared before her. Facing the wall, the hag wore a ragged dress that might have been white long ago, but was now a dirty gray. Stringy white hair hung down her back and a withered arm hung limply at her side. The hag turned, revealing a ruined face and a hideous milky-white eye. The hair on the back of Abby's neck stood on end. She backed away, terrified, stumbling over a thick root jutting out from beneath the labyrinth wall, then pressed up against the hedge to keep from falling.

The old woman bent down and the raven hopped into her arms, his golden eyes beckoning to Abby. Abby searched the woman's face—wretched as it was, the face was kind, and the woman did not seem to intend harm. The woman's good eye was a piercing blue, and Abby recognized it as belonging to the beautiful raven-haired woman from her dream.

"Hello, Abigail," the woman croaked. "I have been expecting you."

DREAMWALKING

"Come," the woman motioned. "We have much to discuss." With a slight limp, she slid past Abby and began making her way to the labyrinth's entrance.

When she exited the dark maze, Abby's eyes stung as she stepped into the sunlight. The ruin that was left of the mansion looked like it was straight from the pages of *Great Expectations*, and the woman bore a fearsome resemblance to mad Miss Havisham in a tattered bridal dress. All that was missing was a moldy wedding cake.

"What happened to you?" Abby whispered, taking in her surroundings with wide eyes, her curiosity overcoming rudeness.

"I will tell you everything soon," the woman assured her. "But first, we need to get inside, away from spying eyes." She nodded toward the estate's gate, where Abby could see the large alley cats had returned and were watching intently, tails twitching. After Abby's encounter with the shadow thing that had turned into a black cat, the woman's statement didn't sound crazy at all.

They entered the damaged mansion, and the woman led Abby into a long, wood-paneled hall. Broken glass littered the floor from the remains of the tall, gilded mirrors on the walls. A shaft of light illuminated the room, highlighting particles of dust floating in the air. Looking up, Abby could see the source of the light—a framed dome of glass, now with fine cracks spreading like a spider's web, but still intact.

This used to be some kind of grand ballroom, Abby thought. *Now I know I've been here before—the first dream with the little boy. But the room looked different—the mirrors were still whole.*

The mansion must have been all but destroyed in the infamous Newcastle Beach Quake decades before. What was strange was that while most buildings in Newcastle had sustained only minor damage, this one was almost leveled. It looked as though one wing had collapsed. Maybe the mansion was resting on a sandy foundation, since it was so close to the beach. But then again, the inn was right across the street and was hardly affected.

The woman pulled open a set of doors, and Abby followed her into a room filled with a large swimming pool; the air felt warm and moist. Surrounding the pool were large ceramic pots glazed in a multitude of rich colors—cobalt, scarlet, tangerine, and chartreuse. After the quake, the mansion had suffered years of neglect. Against those odds, this room was surprisingly well-preserved. It had become its own ecosystem, and the plants were thriving, feeding off the pool's condensation. Rays of sunlight filtered through the dirty glass panes stretching floor to ceiling on each of the three walls opposite the room's entrance. The glass appeared frosted, covered with tiny droplets of moisture. The woman pushed the heavy doors closed, blocking the cool air wafting in from the ballroom, and Abby felt a dizzying wave of heat as the temperature increased.

A giant seashell-shaped bowl encrusted with algae sat at the far end of the pool, and though water no longer coursed over its scalloped edges, Abby could hear dripping liquid echoing and reverberating off the walls. The pool was half empty, but still deep, and under the thick slime of algae on its walls, Abby could make out an art nouveau pattern embossed on the tiles.

Overhead, waves of light undulated on the ceiling, reflected from the surface of the water. The ceiling showcased a mural with an undersea motif, also in the art nouveau style. A beautiful mermaid floated serenely in a coral bed. Her delicate features, the scales on her tail, and her flowing green hair were highlighted in gold leaf. Behind her, in a deep cobalt and teal sea, was the outline of an underwater doorway on a mound of rocks. The frame of the doorway was intricate and exotic, Asian-looking.

The woman gestured to an antique pair of Chinese garden stools by the edge of the pool and sat down gracefully, arranging the folds of her ruined dress. Hesitantly, Abby sat beside her and waited.

"My name," the woman said, "is Eulalia, and twenty-two years ago, I did not look like this." Beginning with the assassination of her husband, the queen explained the events leading up to her disfigurement.

ഇരുതരുതരുത

Abby needed some time to take it all in. Eulalia's tale was strange, almost delusional sounding. Even so, there was something about the sincerity in her voice that made her story seem rational, like it was perfectly natural that there should be portals to a magical parallel world filled with mythical creatures, and that she, this person who looked anything but majestic, should be a queen. If it weren't for her own vivid dreams, her visions of David and the powerful connection she felt to him, and the experience she'd had with the shadow boy at the Buchans', Abby might have thought the woman was crazy. But, because of her experiences, Abby found herself giving Eulalia the benefit of the doubt.

"Your own sister did this to you?" Abby asked.

"Yes. She did," Eulalia said, without the tone of self-pity Abby might have expected. "She coveted what she could not have and betrayed me."

"And where is she now?"

"I have not seen her since that fateful night. I know she cannot have crossed back over since she destroyed one portal and closed another. Sometimes I feel her, like she is near, but hidden just out of reach, impossible to find."

"And the baby? He must be grown by now."

Eulalia nodded. "He is. You have met him."

"I have?"

"The boy from your dreams, and the boy I lost, are one and the same. His human parents named him David Corbin."

Abby shook her head. She was the one who had lost her mind—or else she was dreaming again. *That's not possible. Is it?* It wasn't that she couldn't believe what she was hearing— after all the strange things that had happened in the past few weeks it was easy to suspend her disbelief. The idea that David might be connected to this woman made a strange kind of sense, as much sense as any other explanation Abby had gleaned from her dreams. But she felt overwhelmed with questions, like she was trying to solve a puzzle with missing pieces. "If it's David Corbin, why hasn't he come to you? And how do you know about my dreams? Where do I fit into all this?"

"My son has been kept from me all these years. Just as I have been imprisoned within the boundaries of this estate, he has been shielded from my presence. He has no knowledge about who he is or where he comes from. All my efforts to break the barrier myself have proven futile. I have, with some assistance, gotten a message to him, but Lucia's followers made sure those who helped me were punished, and I am sure he has since forgotten all about the Sign of the Throne. I am sure they *made* him forget," she added bitterly.

"The Sign of the Throne?" Abby asked.

"Yes, I will explain that in good time," Eulalia responded. "First, allow me to answer your other two questions. The reason I know about your dreams is that like you, I am a cai aislingstraid—*c'aislingaer* for short. It means, 'soul who walks in dreams'. In our dreams, we have the power to see the future and to connect with other dreamers' souls. In this connection, we can see into their thoughts and know what they have experienced and what they will experience. We do not have the ability to see everything, but the stronger the emotional bond, the more clearly we can see.

"And that is also the reason it is difficult to see those who serve the Dark. Unless they plan to interact directly with someone connected to you, their intentions and actions are veiled. Dreamwalking is like walking in the dark of night with a torch lighting your way. You can only see what is illuminated by the light. And because we have free will, the

91

future is always changing. Nevertheless, once something is set in motion and gains momentum, it does tend to occur. Because of this, and because people tend to act within certain patterns, you can make fairly accurate predictions about what will happen. Do you understand?"

Abby nodded. She wasn't sure she really understood about dreamwalking, but she saw no other alternative than to agree.

"I will try to teach you all I know about being a c'aislingaer. Now, as to your second question. The reason you are here is that I need your help. With each passing hour, the Darkness grows stronger. You have seen it yourself. If David does not take the throne of our kingdom before his twenty-third birthday, the dark lord Tynan Tierney, the Kruor um Beir, will be freed from the Wasteland and will rule. If that happens, both our worlds will be thrust into darkness, and there will be no stopping him. Monstrous creatures will enter your world, feeding off everyone they find. You have already connected with David—now your task is to remind him who he is."

"How?" Abby asked. It wasn't that she didn't want to believe, to help, but how in the world could she relate this story to David? She couldn't even hold a normal conversation with him, much less one like this. *Impossible,* she thought. *Just impossible. Hi David, you don't know me, but it's the craziest thing...*

"I can see that you have doubts. It will not be easy. For thousands of years, my people, the People of the Light, have kept the Darkness at bay in a world hidden from yours."

"Hidden how?"

92

"There are many other worlds you cannot see. Mine is only one of them, hidden behind the veils of time and space, a parallel universe—another planet, if you will. It is a place much different than your world—smaller, but much older."

"What is it called?" Abby queried.

"Cai Terenmare. The name has great meaning to me, but I am afraid such an old name does not translate well literally. Metaphorically, however, it means 'the soul, resting at sea.'"

"That sounds beautiful," Abby said. "You miss it?"

Eulalia laughed, but Abby could hear no joy in her voice. "Horribly. It *is* a beautiful place. The view of the Western Sea from the Solas Beir's castle where I lived…my heart aches to think of it. That word, *cai*, has several meanings—'soul,' 'heart,' 'home.' The name of the castle, Caislucis, literally means 'house of light.'"

"But if another language is spoken there, how is it you speak English?"

Eulalia laughed again, and this time she seemed genuinely amused. "So many questions, young one, and rightly so. I speak many languages. It is the gift of tongues, passed down through the blood of my people. Wherever our journeys take us, we are able to converse in the languages of other worlds. And some of our words have even become part of your world, influencing your languages, your cultures. There are stories about us that remain in your world, even if time has muddied the truth about what we are."

"So, you're not human, but that means you are…?"

"My people are powerful shape-shifters, nearly immortal, waging battle in forms representative of our true nature, our souls. That is why you first saw me as a white doe in your dream. Once we reach maturity, we never grow old. We *can*

93

die—if we drown or are consumed by fire, poisoned by silver, or torn apart by those who serve the Dark. Still, as long as we can return to the pool of healing at Caislucis, we can heal from almost any wound."

"So, once you return home, you'll be okay?"

Eulalia nodded. "Yes. I will be restored, if only I can return."

"Tell me about the Darkness." Abby urged, finally giving in and accepting the odd turn her life was taking. If there was any chance to help, any hope for success, she would need to know as much as possible about what she was up against.

"Like my people, those who dwell in Darkness change shape to match their nature—but they are twisted, deceptive creatures who thirst for blood and power. They feed off those in the Light and all living creatures in your world. They are the Kruorumbrae, the Blood Shadows, and they have the ability to drain the life force from a body. They can even change into someone who looks and acts familiar to you, stealing that person's body and using it as a disguise. Make no mistake— the Darkness *is* strong. Up until now, we have always had a Solas Beir among us who has kept the balance of power."

"What is a Solas Beir?" Abby asked, mesmerized.

"There is only one Solas Beir in each generation of my people. The Solas Beir is our ruler, the one who serves as the Light's representative, who bears the Light. The term *lightbearer* is used in more casual settings, but Solas Beir is a formal title, and therefore preferred, particularly in affairs of state. The other reason that the term *Solas Beir* is preferred is that the term *lightbearer* is sometimes used to refer to a future ruler, one who has not yet ascended to the throne, who does not yet possess the power of the Solas Beir. Do you understand?"

Abby nodded. "But what do you mean by power? Political authority?"

"That, and power that comes directly from the Light. The Solas Beir is the strongest of us, unbound by the natural laws of our worlds. He can move and manipulate objects by sheer force of will, defy gravity, and heal others. He also has the power to shape-shift and heal himself. In representing the Light, he has the power to destroy those who walk in Darkness merely by speaking a word. But although he has great power, he cannot use it for his own gain. He has a heavy burden to bear—he is a servant of his people, leading them, protecting them, and if necessary, sacrificing himself for them."

"Is the Solas Beir always male?"

"The power of the Solas Beir comes from the Light, and is passed from parent to child. It may be possible for a daughter of a Solas Beir to someday inherit the gift and rule. However, all of the Solas Beirs in our history have been male," Eulalia said.

"So then, if Tynan Tierney were to gain power and rule Cai Terenmare, he wouldn't be a Solas Beir," Abby reasoned.

"Not a *true* Solas Beir," Eulalia explained. "He might call himself Solas Beir, and he might have great power, but his power does not come from the Light."

"But the last king, your husband, was a true Solas Beir?"

"Yes."

"And David...?"

"Is the next one. *If* he returns," Eulalia continued. "That is why Lucia's plan was so brilliant, you see. Even though Tierney failed in his attempt for the throne and has been imprisoned, Lucia was able to remove the one person who can keep him there. If she can keep David from coming home, she still wins. And if Tierney rules Cai Terenmare, he will have access to your world. None of us will be safe from his tyranny."

Abby cringed at the thought of Tierney entering her world with an army of bloodthirsty monsters. She imagined a wave of darkness pouring in from the sea like fog, destroying everyone she loved. She had to know more. "So, after you were injured and were trapped here, what happened? Did Fergal make it back through the portal?"

"He did. He informed Cael of my plight." The queen sighed and paused, as though she were lost in thoughts of another world. "It has been so long since I have seen Cael..."

Abby stared at her. "You and Cael are very close." It was a statement, not a question.

"Yes." Eulalia met Abby's gaze. She smiled weakly. "Another story for another time. Suffice it to say that I can see his dreams *very* clearly. When Cael learned what happened, he gathered his best soldiers. Half were left to guard the kingdom, and half went with him to find the Sign of the Throne. With the greatest haste, they rode on horseback to the snow-covered mountains in the northernmost reaches of my world, seeking the Northern Oracle."

"The Northern Oracle? What is that?" Abby asked.

"*Who*, actually. The Northern Oracle is one of four principalities governing the outermost realms of my world. Oracles are people, but they are not like us. They are like forces of nature—they do not bow to the Solas Beir's authority, but by working in harmony with them, the Solas Beir can tap into their power, much like a ship sails with the wind. Cael's journey north took many months. Although he and his men could have traveled as swiftly in their totem forms, going by horseback allowed them to conserve the energy required for battle. And they battled often.

"Tierney's forces delayed them at every turn with frequent attacks. The journey was treacherous. Countless times they encountered beasts of darkness, terrible creatures thirsting for their blood.

"Many of Cael's men suffered grievous injuries, but they fought off each attack courageously, giving their enemies many more wounds than they bore. However, with such short intervals between conflicts, the men grew weak, having so little time to heal. As they grew weaker, it became impossible to transform to their animal forms to fight. And still, the nightmarish creatures seemed to multiply—with each monster they cut down, two more appeared, more massive than the last."

Abby shuddered and wrapped her arms around herself.

Eulalia paused and studied her face. "Are you all right, dear? You are shivering."

Abby smiled grimly. "I'm fine."

Eulalia looked skeptical.

"Really. I'm just picturing your story in my head, and it's terrifying. I can't imagine being in Cael's shoes, fighting creatures like that."

Eulalia patted Abby's hand. "I pray you shall never have to. Shall I continue?"

Abby nodded. "Please."

Eulalia shifted in her seat, smoothing out her skirt. She gazed into Abby's eyes and continued her story. "The worst attack came in the form of an ambush as they neared their destination. The house of the Northern Oracle stands on top of a mountain, and the forces of darkness were laying siege to the snow-covered fortress. There was no telling how long the creatures had been there or if anyone remained alive within the walls. The only road leading to the fortress was through the Gauntlet, an icy canyon so narrow and deep it seemed to expel light. As Cael and his soldiers made their way, they could hear the hellish howls of the beasts on the ledges above, crying out for blood to be spilled.

"In the darkness, they could hear the creatures descend behind and before them, their claws scratching on frozen rocks. Through a dense fog, the men could see the dark outlines of hulking feline forms, some stalking on two legs like men, some creeping closer on all fours, all with bristling hair standing on end.

"As the creatures got closer, the soldiers could see their evil, murderous grins. Cael and his troops were trapped—their only chance for escape was to fight. The horses upon which they rode, steady in battle up to this point, panicked, tossing many of their riders to the ground. The horses knew death was imminent and they were mad with fright.

"The monsters attacked from all sides. A creature leapt onto the back of a riderless horse, sinking its claws into the stallion's hide, locking its teeth onto the terrified animal's neck. The rider, recovered from being tossed from his mount, made the mistake of watching his horse's demise. He stood frozen in horror as the horse crumpled under the weight of the monster and the blood drained from the dead animal's body. Another beast grabbed the man's ankles, dragging him away screaming into the darkness.

"Cael heard his cries, but could not help—he had too much trouble of his own. He was trying to push the monsters forward, toward the fortress. With a sword in each hand, he slashed and sliced, cutting through beast after beast, and still they came. He fought astride his stallion, the brave horse striving to kick down the monsters, until he was too overwhelmed and too exhausted to go further.

"The creatures pulled the stallion down. Cael leapt clear and tried to free his horse, but there were just too many monsters to save the valiant steed. Cael did not dare stop to grieve. To lose concentration for a second was to lose altogether.

"As men and horses were lost in the battle, those who remained formed a tighter circle, fighting the monsters on all sides. No man was without injury. The soldiers' armor was little more than useless against the claws and teeth of the beasts. Cael bore a gaping wound at his neck and the armor protecting his chest was slashed. There were deep gashes on his chest and thighs, and he was losing blood quickly. He felt faint but managed to keep his feet, knowing that if he fell, he would not get up again. All seemed lost.

"And then, the tide turned. Cael heard horrible shrieks from the furthest ends of the canyon on either side of the battle, and to his surprise, the monsters seemed to be catching on fire. In the glow of their burning flesh, he saw masked figures clad in tight-fitting black clothing on the ledges, pouring liquid from large clay pots onto the monsters below. Other figures shot flaming arrows into the crowded canyon, igniting the oil-covered beasts.

"A rope ladder was tossed down the side of the canyon where the soldiers were fighting in a tight band. One of the masked warriors descended, beckoning the men to climb out of the fray. With the oily beasts battling in such close proximity to each other, it was little wonder that the fire spread quickly. Cael ordered his men up the ladder before they too succumbed to the flames. The mysterious warrior waited at the bottom with Cael, standing guard while the wounded soldiers ascended out of harm's way.

"One of the monsters, burning and shrieking, lunged for Cael. In a flash of fluid motion, the warrior unsheathed a long, elegant sword from his back, and sliced through the beast, cutting it neatly in half, seemingly without effort. The warrior then calmly wiped the sword clean and offered Cael the ladder, climbing up after him.

"As Cael reached the top of the canyon, he looked down. The fire had consumed everything below and was now inching up the rope ladder, licking up what remained.

"The masked warrior who had guided them up the canyon walls seemed to be in authority; he gestured with a gloved hand toward the fortress, silently motioning for them to follow. Beaten by an icy wind whipping over the ridge, blowing snow over their exhausted, wounded bodies, the men willingly followed the warrior, relieved to enter safe shelter.

"The towering walls of the circular fortress were thick, made of smooth black stone, and devoid of any decorative architecture that might provide a foothold and assist an enemy in gaining access. Although the gates were made of wood, they too were solid and smooth, built to withstand any blow. Sentries were stationed at towers on either side of the gate, their gazes and arrows trained on the canyon below, ready to fire through narrow slits in the walls should any of the beasts prove to have survived. Cael and his men followed the masked warriors across a small courtyard, paved with frost-covered black pebbles, into a single massive building, circular like the outer wall.

"Inside, the soldiers were greeted by the warmth of a hearth and the welcome smell of food. The room was minimalist in decor, stoically furnished with long, low tables for meals and cushions as seating on the black slate floor. No paintings or tapestries graced the walls. Functional items, weapons and tools for carpentry and for tilling soil, hung neatly on hooks, serving as decoration. Clay pots and woven baskets rested on the floor against the walls. Along one wall were shelves of rolled parchment scrolls, reaching from the floor to the wood-beamed ceiling. Other than that, the room was barren, an empty hall ruled by order.

"The leader of the warriors motioned for Cael and the soldiers to be seated and take refreshment. Monks with shaved heads, wearing simple, long-sleeved black robes, entered the room. They carried trays with bowls of clean water, towels, cloth bandages, and various healing herbs. They began to tend the men, dressing wounds.

"Cael flinched as he removed his armor; the gashes in his chest and thighs stung. The wound stretching from his jaw down his neck would take a long time to heal—it was deep and had already festered from its contact with saliva from the creature's nasty bite. He could feel himself growing feverish from the bite and blood loss. He had been wounded in battle many times before, but this time, his skin would be scarred.

"Removing thick leather gloves, the leader pulled away the mask to reveal a feminine face with delicate features that were in stark contrast to fierce, almond-shaped eyes. Cael gasped in surprise and then quickly lowered his gaze to hide his shock. He had known the Northern Oracle was a woman, but he never would have imagined a woman or an oracle on the front lines of a battle, leading a rescue effort with the courage and skill of a seasoned warrior.

"She smiled, enjoying his reaction. 'Knights of the Solas Beir,' she pronounced, 'I welcome you to the house of the Northern Oracle.' Then she removed her leather hood, unleashing long, straight, black hair. She unbuckled the strap of the sheathed sword she carried on her back and hung it from a hook. Her thick leather jacket had a high collar that protected her neck from enemies' blades and the cold. She unfastened the clasps that ran down the side and removed it.

"Without her protective armor, she was petite. She wore a scarlet sleeveless tunic with a mandarin collar that fell just below the waist of her thick leather leggings. The thin, red fabric clung to her small frame, making her appear deceptively frail.

"Cael knew how strong she was—he had seen her use her sword. 'Thank you, Northern Oracle,' he replied. 'We appreciate your rescue and your hospitality.'

'It is we who owe thanks,' she said. 'We have been under siege for many months. If you had not drawn the creatures away from our gates, we would still be so. Our supplies are depleted, but you are welcome to share what we have and stay as long as you wish.'

'Thank you, but we dare not stay long,' responded Cael. 'Our kingdom is in grave danger.'

"The Northern Oracle nodded. 'Yes, I have seen this. You seek the Sign of the Throne.'

'You have seen true,' Cael said. 'Our queen is in dire need of the Solas Beir's sigil.'

'I cannot help you,' the Northern Oracle replied. 'The sigil is not here. I am afraid your journey has been in vain.'

"Cael was distraught. Such a long and treacherous journey all for nothing. 'If the Sign of the Throne is not with you, where can it be?'"

"It really wasn't there?" Abby asked.

Eulalia rose from the garden stool and stretched as though she had been sitting too long. She walked over to the edge of the pool and stared into its murky depths. "No. Unfortunately, it was not. The Northern Oracle has always been our ally. I assumed, incorrectly, that she would be the keeper of the Sign of the Throne. She has been ever constant and true to the Light, but of course that was why she could not protect the sigil. Were Tierney to seek it, the house of the Northern Oracle would be the first place he would look—and indeed, that was the reason for the siege. His followers were determined to free him from the Wasteland. I am afraid that because of my assumption, I sent Cael to the wrong oracle. It appears that my husband kept secrets even from me."

Abby stood up and stretched as well. "So all those men who were killed in the Gauntlet, didn't have to die."

Eulalia nodded. "You speak true."

Abby sank down onto the garden stool, thinking about it. She looked up at Eulalia. "Then what happened?"

Eulalia began to pace along the pool's edge. "After Cael learned that the Northern Oracle did not possess the Sign of the Throne, the Northern Oracle insisted that he and his soldiers stay until they had recovered enough for the long journey home. As it turned out, they had no choice—as they were healing, a storm rendered the canyon impassable, and they were forced to wait almost a year before the ice receded.

"Although frustrated by this turn of events, Cael and his men made the most of their time in the north. The Northern Oracle and her people prided themselves on self-reliance. They infused discipline and spirituality into every task, caring for domesticated deer, tending indoor gardens, and refining their skills as warriors while gaining edification from the ancient texts. The people of the north kept owls, which they used for hunting the small hares that inhabited the ridge, and in this practice, their spiritual connection with their birds of prey and the world around them was particularly salient.

"Cael was greatly humbled by his observations and found he had much to learn. When at long last the snow melted, he had become a stronger warrior and a more disciplined man.

"The Northern Oracle equipped Cael and his men with fresh horses and supplies. Most noteworthy was a small leather satchel filled with a combustible powder.

'Keep it dry,' she urged. 'You will have need for it soon.'

"Cael pressed her for further explanation, but she simply shook her head, unwilling to share all she had foreseen. Instead, she instructed Cael to voyage west to the island of the Western Oracle.

"My husband had good reason for entrusting the Sign to the Western Oracle. She was loyal to no one, narcissistic, and absolutely lethal. Tierney would surely have met his match in seeking the Sign in her care. They made a secret arrangement, so secret that not even I was privy to it. Ardal himself consulted with the Oracle to seal the pact; this was his insurance to protect our people, should anything happen to him before our son Artan could take the throne. The Northern

Oracle told Cael that he must take the diadem of the Solas Beir and present it to the Western Oracle. Only then would she relinquish the Sign of the Throne.

"Cael journeyed home as quickly as he could. He testified before the council that governed the kingdom in the absence of a Solas Beir, and they granted him use of the crown.

"He replenished his provisions and packed gifts of treasure to flatter the Western Oracle. The soldiers who had joined him in seeking the assistance of the Northern Oracle continued with him west. They sailed for many months to reach the island.

"One evening, at sunset, they heard singing. The song was so sweet that one of the men immediately dove overboard. Cael tried to stop him, but it was too late. All that was left of the man was blood in the water.

"The siren surfaced, a beautiful, sensuous woman, beckoning the men to join her. She wiped blood from her lips and resumed her song. As she sang, many of the men fell into a trance, captivated by her beauty and bewitched by her voice. Her song summoned dark clouds and below her, the sea boiled as something writhed beneath the waves.

"As lightning flashed across the sky, a scale-covered arm scooped a man from the deck and pulled him under the surface. A black-and-white striped tail smashed the mast with its paddled fin and sent the men scattering, knocking several overboard. All were gone in seconds.

"More sirens surfaced, beautiful from the waist up, lethal below, with a second pair of muscled, hungry arms stemming from their scaly, serpentine tails. Each arm was tipped with the head of a viper, a venomous sea krait. Clinging to the sides of the boat, the sirens began to rock the vessel violently, attempting to capsize it.

'Join us,' they hissed.

"Cael hung on with all his strength and shouted, 'I seek the Western Oracle by order of the Solas Beir! You must grant us safe passage!'

"At this, the sea became calm, and the sirens ceased their rocking. Their strong arms guided the ship through the darkness until it bumped lightly on the shore of a tremendous island, a mountain looming ominously over the sea. Near the edge of the water was a marble temple.

"Cael and the few remaining soldiers disembarked, carrying a strongbox holding the crown and gifts for the Western Oracle. The sirens slithered up the sand, but kept their distance. Cautiously, Cael turned his back on them and walked forward, up stone steps into the towering edifice supported by marble pillars. A strange, sweet-smelling mist filled the air, and Cael remained on his guard, signaling the men to keep their swords ready.

'Come forward, Cael,' a musical voice called invitingly. 'I have been waiting for you for such a long time.'

"The mist cleared slightly, and sitting on a carved marble throne was a beautiful woman with voluptuous curves, long, finely-turned legs, flowing tresses, full lips, and bewitching eyes. She was a goddess in a pure white silken robe that flowed around her perfect form, as though it too were made of mist. Hers was a form meant for seduction, and Cael found himself irresistibly drawn to her, letting down his guard.

"But my connection with him is powerful, and I sensed his will slipping away. 'Cael,' I called out in his mind. 'Finish this and come home. I need you. We all do.'

"As if waking from a dream, he gathered his strength and his wit. 'Western Oracle,' he crooned, 'I come in the name of the Solas Beir, who thanks you for your honorable service to our kingdom. You are as beautiful as you are kind and generous. Please, allow me to present you with gifts to demonstrate our gratitude.' At this, he opened the strongbox, scooping up lengths of jeweled necklaces. Bowing nobly, he presented them to her.

"She took the gifts from him and smiled. 'Thank you, Cael. They are lovely.' She placed the necklaces around her neck and gazed down at him seductively. 'I am pleased that you came to present them personally. I hope you will stay with me.'

"Cael returned her smile. 'Your beauty does entice me, Oracle. It pains me to leave your presence, but I must return home.'

"The Western Oracle frowned, pouting. 'But, my dear Cael, you must stay. I have waited only for you. And you have kept me waiting for so, so very long.' Then, leaning forward as if he were her confidant, she whispered, 'Have my daughters offended you in their welcome? I am certain they can make it up to your men,' she beamed as the sirens slithered into the room, wrapping their lovely upper arms seductively around Cael's soldiers. Cael's men dropped their guard, entranced once again.

"Cael resisted her advances. 'I am sure my soldiers would welcome such hospitality. Unfortunately, I come on a mission from my king, not of my own wishes. Were I here of my own accord, I would happily stay with you forever. The Solas Beir asked me to retrieve the Sign of the Throne. I have brought his diadem as a sign of goodwill and as proof I come on his authority.'

"The Western Oracle looked scornful. 'Ah, that,' she spat.

"Cael held up the shining crown. It was a simple silver circlet, a perfect circle, void of decoration.

"The Western Oracle winced, as if it were physically painful to be so close to the object. Then, regaining her composure, she smiled graciously. 'I see that you are true to your king, dear one. An admirable quality. How I wish you could stay with me and be so true.' She sighed sadly. 'I see I have no choice but to honor your request and let you return. I will give you the Sign of the Throne.'

"With a flick of her wrist, she signaled for one of her daughters to bring the sigil of the Solas Beir. The siren disappeared briefly and returned, solemnly carrying a small wooden box, ornately carved with symbols of the kingdom.

"Cael thanked her and opened the box. Inside he found two halves of a silver nautilus shell, joined by a seam of silvery blue light. With great respect, Cael closed the lid and thanked the Western Oracle.

"She smiled sweetly. 'And now, my love, let me offer you a token of my affection, a blessing for your journey home.' She beckoned for him to come forward, cupping something small and round in her hands. When he drew close, she held up a tiny silver hand mirror. 'Do you know what this is?' she asked.

"Cael shook his head. Gazing into her eyes, he felt a strange sense of vertigo—he could feel his will slipping away.

'This, sweet child, is a powerful instrument. In the right hands, it can open doors to many worlds,' said the Western Oracle.

"Cael was fascinated by the mirror. He could feel it drawing him in, pulsing, almost as if it were alive. He let down his guard, his hand falling slack from the hilt of his sword. The Western Oracle placed the mirror in his hand and smiled. She leaned forward to kiss his lips, and his eyes closed.

"There was a sickening rip, and Cael came to his senses. Before his eyes, he saw a line of blood part the Western Oracle from the crown of her head to the hem of her flowing robe. Her female form deflated like a fleshy rag doll, each half limp and cast to the side, as a huge pair of hideous lips parted. Row upon row of teeth was revealed, curved like cutlasses toward the throat, preventing escape for any man unfortunate enough to be prey. The entire island shook as the mountainous frogfish rose up, a giant pair of yellow eyes glowing like lanterns as they opened in the rocky hillside on which the temple was built. Cael recoiled in horror, rapidly backing away.

"The Western Oracle laughed mockingly, her voice still musically sweet. 'You do not like my lady puppet?' she asked.

"*A lure,* he thought, his mind reeling madly. *It was a LURE.*

"The beast's grin widened. She cackled, a slushing, throaty sound that threatened Cael's sanity. 'I use my lady puppet to catch lovers! COME TO ME, LOVERBOY!'

"The beast's mouth opened impossibly wide. On the wet, fleshy inside of the mouth, Cael saw the remains of her former lovers—heads with blind eyes, gaping hungry mouths, and reaching arms sprouting from bony shoulders, dissolving flesh stripped and hanging. Each man was planted on the inside of the monster's mouth like a crop in the ground, his rib cage and lower half absorbed by the beast. Not quite alive and not quite dead, the creature's lovers moaned in agony and thirst.

"Cael's hand flashed to his sword. Behind him, he heard the sickening crunch of bones, as the beast's daughters crushed each of his remaining soldiers, ripping out their throats before there was time to scream. Cael tried to block out the slurping sounds of their feeding. There wasn't much time before they came for him, bearing him up to the beast like a murderous gift. He had one chance for escape and one chance only. He drew his silver sword and launched it deep into the beast's throat. She gagged, choking on the poison weapon.

"Then, while she was occupied and the sirens were still feeding, he scooped up the Sign of the Throne, the diadem, and the hand mirror into the strongbox. Carrying the box under one arm, he ran swiftly down what was left of the beach, hiding his steps in the surf.

"Once the sirens had fed, he knew they would come for him. They would search the ship first. It would never sail again, but it was defensible.

"*A reasonable man would barricade himself in the ship, creating a bottleneck, so that when they come, he could pick them off one by one until they finally overpowered him*, he thought. But Cael was not a reasonable man. *I will not give them the pleasure of killing me in my own cursed boat*, he vowed.

"Instead, he crept along the shore silently, until he was behind the enormous beast. With a final, pathetic gag, the Oracle stopped shaking, and the island was still. In death, her body swelled like a bladder, the wound from the sword releasing toxic, flammable gases within her.

"Cael pulled the small leather satchel from around his neck. Inside was the Northern Oracle's potent fire powder wrapped within a woven cloth. With his silver dagger, he made a small slit in the beast's side and poured in the powder. He stuffed the cloth in the tiny wound, sealing it, and created a spark with a bit of flint, lighting the makeshift wick. Then, holding the strongbox against his chest, he dove into the sea and swam for his life.

"On shore, one of the sirens sensed he was gone. She paused from her feeding frenzy and looked up. She tried to alert the others. 'Mother…'

"And then, the beast exploded, rocketing bits of flaming flesh into the air, before they arched back down into the sea. The blast overtook the sirens, reducing them to ash, and flames licked up what little was left of their victims. The marble temple was reduced to sinking rubble, and the ship shattered into millions of splinters, consumed by the fire. The island of the Western Oracle was no more.

"As the blast spread outward, Cael dove deep, hoping the water would shield him. Underwater, the sound of the explosion was magnified, and his ears began to bleed. The force of the blast was so strong, it created a wave that violently lifted him to the surface.

"As the wave crashed over him, he tumbled and rolled downward, hitting rocks and coral as he was dragged along the bottom of the ocean. Somehow he managed to hold onto the strongbox, and when the strength of the wave dissipated, he bobbed to the surface, his body draped over the box, which floated gently.

"He was bruised and battered, and blood flowed from a slash on his forehead and from his burst eardrums. He was spent. He could keep his eyes open no longer. He faded into unconsciousness, his grip on the strongbox slipping. Deep below, several dark figures drifted upward toward his limp body.

"Eyes still closed, Cael first heard the sound of waves. He felt a strange rocking sensation pulsing through his body, as though he were still at sea. He realized he was lying on his back on cool sand, and small remnants of waves were racing up the shore, coursing over his body, lifting him slightly before sliding back into the ocean. He felt refreshed, his wounds already healed.

"He opened his eyes, wondering where he was. A female figure was leaning over him, backlit by the sun, making it difficult to distinguish her features. Cael froze—one of the sirens must have escaped the blast and found him. But if that were true, why was he still in one piece?

"The creature sensed his fear and confusion. 'Do not fear,' she whispered. 'They are all gone and you are safe.'

"Cael sat up. His companion resembled a siren—from the waist up, she was a beautiful woman, and below, she had a tail rather than legs. But there the similarity ended. While a siren was equipped with a serpentine tail and secondary venomous appendages, this mermaid-like creature had more in common with a dolphin. Her tail was a dark, mottled grey, smooth and muscled, punctuated by powerful flukes. Her upper body was strong and smooth as well, although a lighter grey that was mirrored in her eyes. Her hair was snow white and fell to her waist, still wet and slightly tangled.

'Where am I?' asked Cael.

'Not far from home,' the mermaid replied. 'We found you after the explosion that destroyed the monsters. You have been asleep for a great while, so we healed you and carried you here.'

"Cael looked around. 'We?'

"She nodded and gestured out to sea toward a familiar rock archway carved from the waves. Peeking shyly around the boulders were more merpeople.

'Who are you?' he queried.

'My name is Nerine, and I am a daughter of the sea,' she replied. 'My family and I serve the Light. The sirens have preyed on my family for many generations. Now that you have destroyed them, we are free. We give you our thanks.'

'And I thank you for keeping me from drowning,' Cael expressed in gratitude. He reached for the strongbox and checked to make sure its contents were secure.

'What is that?' asked Nerine.

'I am on a quest for the Solas Beir and have been long in completing my mission,' explained Cael. 'Please thank your family for saving me. I shall be forever grateful to you all. And now, I must go home.'

"Nerine nodded. 'Safe travels, my friend. May your journey not have been in vain.'

"Cael collected the strongbox, and with a smile, waved his thanks to Nerine's family.

"Caislucis was not far. He could see the castle overlooking the beach, its clean, white turrets spiraling skyward, perched on the foliage-covered cliff above him. His heart leapt with hope. Only a couple hundred more steps and he would be home. A familiar and ancient stairway was carved into the side of the cliff, twisting and turning, stone steps narrow and worn.

"His mind flashed to a childhood memory, returning to a happier time, before the loss of so many friends, before the darkness that heralded the tyranny of the Kruor um Beir, before the love of his life married his best friend and became queen. He could see the two of them together—a small boy throwing pebbles into the sea and a beautiful little girl with raven colored hair, running from waves that rushed up the sand, chasing them as they retreated; a child without a care in the world. He mourned for that child, for the dark days she could not yet see. 'I am coming, Eulalia,' he whispered. 'You will be home soon.'

"Cael looked down at the strongbox he carried. Maybe there was still time. Maybe he could still save her and her child. With that thought in mind, the last few steps home took no time at all.

"Despite his solemn, worn face and ragged clothes, the sentry standing guard at the castle gate recognized Cael, even from a distance. The soldier dispatched a page to gather the council.

"As Cael entered the grand hall with its towering ivory ceiling of pointed arches and ribbed vaults, two pages greeted him, one holding a tray with food and drink, and the other waiting with a clean, warm robe. They bowed and offered their gifts of welcome. He smiled, but took only the drink. 'Thank you,' he said, 'but my comfort will have to wait.' He dismissed them and turned to address the council.

'Welcome home, Cael,' said Obelia, the oldest member of the council. 'We are glad you have returned safely.' Obelia is like a grandmother to Cael. She has served the Light for centuries. In spite of her many years, she still appears young and vibrant, her dark skin smooth, her golden brown eyes twinkling.

"The other six members of the council nodded their welcome. The council members are diverse in appearance. Gorman, the kingdom's chief historian and librarian, is a tiny man with indigo skin, violet eyes, and a tuft of frizzy green hair sprouting from the center of his head. On the other hand, there's Erela, a regal and towering figure, a dignified woman with the face of a warrior and the wings of an angel. Despite their differences, however, they were united in their purpose.

"Cael bowed. 'Thank you, Obelia. I give my thanks to the council for gathering on such short notice. I have recovered the Sign of the Throne, but at a great price. All of the brave men who offered their service for this mission have perished. I am the only survivor.'

"Cael studied the faces of the council members. Some wore expressions of shock, and others, grief. The men who had sacrificed their lives were their fathers, their husbands, their brothers, their sons. No one on the council was untouched by the magnitude of the loss.

"For those who live as long as the people of the Light, who rest in the comfort of being nearly immortal, such loss is rare. But loss has become increasingly common since the wars against the Kruorumbrae. Tynan Tierney's reign of terror has taken its toll on my people.

"The men who followed Cael in search of the Solas Beir's sigil, his closest friends, knew the risk. They went willingly. Cael told the council of their sacrifice, a selfless gift to his people that would be legendary throughout the generations.

"As much as he respected Ardal and understood the king's reasons for entrusting the Sign of the Throne to the Western Oracle, he couldn't help but feel angry and resentful about the loss of so many friends. The fact that the sign had been protected from Tierney these many years did little to ease his pain, or the pain he felt for the families of his friends. He vowed that their great sacrifice would not be for naught.

"In his appeal to the council, he emphasized the need to make haste in getting the Sign to the queen so the Solas Beir could return. Artan was their only hope for a victory against Tierney's forces of darkness. There was nothing to debate—the council came to a decision quickly.

"Cael summoned Fergal. The tiny amphibious faery would bear the responsibility for carrying the sigil to me and delivering one of the halves to my son for his protection. The crown and the silver hand mirror would be placed in a vault to await the return of the Solas Beir. Fergal valiantly accepted his mission, and he and Cael proceeded to the pool of light that was the portal's entrance.

"Cael wished Fergal well. 'Good journey, my friend. Thank you for helping our queen and our people.'

"Fergal disappeared beneath the surface of the water, carrying the two halves of the Sign of the Throne, which seemed enormous in his tiny arms. He was well equipped for the task, slipping through the minuscule rift in the portal, and delivering the sign to me without incident."

At this point in her story, Eulalia paused, retrieving something from the folds of her gown. It was half of a silver nautilus shell. It was lovely—its beauty was in the simplicity of a perfect spiral.

"That's it, isn't it?" Abby asked.

"Yes. This is the Sign of the Throne. It is an object of great power that will allow my son to return. I do not say lightly that you must protect it with your life. You must wear it around your neck at all times, and it will protect you from the Darkness as long as you guard it. Only one who bears the Light and one who walks in dreams can join the two halves. Once they are joined, you will be able to open the portal together."

Eulalia placed the sign in Abby's hand. To Abby's surprise, the shell seemed alive, pulsing with silver-blue light as it touched her palm. It was almost as if all the magic and mystery of the universe had been encased within this one small object, exuding potency beyond definition. Abby unclasped the silver chain of the necklace she always wore and slid the seashell pendant onto the chain. As she refastened the clasp, she felt the subtle pulsing of the shell fall into rhythm with her own heartbeat. She looked questioningly at Eulalia, who nodded knowingly.

"The power of the Light is revealed in the Sign. The Light *will* protect you. And I think you have already had a taste of the need for protection against the Darkness," Eulalia said.

Abby's thoughts returned to the shadow boy she had seen in the Buchans' home. She looked at Eulalia. "You know about the creature I encountered?"

"Yes, Abby. I saw what you experienced in my dreams," Eulalia said, returning to her seat on the garden stool. "You are right to be afraid. Your life was very much in danger from the Blood Shadows that evening. The boy you saw is Malden, one of Tierney's closest disciples. He is sadistic and mischievous, and very much enjoys invoking fear. It inspires him—he feeds on it. That is probably the reason why he only toyed with you and did not attack. Had you encountered another of Tierney's followers, Calder, you probably would not have survived. Although Calder is loyal to Tierney, he has a reputation for being impulsive and unpredictably violent. You should avoid him at all costs.

"For now, if you encounter anyone who serves the Darkness, crossing the boundaries of Newcastle Beach should offer additional protection. However, if the Darkness gains strength, not even the stone circle will be able to contain it."

"How do we stop the Darkness?"

"You are the key, the one who can reach David, who can remind him of who he is. Connect with him, and help him remember. You must convince him to come to me, and then we can restore the portal."

"But what can I say to remind him?"

"You will know what to say when the time is right," Eulalia said. "Trust yourself, and let go of your fear. The Light will guide you."

The Force, Abby, use the Force, Abby thought. *Alrighty then, Obi-Wan. Sure thing.* "So, uh…not to be skeptical, but how is it there's this window to a whole other world, and nobody in Santa Linda knows about it?"

Eulalia laughed. "People in Newcastle Beach know about it. Or at least they used to."

"What does that mean?"

"In days of old, there were many portals all over your world. The evidence still exists within the mythology of every human society—your Egyptians with their half-man, half-animal deities, or your Greeks with the sea monsters, Scilla and Charybdis."

"Wait—Scilla and Charybdis? From Homer's, *Odyssey*?" Abby asked.

Eulalia nodded. "Yes."

"But that's just a story."

"Are you certain of this?"

"Of course—it's fiction. It's just a myth," Abby insisted.

"Is it? No, it is based on truth," Eulalia corrected her. "Why do you suppose it took Odysseus so long to return home? He slipped through a portal in the sea. Those monsters were from my world, not yours."

Abby was speechless.

Eulalia continued. "Modern humans may discount such creatures as myths, but long ago, people understood that they were very real, and sometimes they could be found in your world. If you doubt, you need only look at how the lore in your world connects between different cultures. There are a great many similarities between the creatures, even if they are called by different names. It was not just that humans traveled the earth sharing the same stories, or even that they had similar fears. It was the creatures who were the same, and they came from the same place. In the case of monsters like the ones Odysseus encountered, old seafaring maps bear the evidence. Humans did mark their existence—they marked it very well, and gave warning for others who might pass that way."

"So you mean like those antique maps that have sea monsters and mermaids on them?" Abby asked.

"Yes."

"But with the mermaids—it's just—what I've always heard is that sailors didn't really see women with fish tails, they saw seals, or manatees, or whatever. And I guess they had been at sea too long or were really, *really* drunk…"

119

"And have *you* ever seen a manatee?" Eulalia asked.

"Yes—they have one at the university's aquarium," Abby said. "They're huge! And not terribly attractive," she added, laughing.

"Exactly. Do you really think someone would mistake *that* for a beautiful woman? That is the most ridiculous thing I have ever heard," Eulalia laughed. "I also realize, however, that belief in creatures such as mermaids would be very frightening for some humans. I daresay it would shake the very foundation of their world. Sometimes it is easier for people to discount than to believe."

"I see your point," Abby nodded. "But then, where did the monsters go? I mean, humans have pretty much explored the entire planet, and with cameras you'd think there would be *some* kind of evidence." Abby paused, thinking back to how she felt telling Cassandra what was happening to her, worrying that Cassandra's skepticism would keep her from believing the story. She realized she was sitting with her arms crossed. Abby didn't want Eulalia to think she wasn't open to belief, so she uncrossed her arms and placed them in her lap. When she looked up again, she found Eulalia watching her and hiding a small, amused smile, as if she understood what Abby was thinking. Abby sincerely hoped the queen could not read her mind.

"There is a reason for an absence of modern evidence," Eulalia explained. "Long ago, both those who served the Light and those who walked in Darkness traversed freely through portals all over your world. But as the Darkness grew more powerful, the thirst of the Kruorumbrae became insatiable; the balance shifted. That shift in power was paid for by the humans—with their lives. It was not just that the Blood

Shadows preyed on a few humans to survive. They became greedy. Some Shadows claimed to be gods, demanding human sacrifice. And, for the promise of power, there were those who were willing to pacify them, offering up their human brothers and sisters in droves. It was a time of great fear and bloodshed. A few opposed the slaughter and rebelled, but they were indiscriminant hunters, killing those in Darkness *and* those in the Light. Frightened men are quick to kill. To protect both the humans and those who serve the Light, the Solas Beir began closing portals."

"In that case, isn't fixing your portal a bad idea? Won't the Shadows be able to travel freely again?"

"No, not this time. We will not open all of the portals, and those we open will be guarded closely. The portals themselves were not evil. Those places where our worlds intersected were magical places, hidden way stations where many who served the Light chose to abide. Humans who lived near those places soon learned that they were prosperous places, places where they were blessed by the presence of my people.

"Long ago in your world, there were two such humans, twin brothers who loved to explore seaside caves carved by wind and waves into the cliffs near their home. In one of these caves, they found a silver hand mirror that had the remarkable ability to transport a person from one place to another. At first, their journeys were short, no more than a trip from the cave to a faery ring in the forest outside their village. But soon, they found that they were able to travel greater distances within their world, which proved very profitable. They could journey from their homeland in Scotland to anywhere in your world in seconds, bringing back valuable goods, mostly from the Mediterranean, Africa, and Asia.

"Without a restraint on time or the perils of moving goods by ship, they had an advantage over any importer who had to rely on more conventional methods of trade. They were young and enterprising, and they longed for adventure, so they traveled the world and became very wealthy. Eventually, they immigrated to the place you know as Santa Linda, together with their younger sister. Although they were already very rich, they profited from others who had dreams of finding gold.

"And still, even in their great success, their wanderlust was insatiable. It was only a matter of time before their ever-widening circle of travel expanded so much that they broke through the membrane separating our worlds. They were welcome among those in the Light, but they were warned as well. The mirror had a dual nature—while it initially showered them with good fortune, sustained use would reveal its darker side.

"You see, my people had encountered the mirror before. It was created by the ancient one who first dwelt in Darkness and took pleasure in the destruction of others. The mirror, like the Sign, is alive in its own way and testifies to the nature of the one who made it. It seduces the traveler, and once the traveler falls under its spell of addiction, the mirror displays rather nasty tendencies."

"What kind of tendencies?" Abby asked.

"The kind that lulls the traveler into a false sense of security, that he or she has control over the destination. Then, once the traveler gains this confidence, the mirror abandons the traveler in some savage land ruled by teeth and claws."

Abby cringed.

Eulalia shrugged. "You have a saying in your world: there is no such thing as a free lunch. Correct?"

The familiar saying sounded weird coming from Eulalia.

"Yes…" Abby acknowledged.

"Well, the same principle applies. Nothing is acquired without a price."

"I guess so. What happened to those men?"

"The Solas Beir and the brothers made a covenant. He asked them to stop using the mirror out of fear that they would create a rift in time and space that would allow the Darkness to regain power in both our worlds. Instead, the Solas Beir would create another portal between our two worlds, and the men's family would be charged with guarding it, in exchange for continued prosperity. Under the guidance of the Solas Beir, the brothers commissioned the construction of two mansions, side by side, one for each brother, and the stone circle was laid, establishing what has become Newcastle Beach.

"The first brother, Thaddeus, was able to forget about the mirror. He went on to live a long life, and had many descendents, whose collective wealth now spans the globe. Eventually the mansion was deeded to the community and became the inn.

"The other brother, Samuel, met a very different fate. Perhaps it was because his home, the very place in which we stand, was the one housing the portal. Samuel traveled frequently between worlds, and instead of satisfying his curious nature, his journeys fueled his desire for discovery. At night, he could feel the mirror calling to him, seducing him to break his promise to the Solas Beir, even though it was locked away by his sister, Adelae.

"One night he could take it no more—he forced Adelae to give him the mirror, and with a mad wink, he disappeared. Unfortunately, it was then that the mirror chose to betray him. He found himself at the feet of the Western Oracle, who took the mirror for her own and consumed him as a lover."

"Ewwww. So the half-dead men Cael saw, the ones in her mouth...one of them was..."

"Yes. One of them was Samuel Buchan."

"Buchan? Like Riordan and Cassandra?" Abby asked, her mouth dropping open in shock. *It's just another coincidence,* she told herself.

Eulalia nodded. "Yes, from the same clan."

"Do they know about all this?"

"No. They know little about the family's true history. The connection with my people has remained hidden from all but a select few from the Buchan lineage, most of whom have since passed on. However, there is the matter of the property itself. Currently, ownership of the mansion lies with Riordan's aunt, but when she dies, it will fall to him."

"I'm guessing she knows that, and that is why she is so nasty to him," Abby said.

"It is possible."

"But why hasn't she done anything with this place? You know, fixed it up? Don't you need someone to be living here, guarding things?"

"Someone *was* living here, up until the time the portal was destroyed."

"Who?"

"Adelae. She blamed herself for Samuel's disappearance, so she waited at the portal every night until her death. And while her visits to my world extended her years beyond the usual life expectancy for humans, her exposure to the mirror and her own guilt drove her mad. Quite mad. She became but another victim of the mirror.

"She died the night the portal was destroyed. When Lucia smashed the mirrored portal in the ballroom, the earth shook, and part of this mansion collapsed. Adelae was crushed in the rubble. That, in itself, was a sad end to a tragic life. But what is worse is that, in her madness, Adelae had distanced herself from her family. There was no one to mourn her. She had become a ghost of herself in life, and in death, her tale lived on through the stories children tell," Eulalia concluded.

"The lady in white haunting the mansion? I guess I assumed you were the inspiration for that story, given your situation," Abby noted.

"No, that story predates my haunting of this place, although it is a story I use to my advantage to keep humans away. It is an unhappy coincidence that we should share similar fates marred by evil."

"So when did the Shadows come to Newcastle Beach? Or were they always here?" Abby queried.

"Those who serve the Darkness took up residence in this neighborhood between the time the portal was built and the time it was destroyed," Eulalia said. "But evil has always existed in your world—humans can be just as ruthless as the Kruorumbrae.

"However, my people taught the humans how to keep this particular genus of evil at bay. Silver, as you already know, can be an effective weapon. Sea salt or even common table salt can also be helpful in creating circles of protection or blocking passage from windows and doors. And, while my people are satisfied with sustenance similar to the foods in your world, the feeding habits of those who dwell in Darkness are more complex. They feast on blood and flesh, but they are also parasites, and they feed off the psychic energy and fear of humans and those in the Light. The victim falls into a depressive state, and may develop suicidal or homicidal tendencies. As a preventative measure, gifts are presented to appease the appetites of these predators. Not any gift will do. It is tradition to offer milk and honey, as these foods are more potent than others, having been obtained from creatures who expended great energy in producing them."

"It's like the promised land," Abby whispered to herself. She thought about what Riordan had said about his aunt and her offerings. It made so much sense now.

"What was that?" asked Eulalia.

"Nothing—just that this place is literally a land flowing with milk and honey," Abby explained.

"I suppose it is. As the borderland between parallel worlds, it has been a promised land for many. And yet, there are some who have been less fortunate," Eulalia noted.

"Like yourself."

Eulalia nodded.

"So all these years, living in this place—how is it that you were—" Abby searched for the right word, "sustained?"

Eulalia smiled. "I've had friends. You met a few of them."

Abby raised an eyebrow in question.

"The ravens have been my constant companions, guarding me and bringing me food. Granted, they never brought a feast, but it has been enough for me to survive."

"Are they faeries?" Abby asked, wide-eyed.

Eulalia shook her head. "No, they are just very intelligent, perceptive animals with a talent for transcending the boundaries between worlds. Some say ravens can even pass through the veil of death, but this I have not seen. When the portal was destroyed here, they were no longer able to cross to my world, transcendent though they may be. Aside from visits from Fergal and dreamwalking with Cael, the only contact I've had with someone from my world is with Nysa, a water sprite who lives in the reflecting pool. She has been a loyal and comforting friend."

Abby's mouth dropped open. "No way. There's a *mermaid* in the pond?"

Eulalia laughed. "She is actually a nixie—similar to a mermaid in that she is a water faery, but different in that she is a smaller shape-shifter. She can appear as a small girl or as a golden-orange koi. Sometimes in the middle of changing forms, she gets distracted and ends up half girl, half fish, and it is anyone's guess which half will be the girl. Would you like to meet her?"

Abby's eyes lit up. "Of course!"

"All right. But there are a few things you should know about nixies. Over the years, there has been a great deal of confusion in the human world regarding the nomenclature of the water faeries—that is, between nixies, mermaids, and their predatory cousins, the sirens. Nixies have gotten a bad reputation for singing songs and luring humans to a death by drowning. Understandably, nixies tend to be rather sensitive about this, since only sirens have such dark tendencies. Also, you should note that appearances are deceiving—she may look like a small child, but she is almost one hundred years older than you."

"Duly noted," Abby assured her.

"Good. Do you have a coin with you?"

Abby searched her pockets. "Um—all I have is a penny."

"Is it shiny?"

Abby nodded. "Yes."

"Excellent—she will like that," Eulalia smiled. "Drop it into the pool. When she hears it hit the bottom, she will swim up the plumbing that connects the reflecting pool with this one."

Abby did as she was told and waited. She watched the coin splash as it hit the water, drifting down to rest on the tile bottom of the pool. Then, she heard the metallic rattle of the grate at the end of the pool, and a noisy splash as something broke the surface of the water. Abby could see something orange streaking through the water toward them, and suddenly, there she was, standing beside Eulalia, shaking off a few drops of water, and proudly holding up the penny.

"Got it!" the nixie exclaimed. "Shiny!" She happily admired her find.

Abby's first impression of the water sprite was that she was a Kewpie doll come to life—she had a sweet baby face with round, rosy cheeks, bright amber eyes, full lips, and the body of a chubby cherub, including a little potbelly stomach sticking out. She stood about a foot high, bigger than she was as a fish. Her skin had an orange tinge, and her cropped hair, in varying shades of orange and yellow, resembled a dandelion fluff set aflame. She wore a simple, one-shouldered shift of a silky texture that made Abby think of water lilies. Around her neck was a collection of other treasures she had found— several lost keys, a metal teaspoon, and a ring with an oversized plastic jewel, most likely acquired from a gumball machine and lost by some curious child peeking through the estate's gate. Her large golden eyes studied the penny, looking for a way to string it with the rest of her collection. She shrugged, apparently giving up, and placed it in some unseen pocket in her short, white dress.

Eulalia made the introductions. "Abby, this is my friend Nysa. Nysa, this is Abby, the c'aislingaer we have been waiting for."

"I'm very pleased to meet you," Abby said formally, unsure of the most appropriate way to greet a water sprite.

Nysa beamed. "Nice to meet you. Thanks for the shiny." Her eyes grew unbelievably wider as she noticed Abby's necklace. "Ooooh, pretty," she cooed.

Abby touched the silver seashell. "The Sign of the Throne," she explained. "It *is* beautiful, isn't it?"

"Yes," the nixie agreed. She pointed to the silver cross that rested against Abby's skin beside the seashell. "That one, too."

"My cross pendant? I like it, too—it's always brought me comfort."

Nysa smiled and nodded.

Abby chuckled—she understood how the nixie could be mistaken for a child. There was a sweet innocence about her, an aura of trust and goodwill. She looked from Eulalia to Nysa, noting the way they looked at each other with adoration, suddenly gaining insight: in spite of Eulalia's admonition to Abby regarding the nixie's age, the queen seemed to have adopted the water sprite as a surrogate child for the one she'd lost.

"Would you...would you like to have my cross pendant?" Abby offered. "It's silver," she added, looking to

Eulalia, concerned that the nixie might find the precious metal offensive. Eulalia nodded her approval.

Nysa grinned with joy and clapped her hands, in no way containing her excitement. Abby unclasped the chain around her neck and removed the pendant, leaving the seashell centered on the chain. She presented the silver cross to the nixie, who eagerly added it to her collection, not at all concerned about the fact that it was silver. Maybe the thing with silver was like an allergy, and there were different degrees of sensitivity to it. Maybe the Shadows were more allergic than creatures of Light, who seemed to be able to touch it without difficulty. Abby thought about how Eulalia's husband had been killed. Those in the Light only seemed to have a problem if silver entered the bloodstream, she concluded.

⁺₃⁺₃⁺₃

"The hour grows late," Eulalia noted, nodding toward the windows.

The light had changed and Abby realized that it was almost sunset. She had spent all afternoon here and had forgotten about her original mission of taking a walk on the beach. So much for clearing her head—her mind was buzzing with an overwhelming load of new things to think about, new questions to ask. But at least she had some answers now.

"I must finish telling you about the Sign before the light is gone," continued Eulalia. "Those who dwell in Darkness are always stronger at night."

Abby grimaced.

"Do not fear. For now, the Sign, even half of it, is strong enough to keep you safe, and I will equip you with an escort of ravens for your walk home, just for your peace of mind."

"Okay," Abby responded, trying to sound brave, but unable to put the shadow boy out of her mind. Personally, she wasn't sure her raven bodyguards would cut it, but she wasn't about to share that thought out loud.

"The last piece of the story is about how we were able to get the other half of the sign to my son. It is really Fergal's tale."

"Mine too," chimed Nysa, settling in comfortably at Abby's feet.

"Yours too." Eulalia smiled at the nixie, and then grew serious. "The ravens had known for some time where David was living. Secretly they watched over him, bringing me news. Once Fergal brought the Sign through the portal, we had to devise a way for him to get it to David undetected. We almost succeeded.

"I separated the pieces—we could not risk both halves falling into the wrong hands. With help from the ravens, Fergal would fly over the Corbin house, landing outside David's second story window, which was open just enough for Fergal to squeeze through. Then, he could silently slip over to David and present him with the sigil of the Solas Beir.

"It had been many years since I lost my son, but I was confident that once he saw the Sign, his memory would be restored and he would come to me. With the element of stealth on our side, we hoped to avoid attention from the continual stream of stray cats that patrolled the Corbin property, Kruorumbrae preventing us from making contact with David—keeping him blind to the magic around him. It was a good plan, but we underestimated the Shadows and their power over him.

"One raven lifted Fergal into the sky, holding him under the arms. A second carried the sign, since it was too heavy for Fergal to carry such a distance. Instead, Fergal carried a silver sewing needle, as a precaution in case he should be discovered. Once on the roof, the pair of ravens kept watch while the tiny faery slipped in through the window.

"At first, things went smoothly. Fergal climbed down the curtain to the bedroom floor without being discovered. But then, the shadow cats sensed something, and they raised the alarm.

"A legion of Kruorumbrae began crawling up the walls of the house toward the ravens, and dozens entered the house, racing up the stairs and down the hall toward David's room. Their combined darkness gained strength and gathered silently behind Fergal as they blended into one giant feline. The creature was as large as a panther, and as dark and empty as a black hole, sucking the light from the room. Evil eyes glowed a dull red in the creature's skull, and a set of needle-sharp teeth flashed white, in contrast to the darkness of its hide.

"With an unearthly scream, it slammed into the window, shutting it with a loud crash, cutting off Fergal's escape, even as he ascended the sheets to the foot of the bed. The ravens frantically beat against the window, trying to find a way inside to protect David and Fergal. Soon, they were too busy to help anyone—the shadow cats reached the roof top and launched an attack, pouncing from every angle. The ravens took flight, circling just out of reach, helpless. They could only watch Fergal's plight from a distance.

"Undeterred by the menacing growl of the creature stalking him, Fergal bravely ran the length of David's limp, sleeping body to his head and slipped the sigil under David's pillow before the monster could see it. Then he turned to face the shadow beast, brandishing the sewing needle like a sword. As the creature leapt onto the bed, Fergal jumped to the floor and slipped out of reach under the bed, running as fast as his little legs could carry him toward the door. The beast followed, circling the bed, trying to reach the door first to cut off Fergal's escape.

"David started in his sleep, on the edge of waking. He moaned and opened his eyes, and then sat bolt upright in bed, staring at the shadow beast crouched low on the floor near the door, ready to pounce. A scream caught in his throat as the monster turned its glowing, blood-red eyes on him.

"Fergal came to a dead stop—he had to get the beast to follow him. He thrust the needle into the creature's paw and it howled in agony, instantly fragmenting into many smaller felines. This cost Fergal valuable time, but the shadow cats were reminded that he was their original target; they forgot about David and the Sign of the Throne.

"Fergal resumed his flight, leaping from the top step to the banister, zipping to the bottom of the stairs. The Kruorumbrae were close on his heels—he could feel hot breath on his back, stinking like sulfur and sour meat.

"Fergal sped toward the back door, sliding through the tiny crack between the door and the floor. The shadow cats burst through the door as if nothing were there, losing density in the mere second they passed through the wood, and becoming menacingly solid on the other side. On the rooftop, the shadow cats lost interest in the ravens and poured like toxic, black oil down the sides of the house, silky and evil. Fergal was surrounded. The shadows savored the moment, ready to strike, confident that their numbers would yield victory.

"As the Kruorumbrae closed in, the ravens dived from the roof in a dead drop. Rocketing down, the first raven, Brarn, dispersed the gang in an explosion of hissing and fur. His mate, Eithne, followed close behind and scooped up Fergal. Then, a shadow cat leapt up and collided with her, knocking her out of the sky. She lost her grasp on Fergal and dropped him. Fergal did not fall far, but he lost the needle as he tumbled down.

"The cats overpowered Eithne, sucking the energy from her body. Weaponless, Fergal stood frozen in horror as he saw the Light leave the raven's eyes. There was a terrible void in the moment the bird's spirit left and her body went still.

"The feeding frenzy provided a long enough distraction for Brarn to circle back and rescue Fergal from an identical fate. Unfortunately, Fergal did not escape unscathed. As the raven bore him upward, one of the shadow cats reared up and slashed at him, shredding his back to ribbons. By the time Brarn landed beside the reflecting pool, Fergal's condition was serious, his breathing shallow and labored because of the pain. If not for Nysa, he would have surely succumbed to his injuries."

"I helped Ferggie," Nysa explained in a serious tone.

"Yes, you did," continued Eulalia, nodding approvingly at the nixie. "Nysa carried Fergal in her arms and dove into the pool. She was small enough to slip through the tiny opening in the portal. Once through, she was able to get the attention of a guard for assistance in taking Fergal to the pool of healing. He made a full recovery, and he and Nysa gave a report to Cael and the council.

"Nysa then returned to me, and Fergal resumed his post delivering messages between worlds. We could not recover the fallen raven, and her mate mourned for many months, flying over the place where the Shadows took her. Even now, he searches for her, though she was lost long ago."

"Brarn is still alive? I didn't know ravens lived that long," Abby mused.

"Yes. He is old, but he is still with us. He is the raven you rescued today."

Abby pictured the raven she had held in her arms, who led her through the labyrinth. She had not realized that ravens mated for life, or that they were capable of such empathy—she could not imagine his grief. "Poor Brarn—how terrible for him. So then, what happened to David? Does he remember anything?"

"Unfortunately, no. Although he found the Sign of the Throne the next morning and instinctively kept it hidden and safe, his mind was too clouded to recognize it for what it was or to remember anything about our world. In a way, this has helped protect the sign. Because David did not recognize the sign as an object of power, the Kruorumbrae did not realize the significance of Fergal's delivery. They assumed that the faery's mission was to talk with David, and they were confident that he failed. They have been so successful at keeping David in a state of oblivion these many years that they have become arrogant and complacent. It is my hope that this will be their undoing."

"And that's where I come in, isn't it?" Abby reasoned, gaining sudden insight into her role. "I'm just a regular, ordinary girl. They don't see me as a threat at all."

Eulalia smiled. "You are anything but ordinary, but yes. That is the plan. Their magic cannot bar you from accessing David, and yet, with luck, they will entirely underestimate you."

Abby nodded, appreciating for the first time her position as a perpetual wallflower.

"A note of caution—you must be very, very careful whom you trust. The Darkness takes many forms—not everyone who appears to be a friend will be. Remember, the Blood Shadows have the ability to steal a human body and appear as that person. And as time grows short, they will get stronger and take more extreme measures."

Abby felt a prickle as the hair on the back of her neck stood up. She nodded in understanding, contemplating the implications. "Got it."

"Good. Now, go home before it gets too dark. You will see David very soon—make the most of your time with him. Trust yourself and follow the signs. You will know what to say when the time is right. He needs to trust you enough to come here, so that together you can use your halves of the Sign to open the portal. His twenty-third birthday is in twelve days, so we must hurry."

"Wait—twelve days?" Abby did a quick calculation. "That's just two days after the Autumn Ball. With all due respect, if you haven't been able to get through to him all this time, how...?"

"I know. Time is short and it seems impossible."

"Well, yes," Abby replied.

"I have been imprisoned here a long time, Abby. These years in your world have made me tired and weak. But I have learned a great many things in that time. One is that I should trust my dreams, and I have seen that this time we will win. The other thing I have learned is that even when I was in my lowest, most desperate state in this place, the universe has provided for me. It is when things seem impossible that miracles happen."

SIGNS

That night, Abby recorded the afternoon's events in her journal and made a few quick sketches of Brarn, Nysa, and the Sign of the Throne. She felt overwhelmed. Given all she had heard in the past hours, she was certain that either she wouldn't be able to sleep at all, or that she would be haunted by nightmares of bloodthirsty sirens and stalking Shadows, all with evil smiles full of gleaming, white teeth.

Fortunately, neither was the case, and she slept peacefully. It was the first time since that initial dream about David and the Shadows that she did not dream at all. *Guess that's how my brain reacts to stress,* she thought as she got ready for school. She felt refreshed and strong.

After school, she headed to the Buchan house. Both Cassandra and Riordan had the night off from teaching, but instead of going out on a date, they had invited Abby over for dinner to sample the world-famous Buchan clan version of manicotti formaggio. She'd been expecting a traditional Scottish dish, given Riordan's love of his culture, but then again, she had learned to expect the unexpected from both Riordan and Cassandra. Neither erred toward the conventional, and she loved that about them.

Although Abby was looking forward to an evening with the Buchan family, she felt nervous. A battle was being waged in her mind. She had agreed to keep Riordan and Cassandra posted if anything strange happened, and yesterday had been beyond strange. It had been supernatural, magical, horrifying, and enlightening. She knew they would be interested in hearing about her afternoon with Eulalia and Nysa, entranced even, and yet she kept hearing Eulalia's warning over and over in her mind. Could she trust them?

Abby knocked on the door and Cassandra answered, wearing an apron dotted with tomato sauce.

"Welcome!" Cassandra grinned. She held out a wooden spoon spilling over with the ricotta and mozzarella cheese filling for the manicotti. "Here—try this."

"Hi there," Abby grinned back. She tasted the filling. "Wow—that's *heaven*."

"I know! If ever I'm on death row and have to choose a last meal, this is it," Cassandra cooed.

"Remind me again—why would you be on death row?" Abby asked.

"Well, you know," Cassandra smiled, "it's good to have a plan, just in case."

Abby laughed. Yes, she could trust Cassandra. Even so, she would take it slow. No need to share everything yet.

"Come on back—we're just busy in the kitchen." Cassandra flitted off with her usual energy, grinning like an imp. Abby couldn't help but find herself at ease, putting the mental battle to rest for the moment.

Riordan was absorbed in the task of stuffing the manicotti, and like Cassandra, he was covered in blossoms of red sauce. The white chef's apron he'd donned bore the brunt of the damage, but Abby could see a smudge of red on his chin and on the kilt he wore, and there was a dollop of cheese filling on the rolled-up cuff of his white long-sleeved shirt. He smiled a hello to Abby and returned to his job, intent on getting the recipe right. Cassandra had told Abby that for Riordan, cooking this meal was serious business—apparently the pride of the entire Buchan clan depended on it. The kids were at the dining room table, Ciaran reading from a picture book to the younger two, who chattered with excitement as the young sage imparted knowledge.

Cassandra drizzled sauce over a finished pan of stuffed manicotti. "Abby, do you mind setting the table?"

"Sure, I'd be happy to," Abby replied, turning to the kitchen cabinet to pull out dishes.

"Thanks—hey, pretty necklace. Is that new?" Cassandra paused en route to placing the pan in the oven.

"Uh, yeah," Abby said, running her fingers over the silver seashell. "It is." She was going to have to share her news soon—Cassandra was observant, and she would know Abby was hiding something. "A, uh, friend gave it to me."

Cassandra appeared oblivious to Abby's inner dilemma. "Very nice—it's the perfect example of a logarithmic spiral."

"Oh. Thank you." Abby had no idea what she was talking about.

"Remember our friend Jakob Bernoulli and his thoughts on synchronicity?" Cassandra asked.

Vaguely, Abby thought. But that wasn't the answer Cassandra was looking for. "Yes...?"

"Well, guess what? He was *obsessed* with spirals like that," Cassandra said.

"Wow," Abby said. "That's an interesting coincidence."

"Synchronicity," Cassandra corrected. "He called it *spira mirabilis,* the marvelous spiral, because it occurs so frequently in nature—sea shells, hurricanes, galaxies, the approach of a hawk to its prey..."

"Hmmm," Abby murmured thoughtfully, one finger stroking the shell. She could feel it pulsing in response.

Cassandra was in her professor role now. "With each turn, the size of the spiral increases, but its shape remains constant. Some scholars even saw it as a sign of the divine, since its proportions are equal to phi, the golden ratio. That is a geometric relationship often found in nature, art, architecture, et cetera, et cetera. It's associated with perfection and beauty. Have you ever seen Leonardo da Vinci's drawing, *The Vitruvian Man*? You know—the drawing with the man in a circle and square, his arms and legs spread out?"

Abby nodded. "Oh, yes, I've seen that one."

"Well, that drawing is a study of symmetry and proportion in an ideal human figure. The golden ratio can even be found in the human body," Cassandra said. "Pretty amazing, no?"

"Fascinating."

"Well said," Cassandra noted, smiling. "It has been a source of fascination for scholars for centuries. In fact, Bernoulli was so amazed by the phenomenon that he chose a logarithmic spiral for his gravestone, accompanied by the motto, *Eadem mutata resurgo*, which means, 'Changed and yet the same, I rise again.'"

"Wow—that is very cool," Abby said.

"Very. Although, the stonemason made a mistake and used an Archimedean spiral instead. I'm sure that made Bernoulli turn in his grave," Cassandra added solemnly.

Not wanting to appear irreverent, Abby simply nodded. While she did not share Cassandra's manic love of mathematics, she could appreciate that the Sign of the Throne represented something greater than she knew, something that spoke of the divine.

Abby's thoughts were interrupted by the ringing of the doorbell.

Cassandra looked at the door and then down at the pan she was still holding. "Oops, guess I forgot to put this in the oven. I'll take care of this if you'll get the door."

Abby shook her head and laughed at Cassandra's absentmindedness. "Nooo problem, Professor." Smiling to herself, she trotted over to the door and opened it.

David Corbin stood in front of her.

Seeing her smile, he smiled back. "Hello, Abby. Is Aunt Moira here?"

Abby was so caught off guard by David's sudden appearance that it took her a full second to remember who Moira was and that he was somehow connected to her. "Oh! Of course. Please, come in, and I'll let her know you're here." Abby gestured to the living room and turned toward the kitchen, almost colliding with Cassandra, who had emerged to greet their visitor.

"David," Cassandra said warmly. "How sweet of you to pay Aunt Moira a visit. I'm sure she will be happy to see you. Abby—why don't you keep David entertained, and I'll get Moira."

"Oh," Abby said. "Sure."

Cassandra disappeared down the hallway, leaving Abby and David to stare awkwardly at each other.

"So..." Abby began. She racked her brain, desperately searching for something to say, and drew a complete blank. It was all his fault. He looked amazing, standing there in his leather jacket and jeans, his blue eyes burning into hers.

"So?" David smiled, waiting.

Abby put her hands in her jean pockets. "So, I guess I'm supposed to keep you entertained."

He nodded. "Guess so."

And it's going very *well so far,* Abby thought. "So, um, that's really nice of you to visit your aunt. I'm sure she has missed you."

"Technically, she's not my aunt," David said.

"Oh?"

"She's been a part of my life forever," he replied, "but we're not actually related."

"I see." Abby paused, unsure of where to go next with the conversation. David was not being terribly helpful either. "Well, I imagine she will want to hear all about your trip. You were in the South Pacific?"

"Yes, in Thailand and Australia," David said.

"And what was your favorite part?"

"Hmmm, good question," he said. "It was all beautiful and amazing, but I guess I'd have to say diving off the Great Barrier Reef. That was incredible—there was just so much life down there."

"Wow—what did you see?" Abby asked.

"More than I would have imagined," David reminisced. "Sea turtles, feather stars, lion fish, sharks—"

She stared at him, widening her eyes. "Sharks?"

"Just little ones on the reef," David said.

"Define *little*," Abby said.

"Black-tip reef sharks, maybe four or five feet long—no big deal," David said.

"Four or five feet? I'm like, five foot seven—that would be a *big* deal to me."

David laughed. "Well, they're not really a threat to divers. They tend to keep their distance. Anyway, I enjoyed that so much that I went on a cage diving expedition with great whites."

"No way."

"Way." David grinned. He seemed to be enjoying the look of shock on Abby's face.

"*Why* would you do that?" she asked, incredulous.

"Why *wouldn't* I do that?"

"Um, let's see, where do I start?" she asked, putting her hands on her hips.

David chuckled. "It's not as scary as you might think. Sure, they're these huge, powerful creatures—"

"With a reputation for eating people..."

"That *is* a consideration," he conceded. "But they are also beautiful and amazing. You just have to stay away from the bitey end and try not to look like prey."

"Oh, is that all?" Abby asked, raising her eyebrows.

"Actually, yes," David said, nodding. "I mean, they cruise by the cage and check you out, but they don't automatically attack you. They're curious, not ruthless. When they attack, they are just doing what they were built to do. And they don't attack people that often."

"No big deal." Abby shook her head in disbelief. *This boy is crazy. Cute, but crazy.*

David laughed. "Have you ever traveled abroad, Abby?"

She frowned. "I've never had the opportunity."

"Well, if you ever do, don't be afraid to seize the day," David said. "Travel opens you up to new perspectives, new opportunities that you might never ordinarily enjoy."

"I'm not *afraid* of taking risks," Abby protested. "I just don't see the point of putting my life in danger for no good reason."

"I didn't put my life in danger," David argued, stepping closer to her and staring into her eyes. "It's just when you immerse yourself in another culture, you let go of some of your former inhibitions. The thing about Australia is that there are so many things that can maim or kill you there—sharks, crocs, snakes, spiders—BIG freakin' spiders—even the duck-billed platypus is venomous. So you kind of make peace with that and enjoy yourself. Life is too short not to have a good time."

Abby found herself caught in his gaze—she couldn't look away. She hoped David wouldn't quiz her on the many ways she could die Down Under, because she had gotten bewitched by the sound of his voice and had failed to catch the details of what he'd said. His voice had a rough, gravely edge, but it wasn't unpleasant. It was deep and seductive, even when she thought he might have said something about a potentially lethal platypus. She'd have to look up that tidbit of trivia later—it sounded like something important to know if she ever found herself ambushed by egg-laying mammals. Or she'd ask Ciaran—he would know.

"Carpe diem," Abby said, laughing nervously, less because she was worried about death by Australian fauna and more because of her awareness of how close he was.

David nodded, "Exactly." He took yet another step closer.

Abby felt her breath catch—he wasn't touching her, but she could feel him. It was as if some kind of warmth radiated from him, washing over her skin, drawing her to him like the pull of a magnet.

"David!" Moira called as she emerged from the hallway, Cassandra at her side.

Abby suddenly felt awkward about David's closeness and prayed he didn't notice the sly smile that Cassandra was giving her. She also hoped he missed the brief scowl Moira directed at Abby before turning her attention back to David.

"It's about time you came to see me, boy," Moira said.

"Hello, Aunt Moira." David smiled and stepped away from Abby. "You look lovely as ever."

"You are a *terrible* liar. I'm old," Moira replied, putting her hands on her hips.

"Well, you'll always look lovely to me," he said.

Moira smiled—a genuine smile. Abby was shocked. The woman was so cranky around her and the Buchans that Abby would not have believed her capable of that kind of affection. The smile actually softened her and took about twenty years off her face. There truly was something special about David Corbin.

"So, did Abby keep you entertained?" Cassandra asked.

"Most definitely." David shot Abby a grin hinting at conspiracy.

As Abby returned his smile, she couldn't help noticing that the smile on Moira's face vanished. *Oh well, can't win 'em all,* Abby thought. At least she had made progress with David.

"And I hope you are staying for dinner?" Cassandra asked.

"I'd love to. Thank you," he replied.

"David," said Moira, taking his hands in hers, "we have a great deal of catching up to do."

"Of course," David smiled. "Why don't we sit in here and talk until dinner is ready?" He led Moira to a comfortable chair in the living room, and the smile returned to her face.

"Cassandra, I'll come help you," Abby offered.

"Thanks—that would be great," Cassandra said. "Could you round up the kids and get their hands washed? The meal is almost done."

"Certainly." Abby was glad to have an excuse to be out of the way and doing something productive. She was happy David had decided to stay, but she was unnerved by Moira's reaction to her. It was frustrating that the woman despised her so much for no apparent reason.

 ∠∞∠∞∠∞

As she shut the Buchans' door behind her, Abby thought, *Overall, dinner went well.* David seemed to have worked his charm on Moira, and she tolerated Abby during the meal. Or at least, she pretended like Abby didn't exist, instead of glowering at her. At any rate, it was an improvement.

Everyone else had a wonderful time. Ciaran had insisted that Abby sit next to him, and David teased him about having an older girlfriend, which made the little boy giggle shyly. The children wanted to hear about all the animals David had seen in his travels, and he proved to be kind, patiently answering their endless questions.

As Abby watched David interact with the Buchans, she came to realize that he wasn't snobbish, like Jon had said.

There was a part of him that was guarded in initial encounters with people, but another part of him was unexpectedly open and charismatic when he was in a comfortable setting. He was smart and witty, and Abby found herself liking him more and more.

After dinner, David had insisted on helping clean up and then he offered to walk Abby home. Cassandra couldn't resist giving Abby a knowing look, and Abby blushed, embarrassed but thrilled at the same time. It was incredibly difficult to play it cool around David when everything in her was drawn to him. She thought she did okay, accepting his offer with a nonchalant shrug, but even if he didn't notice how appreciative she was to get some time alone with him, Moira did. The fiery look in her eyes said, *I may be old, but I'm not stupid.* There would be no winning the woman over, ever.

ಬಂಚಾಬಂಚಾಬಂಚಾ

Abby felt relieved to be away from Moira's watchful eyes when they left the Buchans' house.

David held the gate open for her and then latched it behind him.

"Thank you for walking me home," Abby said.

"My pleasure," David replied. "So where are we headed?"

"My house is on Orange Blossom Drive, just off of Continental."

"Okay." David turned and headed in the opposite direction.

Abby was confused. "Wait," she called after him. "I'm sorry—my house is in that direction." She pointed toward the eastern gate of Newcastle Beach.

"I know," he said, continuing west.

"Okay...so why are you walking toward the beach?" Abby asked.

David stopped. "I'm not. I was going to grab my bike. Continental is way too far to walk in the dark."

It *was* a long walk in the dark. And thinking about things that could be lurking out there made Abby shudder.

"And," he continued, walking back to where she was standing, "there's a cool breeze coming in from the sea. Look, you're already shivering." He took off his leather jacket and offered it to her.

"Touché. Thank you." Abby put the jacket on. It smelled good—a mixture of butter-soft leather and aftershave. She followed him several streets down to a large Tudor revival not far from the inn. "Wow—your house is gorgeous."

"Thanks." David was busy punching in a code for the garage door. The door rose and a fluorescent light flickered to life. Abby followed him inside.

ഇരുന്നു

"That's *beautiful*," Abby breathed.

David could tell by the awe on her face and in her voice that she genuinely liked the bike. *And I genuinely like this girl,* he thought. He met her eyes and smiled.

She smiled back shyly before returning her attention to his bike.

The motorcycle was a carefully preserved 1961 Harley with clean, shining chrome. The gas tank and fenders gleamed electric blue in the bright lights of the garage. The simplicity in the design spoke of power and freedom without apologizing or overcompensating for anything.

David took a cleaning rag from the workbench beside the bike and reverently wiped away a smudge near the gas tank. He could sense Abby's eyes on him and felt the exciting tension that seemed to be suspended in the air between them. He wondered if she felt it too.

He handed her a black helmet. "Here, put this on."

"What about you?" Abby asked.

He tapped the side of his head. "Thick skull. Besides, if anything happens to you, Cassandra will kill me. Then your folks will kill me. Then Cassandra will kill me again. And I don't see the point of putting my life in danger for no good reason."

"Ha, ha. You're not afraid of man-eating sharks, but a teeny little woman terrifies you," Abby said, fastening the strap on the helmet.

"She may be little, but make no mistake—she could wipe the floor with me." David straddled the bike and grinned. "Shall we?"

"We shall." Abby slid the helmet's visor down, and then settled in behind him, wrapping her arms around his waist.

He could feel her warmth against his back. Having her so close to him, touching him, was electric. He just felt so aware of her, like the tension in the air had changed and become a tangible connection. David thought about her wearing his jacket and wondered if he'd still be able to sense her closeness later, when she gave it back and he wore it home. "Okay. Hold on tight," he instructed. He started the bike and it roared to life.

Abby wrapped her arms around him tighter.

When he hit the gas, David felt her grasp loosen, like maybe she had been surprised by how powerful the bike was. For a second, he worried she would let go, so he placed his hand over hers, pulling her arms tight around him again. He didn't want to let go of her hand—he felt a warm rush of heat where their skin touched. The connection between them grew.

David needed both hands to drive, so he squeezed her hand and let go. Abby responded by clinging even tighter to him, nestled against his back, her legs pressed against his thighs as she steadied herself. Heat washed over him in a wave. He felt his pulse race, and he wondered if he might catch fire. He didn't think he would mind if he did.

He glanced back at Abby. She was holding him tightly, but she didn't seem scared, so he cranked the throttle, taking things up a notch. He heard her laugh as the bike accelerated. Then she surprised him. She tapped his arm, pointed to the throttle, and gave him a thumbs-up.

He tilted his head back toward her so she could hear him over the roar of the motor. "Faster?"

"Faster!" she yelled, laughing.

David grinned to himself. As he turned onto Continental, he held the throttle down.

The ride was exhilarating—and over much too soon. Before he knew it, he was pulling into Abby's driveway. She pulled off the helmet and set it on the back of the bike. She shook the tangles out of her hair, and then stepped down.

David walked her to her door.

"That was fun," Abby said. "Thanks for the ride."

"Are you working at the inn tomorrow?" he asked.

"My schedule changed. I'm only there on weekends now," she answered. "But I'll be at the Buchans' tomorrow afternoon, babysitting the kids."

"Oh," he said. "Well, maybe I'll stop by."

"I'm sure Moira would love to see you," Abby commented. "The kids took a shine to you too."

David thought about asking her if *she* had taken a shine to him as well, but that seemed too bold a move, considering she was talking about other people wanting to see him and hadn't said anything about herself. It seemed like she had been flirting with him earlier, but he didn't know her well enough to know for sure. Instead, he just smiled and said good night.

"I almost forgot," Abby said. She took off his jacket and handed it back to him. "Thanks for letting me borrow this."

"No problem," David said. He watched her go into her house and shut the door. He slipped the jacket back on. He *could* still feel her. The jacket was warm, but there was more to it than that. It was *her* warmth, and her smell, light and clean, rather than heavy with perfume. He had to see her again.

❧◌❧◌❧◌❧

Abby's dream that night mirrored her time with David and spoke of things to come. She saw herself walking down a stone tunnel. There was something important she needed to do, but she couldn't quite remember what it was. She knew though, that the tunnel led to a cavernous room with a cathedral ceiling, where a large crowd had gathered, waiting for her to make an appearance on some kind of stage.

152

As she neared the tunnel's exit, she saw David leaning casually against the wall, wearing his leather jacket and looking intently at her.

"Come with me," he said. She took his hand and he led her from the tunnel to the stage, then down steps into the midst of the audience. Abby hardly noticed the crowd surrounding her. Her eyes were on him, walking slightly ahead of her as he held her hand, weaving his way through the audience, guiding her through the crowd. A silver thread stretched from the center of his back to her chest. *Our souls are connected,* Abby thought, and woke up.

⁕℃⁕℃⁕℃

The next day, Abby was on babysitting duty again. Riordan was busy working on his book, and Cassandra had taken Moira shopping, so Abby was alone, watching the children. The afternoon was warm for autumn, and Abby decided to take the kids to the backyard to play in the sandbox.

Ciaran had knighted himself and Siobhan had proclaimed herself queen, donning a puffy pink concoction that resembled cotton candy fluff more than a dress, so Abby built them a sand castle. Unfortunately for them, Rowan had chosen to wear his dragon costume, and that spelled certain disaster.

There was little Rowan enjoyed more than destroying a freshly built sand castle, much to his older brother's frustration. Ciaran was Rowan's polar opposite—patiently constructing moats and walls, and painstakingly adding detail, inserting pebbles and sticks for decoration.

To keep the peace, Abby made up a game and recruited Ciaran to help her create a sand city so that Rowan and

Siobhan could level it instead of Ciaran's castle. Once Architect Ciaran declared the city finished, the two younger children became a pair of raging Godzillas, unleashing havoc. Siobhan's dress and auburn ringlets became encrusted with sand, making her look like a grime-covered incarnation of the sugar plum faery. Due to his tendency to plow headlong into the buildings with a wide, open-mouthed grin, Rowan acquired a full, sandy drool beard, channeling his inner garden gnome.

During his third rampage, Rowan launched himself at a sand tower but overshot his target and tackled Abby, who had been sitting, legs crisscrossed, in front of the sandbox. She managed to catch him in a bear hug and they tumbled to the lawn. "Whoa there, Crash," she laughed, lying on her back in the grass.

Rowan thought it was hysterical. "Again!" he roared.

"Uh, maybe not." Abby held Rowan at arm's length and shook her head, hoping to discourage him.

Muffled laughter erupted from behind them, and Abby tilted her head back to see David standing at the edge of the backyard. His hand covered his mouth as he tried, without success, to hide his amusement.

Rowan jumped up and ran toward David, head-butting him in the gut as he leaned down to receive Rowan's enthusiastic, albeit sandy, hug.

"Ow," David groaned, still laughing. "That kid is solid."

Abby thought that was hilarious. "See what you get when you laugh at the misfortune of others? There's karma for you—what goes around comes around."

"I suppose I deserve that," David conceded.

"Oh, you *so* do," she smiled.

"Has he been *eating* that sand?" David asked, brushing sticky goo from his shirt.

"Oh, quite possibly, my friend," Abby said. "I think you've been christened with a cocktail of sand and hyperactive toddler drool."

"Oh. Nice." He flopped down beside her on the grass and grinned at her. "Hi. How are you?" He must have come over on his bike, because his hair was delightfully tousled. She really liked it.

"Well, hello," Abby smiled, trying very hard not to think about what it would be like to run her hands through his messed-up hair. She could feel that magnetic pull again, making her want to move closer to him. She resisted and tried to remain aloof. "I'm good. And you?"

"Not bad, toddler saliva aside. Hey, is Moira around?"

"Sorry—you just missed her," Abby said. "Cassandra took her to find a dress for the ball. Riordan's here, but he's writing, so I thought I would take the kids outside so we didn't disturb him."

"That's okay," David replied. "She wanted to talk to me about something, but I can hang out with you guys until she returns."

"Sure. But you have to help me reconstruct Sand City. The monsters are restless." Abby nodded toward Rowan and Siobhan, who were inching closer to Ciaran's masterpiece.

"So I see." David grabbed a shovel and pail and went to work. "I'm pretty good at this, you know. Years of practice."

"Good," she said. "I'm sure we'll benefit from your expertise."

He patted a mound of sand, shaping it into a tower. "Your necklace—you were wearing it last night."

"Yes. I was." Abby reached up and touched the shell.

"This is going to sound weird, but I've seen something like that before," David said.

"Really? Where?" Maybe this was it, the in she had been waiting for to tell him the truth about his origins.

"That's the weird thing—I can't remember, but I have this nagging feeling it's important that I do," David said.

"Well, maybe it is—" Abby began.

Suddenly he seemed to lose focus and his eyes glazed over. "No, it's nothing. Forget I mentioned it." The words seemed forced, like they were coming from somewhere else.

Abby stared at him. *Wait, what just happened?* Out of the corner of her eye, she saw something black leap down from the garden's rock wall and streak out of sight. She trembled— was it one of the Shadows?

David seemed to regain composure, meeting her eyes and speaking like himself again. "So, you're going to the ball too?"

Pretending like she hadn't noticed anything, Abby played along as she shoveled more sand into a bucket. "I am. Cassandra invited me and my friend Jon to join her family."

"That's cool." David picked up a toy garden rake and ran it over the sand, drawing a moat around the tower he had built.

"And you're going, of course?" she asked.

He nodded. "Wouldn't miss it. My mother is very excited to show off the college graduate."

"That's great—I'm sure she is very proud," Abby said.

"To a fault," he laughed, and then grew serious. "Sometimes I feel like an accessory."

Abby dumped her bucket of sand and used the shovel to put the final embellishments on her tower. "How so?"

"It's just...I know my parents love me, but sometimes it seems like my life is more about what they want than what I want. I know they only want what's best for me, so I've never questioned their judgment. But since I've returned from my trip, I've felt..." David paused, lost in thought, smiling to himself.

"Felt...what?" Abby asked. She put her shovel down and studied him.

He shot her a mischievous grin. "Rebellious. I guess that's what Aunt Moira wants to talk to me about—my mother has not been happy with me lately, and I'm sure she's confided in Moira."

"Moira is close to your family?"

"Yes," David said. "She and my mother are very close, and Mom has always looked to her for advice, especially after I came along. My parents had wanted a baby for a long time, but I think they were a little caught off guard when they suddenly had the chance to adopt me from a private agency. I guess things happened so fast—thank goodness Moira was around to help, or I might have been more screwed up than I already am."

"Wow, is that even possible?" Abby teased.

David flicked sand in Abby's direction. "Ha. Funny."

"Hey—no throwing sand," Abby said, and then smiled and flicked some back at David.

"That sounds like a challenge," he grinned.

Abby looked at the kids. "I think not—trust me when I say you do not want to give Rowan any ideas. We would both be very sorry. Anyway, it sounds like Moira has meant a lot to you."

"Definitely," David said. "She's almost like my second mom. She's the kind of person who gets involved in people's lives. Some people might see that as overbearing, but she has good intentions. She's always been there for me, and in many ways, I think she knows me better than my own mother."

"So then, why is your mother unhappy with you?" Abby asked.

"Well, part if it has to do with my new job. I'm excited about the opportunity, but I'm not sure I'm ready to move so far away," he said.

"How far is far away?" Abby asked.

"London."

So the rumor is true, she thought, disappointed. "Oh," she said. "That's pretty far."

He nodded, and leaned in closer to her, his gaze intense.

"But I'm sure that if you don't want to move away, there are opportunities here," she said, looking back at him, feeling herself leaning into him as well. "You have your degree."

He smiled, but it was bittersweet. "Unfortunately, it's a bit more complicated than just finding a job here. It's my dad's firm, and it's very important to him that I take this position. He's been grooming me for it for a long time. Mom thinks he would be devastated if I don't go."

"Wow," Abby said. "No pressure there, right?"

"Oh no, not at all," he laughed. "But that's not all I've been rebelling about."

Abby raised her eyebrows. "Intriguing. Do tell."

David paused. "We had an argument about my date for the ball."

Abby busied herself working on another tower for Rowan to smash. "Oh. Are you going with Michal?"

David looked surprised. "No. Why would I?"

Now it was Abby's turn to be surprised. "Oh! I'm sorry, I just thought..."

"What?" he asked.

"Well, one time when I saw you at the inn, it looked like the two of you were...together," she replied.

"What gave you that impression?" David asked.

"You were giving her a ride on your bike." Abby felt her face grow hot as she remembered how embarrassed she had been, standing on the steps of the inn, staring at David like an idiot while Michal snuggled up to him. She avoided David's eyes, focusing instead on filling another pail with sand, hoping he wouldn't notice the blush creeping onto her cheeks.

"I gave *you* a ride on my bike too," David said.

Abby was quiet. *Okay,* she thought to herself. *The good news is he's not with Michal. Her riding on his bike was nothing special. The bad news is that last night with me wasn't anything special either.* Apparently this was just something he did with every girl he met.

"Abby?"

She tried to hide her disappointment. "Yes?"

"Is something wrong?" David asked.

Abby looked up at him and forced a smile. "Nope."

"Okay," David said. He seemed confused.

At that moment, Cassandra and Moira pulled up in the car.

"Well, Moira is back," David said, standing and dusting the sand from the knees of his jeans. "I guess I'd better go face the music. See you around, Abby."

"See you," she said, trying to make her smile a bright one. Empty as she felt, she didn't think it was very convincing.

❧☙❧☙❧☙

David stood in the Buchans' kitchen, waiting for Moira to put her purchases away. He looked out the kitchen window at Abby. Her back was to him—she was helping Ciaran with his castle. He hadn't meant to share so much about his mother and Moira, but Abby was easy to talk to and he found himself sharing more with her than he did with most people. She was fun, too—he enjoyed the way she bantered with him, the way they could talk seriously one minute and be laughing the next. He could see why the Buchan kids liked her.

He hated to leave things weird with Abby, but he wasn't sure where things had gone wrong in their conversation, or how to fix it. He would have thought Abby would be happy he wasn't taking Michal to the Autumn Ball. He had grown up with Michal, and although they knew each other well, he couldn't imagine dating her. With their families as close as they were, it would be like dating his kid sister—and besides, with the size of that girl's ego, he didn't think there was much room for anyone else.

Maybe whatever was going on with Abby had nothing to do with him. Or maybe he had read her wrong from the start. Maybe she wasn't interested in him at all. It sure seemed like she was interested the night he took her home, but maybe she was just being friendly. Maybe she was interested in someone else. *She's probably dating that Jon guy, since she's going to the ball with him,* he thought, disappointed.

"David? Did you hear me?" Moira asked. "I said let's go into the living room."

"Oh." David turned to see Moira standing in the doorway of the kitchen. "Sorry. My mind is somewhere else, I guess."

Moira took his hand and led him to a sofa littered with throw pillows. "I can see that. I'm worried about you, darling. Are you nervous about leaving? Philip and James have high hopes for you. They think you will do very well in the London office."

David looked at her. "No, that's not it."

Moira had set out a tray with coffee and cookies on the table in front of the sofa. She held the plate of cookies out to David. "Want one? We baked them this morning."

He nodded and sampled one. "Thanks—they're good."

"Is it because Amelia is James's daughter?" Moira asked. "You really don't need to be concerned about that, dear. I can understand how you might worry, but I can assure you that James approves of you. He told me that, you know. And your mother and I both think Amelia is a lovely girl."

"Yes, she's very nice," David said. He shifted uncomfortably in his seat and then twisted around and removed an overstuffed throw pillow from behind him. He set the velvet-trimmed pillow on the sofa beside him.

"I'm so happy that the two of you will be spending time together—you complement each other," Moira smiled. She picked up her coffee cup and sipped it.

"I'm not so sure about that," David said, absently running his fingers along the velvet of the pillow. "I mean, we get along okay, but we don't really have much in common."

"Nonsense!" Moira said. "You come from similar backgrounds, and you've known each other for years. We used to take the two of you to the beach, and out on the boat—you always had a wonderful time with Amelia. I remember how shy she was when she first visited as a little girl, and how you charmed her into exploring that little clubhouse you built in my backyard. You were such a gentleman even then."

David smiled. "I *was* pretty charming."

Moira laughed. "Do you remember that time, oh, you must have been in middle school? Her family was visiting for the holidays and it was the first time you were old enough to attend the Christmas party at the inn. You escorted Amelia out onto the dance floor and you were so beautiful together—my heart just stopped. That was the moment I knew the two of you were meant to be."

David frowned. "*Are* we meant to be? Because, I mean, I've always liked Amelia, and we've gone on dates when she visits, but I wouldn't say I love her. And how would I really know? I haven't dated anyone else, because, well, Amelia's always been in my life, even at a distance. I don't know if it's my mom's influence, pushing the two of us together when we were young, but there's just never been anyone else. And I think maybe I do love Amelia as a friend, but not in a romantic way."

"Oh David," Moira said. "I know that love can be very confusing, but don't worry too much about romance. A relationship based on a loving friendship is what lasts."

"Yes—but why can't I have a relationship with someone I love romantically *and* as a friend?" David asked. He found himself thinking about Abby again—the way he felt drawn to her. He tried to recall a time he'd felt that way about Amelia. He could remember some romantic moments with her, but even those paled in comparison to the few times he'd interacted with Abby.

"Well, of course you can have that," Moira said. "And I think that as you spend more time with Amelia, your relationship will blossom into a deeper level of love, and you will find that she truly does fulfill you both as a friend and romantically."

"I get that Aunt Moira—I do. But I don't think you understand what I'm saying," David said, frustrated.

"All right, dear," Moira said. She set her coffee cup down. "What are you saying?"

"I'm saying that I don't *want* to be with Amelia. I think I'm interested in someone else."

Moira studied him. "And who might that be?"

David looked at her and his discomfort deepened. He felt cornered. "Well, not that I feel comfortable sharing this with anyone else at the moment, but it's Abby. I think I'd like to get to know her better." His gaze drifted to the back door—it was shut, but he was very aware of how close Abby was at the moment, and he could hear Rowan giggling. He wondered if Abby had gotten tackled again. Maybe after Moira was done with this little talk, he could sneak out there again. It sounded like Abby and the kids were having a lot more fun than he was having with Moira.

Moira's eyes flicked to the back door. "The *babysitter*?"

David quivered at the horror he heard in Moira's voice. He turned to her. "You don't need to say it like *that*," he said. "She's a very nice girl."

"Yes, dear," Moira said. "She *is* a very nice girl. But she is *not* the girl for you."

"And why not?" David could hear anger creeping into his voice—he tried to staunch it, to remain civil.

"David, it's very important to have common ground when you are in a relationship with someone—to have a similar upbringing. You have no idea how many relationships fail because of the conflict that occurs when people come from different backgrounds," Moira said. Her voice was tempered, like she was trying very hard to be patient. "And it's not her fault, of course, that she was raised differently than you were, but she could never successfully navigate our world. I mean, she just doesn't understand the cultural nuances that you and I take for granted."

"She could learn," David insisted. "And honestly, I have so much more in common with Abby than I do with Amelia, and like you said, I've known Amelia for years. And there's no spark with Amelia. I want to feel a spark."

"Sparks fizzle," Moira said. "Right now, you are just infatuated with this Abby. That kind of thing never lasts. You'll see—you'll go to London and forget all about her. And I think that you really need to focus on your future rather than the present. Your father and mother have invested so much in your future, and it would be quite embarrassing for them if you were to have a fling with this girl and hurt Amelia's feelings. You need to treat both Amelia and her father with respect during their visit. And once you're in London, no matter what happens with you and Amelia, you need to deal with her honorably. You can't expect James to place his trust in you professionally if you abuse his trust where his daughter is concerned. And later, if you do decide to end things with Amelia, please, at least find someone from a similar social circle. Find someone you would be proud to share a life with when you take the helm in the London office."

David started to reply and then held his tongue. He was angry, and he didn't want to say something he would regret.

Moira leaned over and took David's hands in hers. "David—you know that your parents and I love you very much, don't you?"

He looked at her and nodded.

"All we want—all we've ever wanted—is for you to have the very best that life has to offer. I love you as if you were my own son," Moira said. "I know what I've said sounds harsh to you, but please know that I only say it because I have your best interests in mind."

"I know you do," David said.

Moira smiled. "Then how about this: think about what I said, and be nice to Amelia when she arrives tomorrow. She's a good girl. Make an effort to spend time with her this week. Hold off on your decision to end the relationship at least until you've had a chance to see what it's like to live in the same city with her. She might just surprise you. Okay?"

"All right, Aunt Moira. I'll spend time with Amelia." David was still angry, but he knew that arguing with Moira wouldn't help. And he also knew that, in her own way, she was trying to look out for him, even if she had a rather narrow-minded perspective. She meant well.

And maybe she was at least a little bit right about Abby. They did come from different backgrounds. Maybe being with Abby would be fun now, but what kinds of issues would come up later? And then there was London to think about. It wasn't a vacation he was going on. He was moving there, and he wasn't planning on coming back anytime soon. How could he manage a long-distance relationship with someone he barely knew, someone who had her own plans for her life?

As far as Amelia was concerned, he wasn't sure she wanted to be with him either. Maybe she felt the same pressure from her family to make the relationship work. Their fathers were close, both as friends and business partners, and David's mom got along well with Amelia's mother. From a logical standpoint, it made sense that David and Amelia would also click, but sometimes their relationship felt forced, like it was less about an emotional connection between the two of them and more about the joining of two kingdoms. It wasn't quite an arranged marriage—no one would disown David or Amelia if things didn't work out—but still, the pressure was there.

Every time Amelia's family visited, David could feel both sets of parents watching them interact, dropping little hints about their hopes for David and Amelia's relationship. Those kind of hopes hung heavy around David's neck, almost to the point of strangulation. The funny thing was, he had never realized just how smothered he felt before now. He suspected that meeting Abby had something to do with that.

⁞♋⁞♋⁞♋

"I think I screwed up," Abby confided to Eulalia several days later. After her strange conversation with David, she needed some advice. She felt an increasing sense of urgency as each day went by, knowing there was little time left. "First, there was this moment in the conversation when he got this dazed look on this face, and I could have sworn I saw one of those shadow things hanging around."

"You most likely did," Eulalia replied. "It sounds like the Shadow was trying to control him, trying to make him forget. The next time you talk with him, be careful. They will be watching you. It is important to take him to a safe place to talk."

"*If* I get to talk to him again," Abby said, her words spilling out in a frustrated rush. "After the weird conversation we had, I think he has been avoiding me. I've wanted to smooth things over, but he hasn't been to the Buchans' house again and I haven't seen him at the inn. It's been days and we're running out of time. I'd go to his house, but I think that would just scare him away. I don't know what to do. And...I hope you won't be mad, but I shared a little bit of our conversation with Cassandra, Riordan, and Jon. I didn't tell them everything, but they've been a part of this, and I trust them."

To Abby's relief, Eulalia responded with understanding. "I am not angry. You are right—they *are* a part of this. You have been wise about who you have chosen for allies. But regarding David, what happened that would make him want to avoid you?"

"Well, I like him so much—it's like there is this magical pull toward him," Abby said, avoiding Eulalia's gaze. "All the talk about lightbearers and dreamwalkers—I guess I assumed it was fate—that we were meant to be. I thought we might be moving toward a closer relationship—we were getting along well, and he was opening up more and more. Then he said something that made me think otherwise. I guess my disappointment got the best of me, and I forgot that my real mission was to help him get home. A relationship with him would be wonderful, but it's only the icing on the cake."

"On the contrary, Abby," Eulalia countered, "how do you think you will gain his trust without a relationship?"

Abby looked up. "What do you mean?"

"I mean you cannot expect him to believe you, if there is no foundation for trust."

"True. I guess that makes sense," Abby said.

"Let go and follow the signs. If you push too hard, you will push him away. The next time you see David, let things happen naturally. You will know when it is time to reveal the truth," Eulalia said, placing her hand on Abby's.

"Yeah, but *how*?" Abby asked.

"It will be very clear to you when the time is right. You will know what you need to do. I have seen the future in my dreams, and this time we *will* reach him."

That was *not* an answer. Abby was more frustrated than before. Eulalia was talking in vague Zen master circles and she seemed unnervingly at ease with the coming deadline, a deadline with a very tight schedule and some pretty hefty consequences. *Well, it's not like it'll be the end of the world or anything,* Abby thought. Why couldn't the universe have brought her into this when there was still plenty of time—years ago, even? *Because,* the universe seemed to answer, *you weren't ready.* Abby knew that was true. *Yeah, okay.* Maybe Eulalia did know more than she was saying, but if she really *had* seen the future, why wasn't she providing concrete answers?

Abby slipped through the estate gate, nodding her goodbye to Brarn, who sat perched on the fence, watching her. She walked home trying not to worry, trying to believe that things would work out as Eulalia had seen.

ଈଔଈଔଈଔ

Eulalia watched Abby walk away. She could sense the girl's frustration and could not blame her. It was not a lie—she *had* dreamed that Abby was the one, the only one, who could reach David, and that he would be restored to his rightful place as the Solas Beir. But the truth was, she could not yet see *how* that was going to happen; the details were blurry. Her visions had grown in clarity over the years, as they would for Abby, but this time it was different—there were too many unknowns just yet.

She felt terrible for urging Abby to simply go on faith, but wasn't that what she had relied on all these years? If not for faith, she would have lost hope long ago. She looked at Brarn, standing guard at the gate, this creature who had served her for so long as a companion, a protector, a provider. They had both lost so much.

Eulalia had felt so hopeful in the beginning, when David was still a young child. She remembered seeing him as a five-year-old boy, dressed up like a miniature man in a suit and tie, his dark, unruly curls tamed. He was standing alone, holding an Easter basket, waiting in anticipation of the inn's annual egg hunt while his distracted replacement parents chatted with friends on the steps in front of the inn.

No one noticed when a raven hopped through the iron bars of the gate across the street, attracting his attention. No one saw when that young boy, curious as young boys are, crossed the street and stood at the gate, hesitant, wanting to follow the raven inside. He wasn't the first boy to stand at that gate—there had been others, curious onlookers, and each time, Eulalia would peek from the windows of the old mansion and wonder if it could be the boy she had lost.

This time there was no wondering—she knew it was him. Her heart leapt to her throat, and it was all she could do to stop herself from bursting out from her hiding place in the mansion and calling out his name, his true name.

The little boy followed the raven up the steps to the ruined mansion's front door and cautiously peered inside. He seemed more curious than afraid, but still, he did not enter at first. Eulalia waited until he was well inside before she revealed herself. That was when the boy got scared. She tried, desperately, to talk to him, to keep him long enough that he would recognize her and know the truth.

It broke her heart when he didn't. The little boy shrieked and ran, ran like he was running for his life, out the door and past the reflecting pool, dropping the basket as he squeezed through the gate, running across the street to the safety of his adoptive mother's arms. It was those arms, not hers, that comforted him, and that woman who told him it was all his imagination, that there were no monsters in the old mansion.

She remembered looking in the broken shards of glass that were all that remained of the mirrored portal and feeling disgusted by her own reflection. Of course he didn't recognize her—what was there left to recognize in her ruined face? She rarely looked at herself anymore, and when she did, she was always surprised at her own hideousness. In spite of her useless arm and blind eye, she remembered herself as she had been, not as this marred creature that even she could not recognize.

He never came back, and the days faded into each other, the seasons blending into one so that she never even noticed the heat, the cold, the wind, or rain. She had grown increasingly numb as the years had passed, especially after things had gone so badly in delivering the Sign of the Throne. The numbness was her way of dealing with her imprisonment. She had almost lost hope completely when she started dreaming about Abby.

The girl was young and naïve, but she was stronger than she knew—when she came into her own, she would be the most powerful seer Cai Terenmare had known for a long time.

AUTUMN MAGIC

Abby was ready for the Autumn Ball long before it was time to leave. After nervously inspecting herself in the mirror for about twenty minutes, she gave up and decided to kill some time playing her mother's antique upright piano in the living room. She hated waiting idly, and needed something to distract her from her building anxiety.

Getting lost in music was just the thing to pass the time. Abby was a decent pianist—she took great pleasure from knowing a song so well that she could just let go and allow her fingers to take over. She had learned that you have to feel music. If you over-think it, you're sure to make mistakes.

Hmmmm, she thought, as the music flowed around her. *Maybe that's what Eulalia meant about knowing and letting go.*

She thought about the sigil of the Solas Beir that she wore around her neck. It might be good for keeping the Darkness at bay, but it did little to settle the butterflies in her stomach.

Social events had never been easy for her—big crowds were unnerving. As much as she was excited about attending her first formal grownup event (attending prom with Jon junior year didn't count—it had been a rite of passage all right, but one filled with teen angst), she feared having to interact with people she didn't know. She was always aware of the subtle undertone in people's emotions. Just because someone was smiling and being polite didn't mean they liked you. Often, the opposite was true.

People followed social conventions, but it didn't mean they cared. She found people with strong, opinionated personalities particularly abrasive. It wasn't so much that they spoke too loud or did things that were obnoxious or rude; it was more a feeling that she got from them, a creeping, intrusive energy that overwhelmed her soul. She could always tell when someone was lying; she could hear subtleties in tone of voice or catch tiny discrepancies in facial expressions that others missed. Her strategy in dealing with people who were not genuine was to play nice and then escape so she could recharge from the encounter.

"Sounds pretty good," Jon said.

Startled, Abby stopped playing and twisted around on the piano bench. "Oh! Hey, Jon. Sorry—I didn't hear you come in." She had been lost in her thoughts and the delicate music-box sound of the piano. With her back to the front door and the music masking Jon's footsteps, she had been oblivious to his arrival.

"Sorry," he said. "I didn't mean to freak you out. Your mom let me in."

"Oh no, it's fine," Abby said. She stood up and smoothed the skirt of her gown.

"Yowza." Jon eyed her up and down. "Wow—you look *great*."

Grinning, Abby turned in a slow circle. She *felt* great. The tailor had done an amazing job altering the strapless dress, and now it hugged her figure in all the right places, giving her a confidence she'd never felt before.

"*And* you did your hair," Jon smiled, stepping closer. "You *are* trying to impress me."

Abby had decided to wear her hair down. Her soft curls framed her face, falling around her shoulders and down her back. She brushed a stray curl from her forehead and smiled. "Thank you. You look pretty fetching yourself."

Jon gave her that mischievous little grin of his, and Abby felt her heart flutter. She almost hated it when he looked at her like that—sometimes he was a little too handsome, and tonight, he looked really, *really* good in that suit, which set off his dark hair and soulful brown eyes, not to mention that fantastic tan of his.

Sometimes she regretted breaking up with him—he was perfect in so many ways. But that devious grin said it all. She could envision herself getting into a lot of trouble with him, and that was a problem. Kissing him again would be fun, yes, but he just wasn't the right fit for her. The thought of being with him in a serious relationship made her stomach twist with unease. She could pretend it didn't, and she could rationalize that yes, logically, being with him made sense. But, much as she adored him, and may have wished things could be different, wishing wouldn't make it so. She knew that from her core, and she couldn't deny it. It was far better for them both not to go down that road again.

Besides, she needed to focus on David. And she wanted to. For the first time, Abby could see herself in a serious relationship; that familiar squirming feeling in her gut wasn't there with David. Just the opposite—everything in her was drawn to him. But even if it turned out she had no future with David, she couldn't afford to get distracted. Not with all of Cai Terenmare at stake, and her own world too, should she fail, and should Tierney decide that he and the Shadows needed to pop over for a slice of human pot pie. *Not to be dramatic here,* she thought, *but the fate of the world is literally in my hands.*

She tried not to fixate on the pressure she felt about David. She hadn't seen him all week, but she'd had plenty of nightmares about the Shadows. She wondered if Eulalia was wrong, if somehow the Kruorumbrae did have magical abilities to prevent her from seeing David, and were keeping them apart. Or maybe he really was avoiding her. She knew that the Autumn Ball could be her last chance to reach out to him. And she still had no idea what she was going to say to him.

The doorbell rang again, announcing the arrival of the Buchans. Abby pushed aside her worries, playfully elbowing Jon's arm as she slid past him toward the front hall. "Time to go," she sang.

As Abby's tall, thin father opened the door to Cassandra, her mother barred Abby's escape, insisting on a flurry of awkward, last-minute photos with Jon. "You'll thank me later," Bethany insisted. "Someday you'll appreciate this." She held up her camera like a paparazzo and motioned for Abby and Jon to stand closer together.

Sorry, Abby mouthed to Jon. *So embarrassing,* she thought, looking at Cassandra, who was hiding a smile but seemed very amused.

It felt strange to see Cassandra in her formal dress, such a contrast with Bethany Brown in her jeans and T-shirt. Some people said Abby looked like her mom had as a teenager, and Abby supposed this was true, even though she had her father's blue eyes and not her mother's green ones. Abby wondered if Cassandra and Riordan would act like her parents when the Buchan kids got older, embarrassing them by dragging out a camera. *Probably.*

Shrugging, Jon slipped his arm around Abby's waist, smiling. It wasn't the first time he'd submitted to torture at the hands of Abby's mother.

Abby thought back to when they'd gone to prom together. Different circumstances, same drill. But she appreciated that Jon was being so good-natured about it. His mom was really cool about giving him space, although Abby knew that Blanca would want to see the photos later.

Abby tried to be patient as Bethany snapped a few more pictures, and then she put her foot down. "*Okay,* Mom. Riordan and Moira are waiting in the car. We *have* to go," Abby said. She gave her parents hurried hugs and grabbed Jon's arm, steering him toward the door. She heard a giggle and spotted Matt hiding out by the stairs. Her little brother seemed very pleased by the annoyed look on Abby's face. Abby stuck her tongue out at him, and then smiled.

"All right, all right, *go,*" Bethany said, waving Abby and Jon on. "Thanks for humoring me. And thanks for inviting them, Cassandra—I *hope* they behave themselves."

"We *will,*" Abby groaned.

Cassandra bid Abby's parents farewell. "Thanks for letting us borrow them, Frank and Bethany."

"Anytime. Thanks for treating them, Cassandra," Abby's mother said. "Have fun, you two," she called to Abby and Jon.

"Thanks, Mom," Abby said, dragging Jon out onto the porch. She let him go briefly so she could use both hands to grasp the silky fabric of her skirt and raise the hem of her gown. The last thing she wanted to do was to trip in her heels going down the porch steps and face plant onto the driveway.

Having successfully navigated the steps, she looked over at Jon. He was walking beside her, watching her. He held out his hand and gave her a sweet smile. Returning his smile, she took his hand, letting him escort her to the car.

ಬಿೞಬಿೞಬಿೞ

The Newcastle Beach Inn was aglow with light. Star-shaped, leaded-glass lanterns hung from the scrolled, wooden beams and corbels that adorned the inn. Soft yellow light emanated from the opaque, almond-colored glass. The steps leading to the heavy, carved wooden doors at the inn's entrance were punctuated by tall, six-sided Moroccan lanterns, embossed with glass in alternating shades of amber and turquoise. Light leaked through the punched metal of the lanterns' frames, casting intricate, ornamental shapes on the brick steps and bathing the arabesque-tiled risers in romantic light. Tiny white lights sparkled in the tree limbs that bowed gracefully over the entrance and in the vines entwined around the tall wrought-iron fence that bounded the inn's grounds.

It was a short walk from the lobby to the open doors of the ballroom. Moira, as matriarch, led the way, her arm in Riordan's for support. Abby watched as Cassandra flanked Moira's other side, just in case she needed assistance navigating the flight of stairs that led down to the ballroom floor. She didn't. Moira walked with a careless but dignified air, wearing a sophisticated gown that wrapped her thin frame in layers of black silk. The capped sleeves and diamond brooch in the center of the bodice channeled the class of old Hollywood. She didn't seem old—she seemed timeless.

At the top of the stairs, Jon offered Abby his arm. She took it, but paused, taking in the scene below. The Moroccan theme continued in the ballroom, with large, star-shaped lanterns hanging from arches between the ornate stone pillars that supported the ceiling. By contrast, a series of more rustic chandeliers hung from the ceiling itself. The metal fixtures, in a dark patina, curved in graceful symmetry, and rather than ornately carved crystals, simple glass spheres hung from each metal branch. Floor to ceiling mirrors covered the walls, the edges of the beveled glass set in frames stained a deep mahogany.

A dance floor was laid out in the center of the room, where travertine tile gave way to parquet flooring. Surrounding this were tables covered in flawlessly white tablecloths. White paper star lanterns floated above each table, suspended by silver ribbons, and in the center of the tables were lavish arrangements of ivory-colored freesia, hydrangea, and orchids in pillared vases of mercury glass. Tiny pumpkins were scattered around the flowers, their creamy, coral-colored shells carved to hold tea lights that emitted a soft glow. Larger, white lumina pumpkins had been placed within floral arrangements on long tables around the edges of the room. Servers drifted between these tables, setting out hors d'oeuvres and filling drinks. Elegantly dressed guests sat in black-lacquered, bamboo chairs, chatting amiably and admiring those daring enough to dance.

Jon noticed Abby's hesitation. "Nervous?" he asked.

"I'm okay," she said. "It's just so beautiful."

"It is. And so are you."

Abby laughed. "*Smooth*, Jonathon. Very smooth."

"I mean it," Jon said, staring into her eyes. "Ready?"

Abby smiled. "Yes. Let's go."

As Abby and Jon descended, she felt as though everyone in the room had stopped what they were doing and were staring at her. They weren't really, of course. Abby could still hear the music playing and still see people dancing. She just felt self-conscious. Jon grinned at her, and his contagious charisma increased her confidence. She beamed back at him. Thank goodness she hadn't come alone.

Abby caught sight of David. He looked dashing. He *was* staring right at her, only her, a slight smile on his lips, despite the fact that he was standing next to a gorgeous blond in a garnet gown. Abby smiled back.

€)ک€)ک€)ک

David had made good on his promise to Moira to spend time with Amelia. Over the past week, he had focused his energy on touring her around town, even driving up the coast to check out an artsy beachside village and treating her to dinner at a restaurant perched on the side of the rocky cliff. They'd had a good time together—and as he was standing in the ballroom, he thought back to that evening.

After the meal, they exited the restaurant and walked out onto the broad viewing deck that jutted out over the tumultuous, crashing waves below. To the north was the beach, and David could see a handful of surfers catching a few last waves before the sun dipped below the horizon. Already, lights had been turned on in the bungalows bordering the beach, and smoke rose from a few chimneys.

It was colder there than in Newcastle Beach. Amelia had bundled up against the crisp fall air, wearing boots with her plaid pencil skirt and cream-colored top, and adding a colorful scarf to her black pea coat. She looked sophisticated, like she'd stepped from the pages of a magazine. David had foregone his leather jacket, instead layering his long-sleeved button up shirt with a tailored wool blazer.

As they walked along the deck, she smiled at him, and he took her hand. It wasn't the first time he'd held her hand, and he had to admit, it felt comfortable. They talked about London, and she told him about the places they would visit. She thanked him for dinner and promised to treat him to her favorite restaurant once he had settled into his new flat. David found himself watching her, trying to imagine what his life with her could be like.

The wind picked up, blowing her long blond hair. She reached up to brush the stray locks back, away from her face, and he stopped her, reaching up to brush the wayward strand away himself. She froze, looking at him as he moved closer. He found himself staring at her eyes, and then her lips. Without planning to, he kissed her.

He had kissed Amelia before. When he was younger, he had stolen a number of kisses from her, experimenting, and she seemed happy to reciprocate. Something had changed. They had grown up, and they hadn't seen each other for over a year. But there was something else. David hadn't known Abby when they were younger. He hadn't known what it was like to touch someone and feel heat radiate across your skin like you might catch fire.

Suddenly he knew for sure—settling for comfortable could never be enough. And it seemed something had changed for Amelia as well. She let him kiss her, and then gently pulled away, turning her gaze to the beach. The sun had almost gone, and the bright lights in the beach houses sparkled.

"What is it?" David asked.

"I'm sorry," she began, resting her arms on the balcony's railing. "I don't think I can do this." She told him that although she enjoyed his friendship, she couldn't pretend to want something more. She had met someone else.

"Do you love him?"

"I thought I did," Amelia answered. "But I never pursued it."

David smiled. "Maybe you *should* pursue it, if you feel that strongly about it. What stopped you?"

Amelia turned to look at him. "You. I was too worried about hurting you."

David laid his hand over hers. "Worrying about my feelings is not a good reason to stay with me, Amelia."

She frowned. "I know. But it wasn't just that. I was terrified of disappointing my parents." Then she smiled, but it was bittersweet. "I guess I'll have to now though—I need to tell them how I feel. It's probably too late for Lucas and me. He's moved on. But I now know that I can't continue as I have. I need to date other people before I settle down with someone. Do you understand?"

David laughed, relieved. "Yes. I understand completely. I met someone too. And I think I'm a goner."

Her eyes widened. "But...if you think you're in love with her, why did you kiss *me*?" She touched her lips absently, as though she could still feel his touch.

"I'm sorry," David said, turning away. "I shouldn't have done that. It wasn't something I thought about, consciously, but I think maybe I needed to know for sure that things couldn't work between us before I said something to you."

Amelia put her hand on his shoulder and he turned back toward her. "Well," she smiled, "I guess we know for sure now. So, where does that leave us? Do we remain friends?"

David nodded. "I would like that. I'm going to need a friend in London. And I would still love to take you to the Autumn Ball, if you'd still like to go."

She agreed to go, and David agreed not to say anything to his parents until Amelia had a chance to chat with hers.

Now, Amelia was standing next to him at the ball, looking beautiful in her gown, and happier than he'd ever seen her. David was happy too—it was as if a great weight had been lifted from his shoulders. He still needed to talk with his parents about Amelia, but he felt free to pursue Abby without guilt.

He caught a glimpse of Moira and the Buchans as they descended the stairs. He looked for Abby, worried for a second that she hadn't come. Then he saw her, at the top of the stairs, and his heart stopped. She was stunning. His eyes locked on hers, and he couldn't look away, couldn't breathe, couldn't stop himself from smiling. When she smiled back at him, he knew he *had* to talk to her tonight, to try to explain what he felt. He couldn't leave town without knowing whether or not she felt the same.

ഇരുഇരുഇരു

Abby felt Jon tense up beside her as he caught the look between her and David, and then felt him relax when he saw Marisol. She was smiling at both Jon and Abby. She looked radiant in a copper gown. Even from a distance, Abby could see that the color complemented her brilliant green eyes, and that they were kind.

Not so kind were the eyes belonging to the girls standing next to Marisol. Abby could feel nothing but disgust oozing from Michal and Monroe. They looked beautiful as usual, but their obvious feelings of ill will diminished their looks.

Abby ignored them—she wasn't going to let their pettiness get the best of her tonight. Whatever negative feelings she'd had about them in the past were irrelevant now. She planned to enjoy the evening to the fullest.

"I know what you're thinking about," Jon whispered, leaning in close.

Abby looked at him. "Do you?"

He smiled slyly. "Yeah. Don't worry about them—they're just jealous. Let's give them something to talk about." He steered her toward the dance floor, spinning her around so her gown whirled dramatically, and then expertly pulled her back into his arms.

"Nicely done," Abby laughed. "But aren't you worried about sending the wrong message to Marisol?"

"Nah. I don't think she would be threatened by our friendship," Jon said. "If she is, I wouldn't want her anyway."

Abby wasn't sure if Jon was talking about Marisol or dropping a hint about his feelings regarding her and David. She decided it was better not to ask.

"Well," she said, "I suppose a little competition will only make her want you more."

Jon grinned mischievously, spinning her again. She laughed. It was so easy to flatter his ego sometimes. She settled into his arms.

Looking over Jon's shoulder, Abby noticed that Riordan and Cassandra had joined them on the dance floor and seemed to be having a wonderful time. They were matched in intelligence and humor, and still seemed to be madly in love after many years of marriage. They looked beautiful together—Riordan in a black tuxedo (he had foregone the kilt for one evening) and Cassandra in the peridot dress Abby had helped her find. Abby hoped she should be so lucky in a relationship someday.

As Abby and Jon circled around the dance floor, she saw that David had started dancing with his date too. The fair-haired young woman was uncommonly beautiful, with delicate features and wide, expressive eyes. She wore a strapless, deep-red dress that flattered her figure and flared out at the hem elegantly. With her fair skin and genteel mannerisms, Abby had a feeling David's date wasn't a Great Outdoors kind of girl, but was familiar with more high-browed pursuits.

Although he was a good dancer and his partner seemed content in his arms, David seemed distracted, not making eye contact with the girl at all. As far as Abby could tell, he was looking straight at *her*. She returned his gaze and smiled, thinking David would acknowledge her and return his attention to his date, but his stare intensified, burning into her. Abby felt mesmerized. She could no more break eye contact with him than a moth could avoid being consumed by the brilliant light of a flame.

The spell was only broken as the song wound to a close. Abby forced herself to look away as David left the dance floor, leading his date back to her seat. She thanked Jon for the dance and turned to walk away, thinking that after such an intense interaction, David would be at her side in seconds.

Jon could see that Abby was itching to go to David, but he pulled her back, one hand gripping hers, the other on the small of her back, keeping her close. "Wait," he whispered in her ear. "I know you want to go to him, but bear with me for just one more song."

Abby jerked back, startled. Jon stared into her wide eyes, pleading, and Abby settled back into his arms as the next song started. "Jon," she said. "I'm not bearing with you—I *love* dancing with you. I'm *so* sorry if I hurt your feelings—I just assumed that you would want to dance with Marisol next."

Jon smiled weakly. "I do. But I know that once I let you go, things with us will change. I don't want to lose you." He realized that they were standing still in the middle of the dance floor while other couples danced around them. He moved his feet, and to his relief, Abby joined him. They swayed back into synch with the music.

"Jon, you're my best friend," Abby reassured him. "Nothing can change that."

She moved closer to him, tightening her arms around his neck.

"You say that now, but things *will* change. It's inevitable," Jon said. Abby was silent. Jon supposed she knew that things would change too. He continued. "We've always had each other—since we were little kids. All the ups and downs—us dating other people—we've always managed to come back to each other. I know as we get into relationships with other people, real ones, I mean, we'll grow apart. But I will always, *always*, be here for you."

"Jon, you're my soul mate," Abby said, placing her hand on his cheek. "No matter what happens, we'll always be in each other's thoughts, no matter where we are."

"You're my soul mate too," Jon said. He took her hand and kissed the palm. "I love you Abby, and I just want you to be happy."

"I love you too. And I want *you* to be happy." She hugged him tight, nestling her head against his chest. Then she looked up at him. "I'm sorry that things never worked out between us in *that* way. I just...as much as I care for you, I couldn't give you want you wanted. I'm sorry."

"Don't be sorry," Jon said, smiling. "I just think the universe has other plans for us. It's okay. And I was wrong about David—he actually seems like a nice guy. Just do me a favor, and be careful."

"Why do you say that?" Abby asked.

Jon frowned. "I can't shake the feeling that there's something dangerous about your being with him. Not that he would *mean* to hurt you, but more like being involved with him could put you in a bad situation—you know, with all that other stuff you've been talking about. I've always been the guy looking out for you, and I guess that will be his job now, but what if he can't? I'm sorry—I just have a bad feeling I can't really explain. You have your bad dreams and I have mine."

"Well, given my bad dreams, I'm inclined to take yours seriously as well. I'll be careful," Abby assured him. "I promise."

"I'll hold you to that." Jon hugged her tight and let her go. "All right, I've said what I needed to say. I give you my blessing to go dance with him now, and I'm going to go find

Marisol." He walked with her back to their table. "Wish me luck."

Abby grinned. "Luck. Thanks, Jon, for everything."

ꙮꙮꙮ

Abby looked for David across the room, but he wasn't at his table. The blond was there, talking to several young men. A man Abby assumed must be David's father, Philip Corbin, was there as well, engaged in conversation with his peers. Abby looked to the dance floor and smiled. David was dancing with his mother, and she was clearly bursting with pride. *Aw, how sweet,* Abby thought. She watched them for a few moments, thinking that David really *was* a nice guy if he were willing to humor his mother like that.

After a while, Abby again felt the strange sensation of someone staring at her. This time, however, when she turned, she realized it wasn't David, and it wasn't a good thing. Somehow she had ended up at the Buchans' table alone with Moira, and the woman was studying her intently. The look on Moira's face reminded Abby of a nature show she had once seen about Central American snakes. An image flashed in her mind of a fer-de-lance viper, a cunning and aggressive predator, coiled up and ready to strike a hapless jungle rodent.

The woman smiled. Her gaze was venomous.

Abby smiled back weakly. Yep, she was the jungle rodent all right. Jungle rodent toast. Completely lost for words, Abby looked away, her eyes finding David on the dance floor.

"You won't win, you know."

Abby turned back around. "Excuse me?"

187

Moira's eyes grew dark, darker than Abby would have imagined possible. "He is already spoken for." She nodded toward the beautiful pale-haired girl. "In a few days' time, he will move to London with Amelia. It's only a matter of time before they announce their engagement. So you see, my dear, you are wasting your time." Moira smiled cruelly.

There was something about Moira's eyes and the dripping, sweet poison in the woman's tone that terrified Abby. Fear washed over her in a nauseating wave, disabling her mind, paralyzing her body. She had always suspected that Moira hated her, but she never thought there would be a confrontation like this.

The suddenness of the conversation and the potency of the woman's hatred made Abby feel weak, like she was traveling down a dark, closing tunnel; she felt like she was about to faint. The music in the ballroom sounded far away. Abby could see little black dots appearing in front of her eyes, and she felt her guts clench up. She was going to be sick. Holding her stomach, Abby stumbled to her feet, her ankles buckling inward on her high heels, her thigh bumping the side of her chair and scooting it backward as she struggled to maintain her balance. "Excuse me," she managed. "I need some air."

೮೦೮೮೦೮೮೦೮

When Abby escaped from the ballroom into the cool night air, the sick twisting in her stomach dissipated, and the spots cleared from her vision. She could hear again, and the sound of the waves on the beach below the ballroom's flagstone patio was soothing, allowing her to slow her breathing and take in a deep drink of oxygen from the moist autumn air. She felt better, albeit a little astounded that the hatred of an old woman could produce such a physically draining effect.

One other time in her life, Abby had been caught off guard like this. She remembered her fifth grade teacher, a cranky crone with the temperament of a troll, screaming full tilt at her the one time she got caught not paying attention in class. Nasty banshee. The woman's disciplinary method was arguably effective, however, because Abby was attentive in class from that point on.

That incident had made an impression, no doubt, but it was nothing compared to this. This was a complete emotional unraveling.

Abby walked across the patio and down the stone steps to the beach, thinking about what had happened with Moira and all the things she could have—should have—said. She started to get annoyed with herself. How could she have come undone so easily? Outside in the night air, it seemed pretty ridiculous.

⮡⣿⮡⣿⮡⣿

As the song ended, David took his mother's arm, escorting her back to the table. She was still beaming when he turned to leave.

"Where are you off to?" she asked, absently sipping her wine.

"I'm going to talk with Abby," David replied.

"Who?"

"Abby Brown, Mother," he said. "You met her several weeks ago. She was with Cassandra."

"Oh. I did? Well, don't stay away too long. The wolves are at the door." Margaret Corbin tilted her wineglass toward the league of young men hovering around Amelia, who looked quite flattered by the attention.

David nodded. "So I see."

He walked over to the Buchan table, surprised to find it empty except for Moira. "Hi, Aunt Moira. Have you seen Abby?"

"Hello, dearest," Moira smiled. "Last I saw that young lady, she was dancing with her boyfriend."

David chose to ignore that last part. "Are you sure? I could have sworn I saw her sitting here with you."

"No, I'm afraid you are mistaken," Moira said. "Why aren't you dancing with Amelia? It's rude to leave her alone."

"I think Amelia is doing just fine on her own. She has plenty of people to keep her amused," David said.

"Obviously," Moira said. "What do you expect when you're *still* chasing after that other girl? We talked about this, David. You need to remember who you are and all that your family has done for you before you go throwing it all away."

David frowned. "I'm not throwing it all away."

"Oh, but you are. You just won't listen to reason, will you? And don't you think it's cruel to lead a young woman on when you're about to leave the country with someone else? It's not fair to her or Amelia. Really, David, I would have thought better of you."

David felt anger blaze in his chest. He spoke slowly, in an effort to contain it. "Aunt Moira, I don't know how to make this any clearer to you. I may be going to London, but I have absolutely no intention of being with Amelia. *It is not going to happen.* This conversation is over." He walked away.

ଧଓଷଧଓଷଧଓଷ

Moira's mouth dropped open as David turned to leave, a storm raging in his pale blue eyes. David had never, *ever,* spoken like that. Not to her. It was that girl—she had ignited a tiny spark that somehow caught fire, and now look what had happened. Moira was going to have to manage the situation and quickly, before David did something foolish. She would get him back on track for his own good.

ଧଓଷଧଓଷଧଓଷ

Abby sat on the stone steps and unbuckled the silver ankle straps of her peacock blue satin shoes, sliding them off her feet and placing them beside her. The full skirt of her ball gown billowed around her, the hem grazing the sand, which soothed her bare feet. Abby wiggled her toes around, creating two shallow troughs, enjoying the cool feel of the sand against her skin.

A full moon illuminated the beach, casting a long beam of light across the water. In the moonlight, Abby could see small mounds of washed-up kelp littering the shore. Tiny crabs ducked and skittered under the cover of darkness from each pile of seaweed, avoiding the predatory shore birds patrolling the wet sand. A cool breeze caressed Abby's bare shoulders, carrying away the last of her anxiety about the confrontation in the ballroom. The brightness of the moon was momentarily veiled by thin clouds caught by the wind. In the darkness, she

191

could see faint flashes of pale green light in the crests of the breaking waves—blooming, bioluminescent algae glowing, agitated by the motion of the water.

"Is that seat taken?" a deep voice asked, interrupting her reverie. Abby looked up to see David coming down the steps above her, gesturing to the empty spot beside her. He was breathtakingly handsome in his tailored suit, his blue eyes as intense as ever, even in the dim moonlight.

"All yours," she managed. It really wasn't fair that he looked *that* good. How could she possibly hold an intelligent conversation with him when he looked like that? He sat down lightly beside her, with a grace that seemed at odds with his build.

"Beautiful night," David said, smiling.

Abby returned his smile. "A perfect autumn night. Like there's magic in the air."

He raised an eyebrow and grinned. "Magic?"

Abby groaned inwardly. *Cheesy. That was so cheesy.* "Well, you know," she laughed.

David had mercy on her. "It *is* magical," he said. "This is one of my favorite places in the whole world. I used to come down here all the time before I left for school."

They sat in silence for a moment, mesmerized by the peaceful, constant motion of the waves.

"So..." he began, as if searching for something to say. "Are you enjoying the Autumn Ball?"

Abby decided it was best not to mention the conversation with Moira. "Very much so. The inn looks beautiful tonight. It's quite a party," she replied.

"Where's your boyfriend?"

"Who, *Jon?*" Abby asked, surprised at the abruptness of his question. What was that in his voice? It couldn't be jealousy. Could it? "Oh, I thought you knew—he's not my boyfriend—just a good friend," she said. "He *is* my date tonight, but he's more like a brother. He's actually interested in someone else, and I'm fine with that. Totally cool with that."

"Aha." David leaned back against the stone steps, seemingly satisfied by her answer.

Abby wasn't going to let him off the hook that easily. "What about you? Where's *your* date?" she asked.

David shifted uncomfortably and cleared his throat, and then laughed. "Turnabout's fair play, I suppose. Amelia is...hmmm, you know, I don't actually know where Amelia is at the moment."

"She's very beautiful," Abby said.

David nodded. "She is. A fact not lost on the legions of young men vying for her attention. Last I saw her, she was surrounded by them, so I thought I'd take a walk."

"Oh." Abby didn't know what to say.

He shrugged. "It's fine, really. I invited her to satisfy my parents. Amelia is the daughter of one of my dad's English business partners, a longtime friend of the family. Our parents have always seemed to think we'd make a good match, but neither of us agree. We tried dating, but decided we're better off as friends."

"I'm sorry. Sounds awkward," Abby said, placing her hand on top of his in sympathy. "So the other day at the Buchans'—that's what Moira's lecture was about?"

"I'm afraid so," David said. He looked down at Abby's hand on his and then turned toward her, taking her hand in his strong ones, placing her palm against his and holding it up as though he was studying how they fit together. Her hand was smaller and more slender than his, but it fit perfectly.

Abby watched him, fascinated. She didn't dare speak, worried that if she said a word, he would stop touching her.

He looked up from their intertwined hands and into her eyes.

Abby smiled.

David returned her smile and then shook his head. "What was I saying? Oh yeah, Moira's lecture. Sorry—I got distracted." He gave Abby's hand a squeeze and let go. "So, my mom thought I was being rude to Amelia and somehow jeopardizing my future working in the London office because her father will be supervising me until I'm ready to take on more responsibility. Even though it's my dad's company, it's good to play nice with his colleagues. In some ways, I'll actually have to work harder *because* I'm his kid—everyone will second-guess me and think I only got the job because of my father. Anyway, suffice it to say, the talk with Moira was about my relationship with Amelia and a rather dated and not-so-gentle reminder that as a Corbin, I have a responsibility to associate with girls from similar social circles." A dark look crossed over his face.

Wincing, Abby looked away. Obviously she was not from the same social circle as the Corbins and Aunt Moira. That must be why the woman despised her so vehemently.

Riotous laughter erupted from above them as a drunken couple burst through the French doors from the ballroom, leaving them propped open to the patio. Music wafted down to the beach.

"Would you like to dance?" David asked. Standing, he held out his hand, holding her eyes with his.

Absolutely! Abby thought. "Sure," she said nonchalantly.

Abby placed one hand in David's and stood up, untangling the folds of her ball gown with her other hand. The dress unfurled gracefully around her, its hem sweeping the sand. Barefoot, she stepped toward him. He pulled her close, one hand still holding hers, the other on the small of her back, dangerously close, she noted, to the bare skin of her back and shoulders. She felt her skin tingle from her shoulder blades to the tips of her fingers. He was several inches taller than her, a perfect fit for slow dancing.

David smiled, his eyes flashing a brilliant blue. Abby returned his gaze and smiled back, trying very hard to calm the mad galloping of her heart hammering in her chest. They shuffled around, dancing in a slow circle, listening to the music. He pulled her closer still. His embrace felt so perfect, like their bodies were two halves of a whole. She rested her head on his shoulder, her face nestled close to his neck. He smelled amazing; she could detect both the subtle musk of cologne and the scent of his skin. His jaw lightly brushed against her forehead.

"You look beautiful tonight, Abby," David whispered.

The way he said her name sent a thrill of electricity coursing through her. Abby felt the Sign of the Throne pulsing against her skin, mirroring the rapid beat of her heart. She responded by holding David tighter. In that moment, no one else existed in the world. There was only the sound of their breathing, synchronized with the music and the waves.

The magic of the moment stretched to several songs. David was completely happy, holding Abby so close, his cheek pressed gently against the soft, warm skin of her forehead. And if he weren't mistaken, Abby was pretty content too, holding onto him just as tightly as he was holding her.

Then he heard someone calling her name. "Abby?" The woman's voice drifted down to them from the patio.

"Oh no," Abby whispered, as she pulled away from David's embrace. She smiled apologetically. "I have to go. Thanks for the dance." She whirled away and up the steps.

"Wait," David called after her. But she was gone.

Out of breath from her hurry, Abby reached the top of the steps where Cassandra was waiting.

"Oh!" Cassandra exclaimed, looking surprised by Abby's sudden appearance. "Hi, Abby. It's almost midnight and Moira is getting tired. We need to get her home."

"I understand," Abby said.

David appeared from behind Abby and placed his hand on the small of her back. He held out her shoes, the ankle straps hooked over one finger. "You forgot these."

Cassandra looked from the shoes down to Abby's bare feet, and then back up to Abby's face. Abby grinned sheepishly.

"Actually, Cassandra," David continued, "I can see Abby safely home." He met Abby's eyes. "If she wants to stay."

Abby smiled. "I'd love to stay a little longer."

Cassandra nodded. "No problem. Jon and Marisol are staying a bit longer too. Well, have a nice night."

"Thanks, Cassandra—I had a wonderful evening," Abby said.

"I'm glad," Cassandra replied. Winking, she turned and walked back into the ballroom, pulling the French doors shut behind her.

"No curfew?" David asked.

"No, my parents trust me," Abby said. "I've always been self-regulating—I don't even think they ever set a bedtime for me. I was just one of those kids who got tired and went to bed at a reasonable hour."

"Really? You must have been an easy kid to live with."

Abby shrugged. "I guess so. Come to think of it, I don't think they ever grounded me either. I think I actually grounded myself once, and my mother told me to go outside and play."

"Wow," David chuckled, taking her hand. "I had no idea I was in the presence of a saint."

"Hardly," Abby laughed.

"Oh?" There was that eyebrow thing of his again.

"I can be delinquent," Abby said.

"*Sure* you can," David teased.

"No really, I can," she insisted.

"Careful—I'll make you prove it." He slipped his arms around her waist. His eyes burned into hers.

She held his gaze, daring him. "Go ahead," she tempted.

"Maybe I will," he replied, and pulled her closer to him. She could feel the warmth of his hands on her skin as he held her tight against his chest. Her pulse quickened. He leaned in close, his lips grazing her neck. "But not tonight," he whispered in her ear.

Her pulse slowed. She pulled away and looked up at him, pouting teasingly. "You're no fun."

David laughed and shook his head in disbelief. "Take a walk with me?"

She smiled. "I'd love to."

He took her hand and they moved to a stone bench on the edge of the patio. "Here, you'll need these." He held out the shoes again. She sat down on the bench and he bent down on one knee. She raised her skirt so her feet were visible under the yards of fabric. He held her foot by the heel in one hand and slipped on the shoe with the other.

"The glass slipper—it fits!" he gasped in mock surprise.

So he's cheesy too. Abby didn't even mind the cliché.

"And I don't even have to run away at the stroke of midnight," she said, trying to be cool and not the giggling dork who threatened to reveal herself at his every touch. She succeeded—mostly—as he slipped on the second shoe and buckled the straps.

"So there *is* magic in the air," David said with a goofy grin, pulling her to her feet. He took her into his arms and kissed her forehead.

Then, taking Abby's hand, David turned toward an opening in the wall of red and pink oleanders that marked the entrance to the inn's garden; passing through, they entered a charming path. Wooly thyme filled the gaps between the path's flagstones, creeping over the surface of the stones like a velvet carpet. They passed under a pergola covered in a canopy of yellow roses and made their way to the center of the garden.

Their route was lit by white lights twinkling among the silvery green leaves of the olive trees lining the twisting path; the branches of the ancient, gnarled trees arched high over the flagstone. The garden was lush, the grounds covered with a variety of shade-loving plants. Blue hydrangea, pink foxglove, and wide-leaved hosta were thriving in the shelter of lavender crepe myrtle and white oleander trees, and ivy was creeping up the trunks of the trees into the branches. The moist sea air carried the fragrance of flowers.

At the center of the garden was a circular Spanish colonial fountain. Bubbling water coursed musically over stones into a pool that reflected the lights in the trees like shimmering stars.

David led Abby to the fountain and encircled her in his arms. "So…" he began.

"So…?" Abby smiled, waiting.

David furrowed his brow. "So, I need to tell you something."

"Okay." The sudden seriousness in his voice worried her.

"I think I—" He stopped mid-sentence. "I don't know how to say this," he said, frustrated.

"It's okay—whatever it is, I won't judge you," Abby said.

David looked at her, doubtful. She smiled, trying to reassure him.

"All right—here it is, dramatic as it may sound. I think I'm having an identity crisis," he said.

"How so?" Abby asked.

"Well, I thought I had my life figured out," David admitted. "You know how I told you that all my life my father has been grooming me to join his firm, to head up one of the branches?" Abby nodded. "I finished school last spring, went off on my own over the summer to travel, and then…" He paused, as if he were unsure he should continue.

"Then?" she prompted.

"Then I came home and met you," he finished.

"Oh." *What does that mean?* Abby thought, frowning.

"No, don't get me wrong—I'm *glad* I did," David reassured her, caressing her cheek. "The thing is, the first time I saw you, it was like something in my mind shook loose. Like there is something really important I need to remember, but I just can't. I started thinking about my life, this plan that has always been laid out for me, that I've always accepted but never actually consented to, and I thought, is this it? Is this all there is? Suddenly everything about my life felt so surreal— totally strange and foreign. You were the only thing that felt familiar—like you're an anchor to something more, something real."

Abby was silent, thinking. *Do I tell him now? Say, 'You know, it's the funniest thing—the reason you feel that way is you're the only heir to the throne in a world you don't even know exists. Your aunt kidnapped you as a baby and kept you from your destiny as a supercharged hero, complete with all kinds of cool powers. You're super strong, practically invincible, and I think you can even fly. Oh, and just a heads-up: if you don't return home soon, evil creatures are going to take over the world and kill us all. Good luck with that.' No, that's not going to freak him out at all...*

He was staring at her. "Abby?"

Okay, baby steps, Abby thought. *Forgive the detour, Eulalia—relationship first, then destiny.* "So, it sounds like you're having this internal conflict—but what about London? Are you still going to move there?"

"Maybe. Maybe not," he said. "I'm supposed to get on a plane in two days, but I don't want to go anymore."

"Why not?" she asked.

David looked at her. Sighing, he cupped her face in his hands, pressing his forehead against hers. "Don't you know?"

Abby placed her hands over his. She closed her eyes. "Maybe. But tell me anyway."

"Because of *you*," he said. He kissed her forehead again, and Abby opened her eyes to look at him. "I know it's crazy. I mean, we haven't known each other very long—"

"I don't think it's crazy," Abby said, shaking her head. She wrapped her arms around him and kissed his cheek.

David smiled. "That's good. But my parents would think it's crazy, which is why I haven't told them anything yet. I really like you, and that's part of why I don't want to leave."

"I like you too," she said. "And I don't want you to leave. But you said that liking me is only part of it. What's the other part?"

"The other part is the *really* crazy part," David said. "When I met you, it was like I'd seen you before, like I'd always known you, when I know, *I know,* I hadn't. I couldn't make sense of it. And all of a sudden, leaving felt wrong. I just had this sense of dread I couldn't explain. And then you were wearing this," he gestured to the silver seashell on the chain around her neck, "and I knew we were somehow connected— that what I feel is real."

She reached up automatically to touch the Sign of the Throne. "You said you'd seen my necklace before. Did you remember where?" she asked.

"I did," he said. "I have a pendant just like that at home. But I don't know where it came from. I never used to dream as a kid, but one night, I had this horrible nightmare—some kind of monster was in my room. When I woke the next morning, the silver seashell was under my pillow. I asked my parents about it, but they had no idea what I was talking about. They swore they didn't put it there and probably figured I made the whole thing up. I put it in a dresser drawer and forgot all about it until I saw your necklace."

"And you still have it?"

David nodded. "Yes. It's still there."

"Did anything else strange happen?" Abby asked.

"No, that's just it," he said. "Everything in my life has been perfect—too perfect. I don't remember any other weird experiences. At all. I feel like my whole life has been some kind of dream, like I've been in a…a fog for the past twenty-two years. I don't think anything bad, *truly* bad, has ever happened to me. I've never broken a bone—I don't even recall ever being sick."

"Everyone gets sick sometimes," Abby said. "Everyone has bad things happen."

"I know," David said. "Everyone but me. It's like my life isn't even real. Like it's all been scripted, contrived."

Now's your chance, Abby. Abby didn't know if that was her own thought or Eulalia's, but she understood—it was time. "David, do you trust me?"

He reached up and gently brushed away a stray curl that had fallen into her face, and then looked into her eyes. "Yes. Yes, I do."

"What if—what if I know what's happening to you?" she asked. "What if I told you a story that may be really hard to believe but is true? Absolutely true."

David looked unsure. "I guess I'm at the point where I need some answers."

"Then promise me—just listen and don't freak out," Abby said.

"Okay," David nodded. "I promise. No freaking out."

"All right," Abby said, staring into his eyes, willing him to believe her. "Then you should know that you weren't exactly adopted."

"What?" he asked. He had been holding her close, but then, as the shock registered on his face, she felt his arms go slack, his hands settling loosely around her waist. That couldn't be good.

Still, she had to press forward. "You were stolen," she said.

He stepped backward, away from her arms. "What?!"

"But not by your parents—they just found you and then had to pretend to adopt you—they didn't know that you were kidnapped." Abby stopped, realizing she was making things worse. "You promised not to freak out," she said. *Like that helps,* she thought. *He is freaking out. I screwed up. Again.*

David stared at her intently, his arms crossed over his chest. "And you said you were going to tell me the truth."

"I *am* telling you the truth," she pleaded, stepping toward him. "I swear I am."

David studied Abby's face. Again, she willed him to please, *please* believe her.

"Sorry," he said, "it's just...no, I'm sorry. Continue. Please." He put his arms around her again.

"Okay," Abby said, relieved that he wasn't going to run away. "I *know* this sounds crazy. I do. But I swear to you, what you have been led to believe about your life is *not* true. It all started...wait..." Abby paused. Out of the corner of her eye, she had seen something move in the olive tree on the other side of the fountain.

There was a dark shadow perched on a branch. Abby stared hard, and then recoiled when she realized that the dark silhouette had a feline shape, and that two of the twinkling lights in the tree were glowing red. Abby shivered with fear.

"Abby, what's wrong?" David stared at her and then looked quickly behind him, following her gaze. "What are you looking at?"

"We have to go—it's not safe to talk here." Abby grabbed David's hand and started tugging him back toward the inn.

He pulled his hand back and stood staring at her. "Abby, you're worrying me. What are you afraid of?"

"Please, David. I promise I'll explain everything," she said. "*Please*—we *have* to go."

"Okay." David looked behind him again. Then he took Abby's hand and they hurried back up the garden path.

She pushed him to go faster, looking frequently behind her and feeling a chill every time she heard the rustle of leaves or crackle of branches behind them. It was no use pretending to be calm—the thing knew she had seen it, and it was coming.

ଓଓଓଓଓଓ

Crossing under the pergola, David could see the lights of the ballroom. He didn't know what was going on, but he hoped that once they were inside, Abby would be able to explain.

When they reached the French doors by the patio, Abby let go of his hand and tried to wrench the doors open. They were stuck. David helped her pull them open and guided her

204

inside, his hand on the small of her back. Then he pulled the doors shut behind him.

In the light of the ballroom, he could see how pale she was—she was visibly shaken. She was staring wide-eyed out through the French doors, as if she were trying to see if they had been followed.

David eyed her seriously. "Abby."

Abby turned to him. "It's gone for now."

He crossed his arms again. "*What* is gone for now? I need to know what's going on." He knew his voice had an edge to it, anger disguising his fear.

"I know you do," she replied quietly. "We need to go someplace safe to talk."

"Okay, fine," David said. He uncrossed his arms. "Let's go to my house. It's just a few streets down."

"No, that's too close—it could get in the house," Abby said. "I think once we get out of Newcastle Beach we'll be okay. Come with me to my house."

"And if I do, you'll stop being so cryptic and tell me what's going on?" David asked, holding out his hand to her.

She took his hand. "I'll tell you everything I know."

ഇരുജ്ഞ

David noticed Abby was very quiet during the car ride to her house. He was too. His mind was on her, trying to figure out what had just happened. Things had seemed so great, and then had gone from zero to crazy in sixty seconds.

He had started it with that stupid identity crisis thing—he probably should have kept that to himself. It sounded so ridiculous now that he'd actually said it out loud. His intention had been to tell her how he felt, that he wanted to be with her, and to find out if she wanted to be with him too. But no, he'd messed it all up, babbling about who knew what.

He was surprised by her reaction to what he'd said. Did she really know what was happening to him? And what did she see in that garden? Was something really there or was she hallucinating? Her reaction was too strong not to be real. He knew one thing for sure—if she turned out to be simply a paranoid schizophrenic, he was going to seriously question his own mental state, not to mention his taste in women.

∞∞∞∞∞∞

Abby sat staring out the window, replaying the scene over and over in her mind. Those red eyes, the dark feline outline of the creature. Was it the shadow boy again? She cringed. If so, why hadn't it attacked? How long had it been there, just watching? And how, how could she possibly explain all this to David?

She looked at him. He was stoically silent, eyes straight ahead, focused on the road. He had actually opened up for a moment and made himself vulnerable, and now he seemed locked away in his fortress of solitude again.

As they crossed over the stone circle that defined the boundaries of Newcastle Beach, it began to rain. Listening to the soft patter of rain against the car's windows, Abby felt a weight lift from her heart. Even though David wasn't talking to her, at least they were safe for the moment.

David kept his eyes on the road, driving slowly. He turned into Abby's driveway, stopped the car, put it in park, and shut it off, taking the keys from the ignition. He sat quietly for a moment, and then moved his hand to rest on hers.

He looked into her eyes and smiled weakly.

Please don't think I'm insane, she thought, returning his look with a humorless smile.

ೞೞೞೞೞೞ

David followed Abby out of the car and up the porch steps, hurrying to avoid getting drenched. He waited while Abby got out her key, opened the door, and locked it behind them once they were inside. Then, she took David's hand and led him upstairs to her room. She closed the bedroom door quietly behind her and lit a candle on her dresser.

In the candlelight, she put a finger to her lips, beckoning him to be quiet and not wake her family. She gestured toward the bed and he sat down, waiting for her. She opened her closet door, retrieved a cylindrical cardboard container of salt, and proceeded to pour a line of salt on the windowsill and in the gap between the bottom of the door and the floor.

He watched, confused. *What is she doing?* he thought. *I knew it. She's nuts. I need to re-evaluate my choices in women.*

"Just in case," she whispered. "Just in case we were followed."

Of course, he thought, *because that explains everything.*

She closed the thin metal top of the salt container and placed it beside the candle. Then she sat down next to him. "Okay. So first, let me explain my behavior in the garden. If you're still here after that, I'll tell you the rest of the story."

ॐ⅋ॐ⅋ॐ⅋

Abby started her story with the creature in the garden, tracing back to her first encounter with it at the Buchans'. She wondered what David was thinking. He seemed to be taking it in, sitting patiently and nodding encouragingly in all the right places. She stopped the story for a moment to gauge his reaction. "Well, what do you think so far? Do you believe me?"

"Honestly?" he asked.

She nodded. "Yes."

"I'm...having this battle in my mind," David said. "It sounds so far-fetched, like something from a horror movie, and yet there's this nagging feeling within me that insists it's for real. Remember the nightmare I told you about? The one I had before finding the seashell under my pillow?"

"Yes," Abby said, feeling a tiny bit hopeful. Maybe he would stay. Maybe he believed her.

"The details of the dream are foggy, but I distinctly remember the monster," David said. "A dark, hulking, shadow thing with red eyes. And there was something banging at my window. Then I heard this unearthly scream. It woke me up. I sat up in bed and looked around my room, but there was nothing there. So, assuming this is real, why does this creature want to kill me?"

"That's where things get complicated," Abby said. "It's a long story—are you willing to hear me out?"

David nodded, taking her hand, and she continued.

ৼ୦ড়ৼ୦ড়ৼ୦ড়

Jon yawned and dragged himself out of bed. He had gotten home well after midnight, and his dreams had been a replay of a rather wonderful evening with Marisol. He couldn't wait to see her again. He had promised to call her the next day, but he needed advice. He didn't want to seem too eager. Better to play it cool. Abby would know what to say. He wondered if she was awake yet.

Pulling on a pair of jeans, he walked over to the window and opened the blinds. He glanced across the fence to Abby's house—her blinds were open too. And she wasn't alone.

He looked down at her driveway and saw David Corbin's car. He frowned, and then he grabbed his phone off the nightstand and dialed Abby.

ৼ୦ড়ৼ୦ড়ৼ୦ড়

Abby was exhausted. She and David had talked until the candle burned out and the first rays of sunlight illuminated the room. Abby even showed him her journal, where she had recorded her dreams and made rough sketches of the creatures from Eulalia's stories. It had been a much longer night than she had expected.

"You must be so tired," David said. "I should go and let you get some sleep."

"I'm not that tired," Abby lied, yawning. "You don't have to go."

He smiled. "You're a bad liar when you've been up too long. I don't want to go, but I'd better get myself gone before your dad finds out I was here all night and kills me."

She laughed. "Good point—he might. So when do I get to see you again?"

"I'll call you this afternoon, by four at the latest." He stood up to leave.

"Does that mean you'll go with me to see Eulalia?"

"Yes, I will," David promised. He took her hands and looked into her eyes. "I *do* believe you, Abby. I won't lie to you though. I'm torn—part of me still says this is crazy." He paused, studying her reaction. "Sorry, I mean, it's illogical. I'm trying to make sense of everything you've told me. But the other part insists that this is real, and everything else has been an illusion. I feel like I'm waking up from a dream."

"I know the feeling."

He smiled. "I know you said time is of the essence here, but don't worry. I plan to go with you today. I can't *not* go, actually. Not if there's even the slightest chance this is real. But if I'm really going to leave everything I know and go to Cai Terenmare, I need to at least say good-bye to my parents and try to explain why I'm going. I owe them that much at least. And if it's true that my so-called adoption was a lie, I think they owe me an explanation, too. The problem is, I have no idea *how* to have this little chat with them. That's why I need to get home to my own bed. I have a lot to think about, but I think a little sleep will help."

"No, you're right," Abby agreed. "We both need a few hours sleep."

On Abby's dresser, her cell phone began to vibrate. She stood up quickly and grabbed it, stopping it from buzzing.

"Somebody's up early," David noted.

Abby looked at the caller ID and put the phone back down. "It's just Jon. I'll call him back after I walk you out."

She put her arms around David. "David, at the risk of sounding paranoid: what if you go home and something bad happens to you?"

He looked out the window. "It's daylight now—I don't think anything will happen." He leaned forward and kissed her cheek. "Don't worry. I'll be fine."

He opened her bedroom door, breaking the line of salt as the door swung open. She scooped up her phone and walked him downstairs to the front porch. David pulled Abby into his arms. "Well, I can safely say that this has been the most interesting night of my life," he chuckled sleepily.

She hugged him, resting her head against his chest. "For what it's worth, I had a nice night, David. Thanks."

"Me too. It was very enlightening. In a lot of ways." He lifted her face to his and kissed her lips softly. She wrapped her arms around his neck, and he pulled her closer, kissing her again, harder. Finally he let her go. "You know," he grinned, "if we keep this up, your dad really *is* going to kill me."

Abby's phone began to vibrate again. She looked at it like it was some alien object—when David pulled her into his arms, she had forgotten that she was still holding it in her hand. His touch had a very distracting affect on her. "Jon, *again*. I'm so sorry," she said. "His timing really sucks."

"He lives next door to you?" David asked.

Abby stopped the phone from buzzing and set it on the porch railing. "Yeah—how did you know that?"

"Because he's staring at us," David said, frowning. He let out a long breath. "And I was worried about your dad wanting to kill me."

Abby looked over at Jon's house. Jon was standing at his second-story bedroom window, holding his cell phone. His eyes were locked on David. Judging by the dark angel of death look on Jon's face, it was clear he was focused on one thought: destroying David in the quickest and most painful manner possible. Abby was fairly certain that had Jon been able to shoot lasers from his eyes at that moment, David would have been reduced to a pile of smoking ash.

"I thought the two of you weren't together," David said.

Abby glared up at Jon. "We're not."

"Does *he* know that?"

"He *does*, but I'll be sure to remind him." She turned back to look into David's eyes. "I'm *really* sorry."

"Don't worry about it," David said, holding her gaze. "If I was him, I wouldn't want someone else kissing you either. Not that his reaction deters me in the least." He grinned and kissed her again.

Abby wondered for a moment if the kiss was for her benefit or Jon's, and then decided she didn't care. She kissed David back, hard.

David pulled away and sighed. "Are you *trying* to make it difficult for me to leave?"

She smiled. "Absolutely."

He shook his head and laughed. "You evil, *evil* girl. I'll talk to you soon."

"Okay." Abby kissed his cheek and let him go, watching him drive away.

When David was out of sight, she looked up at Jon's window. He was still staring at her. Frowning, she picked up her phone from the porch railing and dialed his number. "*What?*" she asked.

"You tell me," Jon said, enraged. "You let him spend the night with you?"

"No! Well, I mean, he was here, but we were just talking. Nothing happened!"

"It didn't look like nothing," Jon growled.

"Why are you even looking?" Abby asked. She walked down the front steps toward his house. "It's *none* of your business!"

"It *is* my business." Jon's tone of voice had taken on a deadly calm. "When someone is trying to take advantage of you, it is my business to protect you."

Abby rolled her eyes. "He is *not* trying to take advantage of me. He just kissed me. It's not a big deal. Besides, what about all that stuff you said about giving me your blessing?"

"I changed my mind."

"You can't change your mind," Abby said.

"I can. I revoke my blessing. I don't want you with him. I want you with *me*."

"No," Abby said, shaking her head. "I'm not going to be with you. I'm with David now, and you're with Marisol. I thought you really liked her."

"I do. But I can't stand the idea of *you* being with *him*."

"Well, you're going to have to deal with it, because I'm in love with him."

Jon's expression darkened and he hung up the phone. He pulled the blinds closed.

"Fine," Abby snarled, glaring at Jon's window. "I'm too tired to talk to you anyway, jerk." She stormed back inside the house, locked the door, and trudged upstairs to finally tumble into bed. She was furious with Jon, but she didn't want to think about him.

Instead, she forced Jon from her mind and thought about David. Telling him the secret had gone better than she expected. David believed her, and at least he was still on speaking terms with her. He had kissed her, and it looked like he wouldn't mind doing it again. And once they got a few hours of sleep, he was coming with her to meet Eulalia. Aside from the conflict with Jon, maybe things were finally coming together.

CHANGELINGS

David dragged himself into his bedroom and glanced at his watch: 5:59 a.m. His parents were still asleep—they'd left the ball long before. Hopefully they would let him sleep for a few hours. He set his alarm clock for one in the afternoon so he would have time to talk with his parents before calling Abby.

He sat on the edge of his bed and pulled off his jacket and shoes. Untucking his dress shirt, he lay on his bed.

Wait. He sat back up. Pulling open the top drawer of the nightstand, he rifled through some loose papers and belongings. *Where is that pendant?* His fingers closed around it, and he retrieved it from the messy drawer. He studied it, fascinated as silvery blue light streaked across the shell, coming to life in response to his touch.

It was true—everything Abby had said was true. His trip to London was off.

He tucked the shell into his pants pocket and settled into bed, his hands folded beneath his head under the pillow. He stared up at the ceiling. He didn't know what fate had in store for him, but knowing that Abby would be there with him gave him peace. Thinking of her, he drifted off to sleep.

Hours later, Abby awoke to a knock on her door. She opened her eyes—the light in the room had shifted. *What time is it? Almost four?* She had slept solidly for ten hours.

Bethany Brown opened the door, her green eyes twinkling mischievously. "Well good *morning*, Sleeping Beauty. Have fun last night?"

Abby realized she had fallen asleep in her dress. "Oops—guess I crashed."

Abby's mother smiled. "Guess so. Jonathon called while you were dead to the world."

Abby frowned. "I don't want to talk to him."

"Why not? Didn't you have fun together?" Bethany asked.

"We did, but then we got into a little argument. Did David call?" Abby asked.

"David?" her mother asked, feigning ignorance. Abby rolled her eyes, and her mother hid a smile.

"Yes, Mom, David Corbin," Abby said. "Did he?"

Bethany shook her head. "Sorry, no. Was your little argument with Jon about David, by chance?"

"Kind of." Abby was disappointed. Why hadn't David called? She looked at the clock again. He had said he would call by four at the latest, so maybe he was still talking to his parents. *Shower first, and then, if he doesn't call, I'm calling him,* she thought, trying to reassure herself. It didn't work. She was worried.

"Sounds like an exciting night. Are you going to fill me in on the details?" her mother asked.

"Yeah, Mom," Abby answered, her mind distracted. She had a bad feeling—something was wrong. She couldn't shake the thought that David was in danger. *If he doesn't call by five, I'm going over there to make sure he's okay.* "Hey Mom, can I borrow the car?"

"No—sorry, honey. Your dad had to run in to the office, and I have to take Matthew to his friend's birthday party, remember?"

"Oh. Yeah, sorry. I was thinking I'd go over to Newcastle Beach," Abby said.

"Hmm, I wonder why," Bethany smiled. "Well, I'd take you over there, but Matt and I have to leave in fifteen minutes. I think you'll take longer than that to get ready, won't you?"

Abby caught a glance of herself in the mirror on her dresser. Her hair was a frizzed-out mess—she definitely needed that shower. "Yeah, I'm afraid so. It's okay, Mom. I can walk like I usually do." *If he doesn't call by five-thirty, I'm walking. No, make that six. Ugh—I sound like a stalker.*

"All right, sweetie," Bethany said. "Take your umbrella though—looks like we're in for more rain."

ಭುಗ್ಯಭುಗ್ಯಭುಗ್ಯ

It was well after dark when David woke from his own dreamless sleep. He looked at the digital clock on the nightstand, which was blinking *12:00*.

No way, he thought. *I did* not *sleep until midnight.* He checked his watch: 6:02 p.m. Twelve hours since he left Abby. He was surprised he had slept so long, but then again, he was exhausted when he finally crawled into bed. He'd set the alarm though, hadn't he? He couldn't remember.

David looked back at the blinking clock. Something must have happened with the electricity. He couldn't remember the power going off, but it must have—why else would the clock need resetting? Maybe there had been a storm and he slept through it. He manually synched the digital clock with his wristwatch and then got out of bed to find his cell phone.

He had promised he would call Abby and he hadn't—she was probably worried. As he pulled the phone from his suit jacket, the cell's lighted screen blinked once and went dead. He tried to turn the phone back on, but the screen remained black. *Great,* he thought. Now the cell wasn't working either. He would just have to use the phone downstairs.

David changed quickly, pulling on his favorite pair of jeans and a T-shirt. Reverently, he transferred his half of the Sign of the Throne from his suit pants pocket to the one in his jeans. He grabbed his leather jacket off the back of a chair and stuffed the useless phone inside.

He made a detour to the upstairs bathroom to splash cold water on his face. Inspecting himself in the mirror, he had to admit that he probably needed a shave, if not a shower. He looked rugged—his hair a little wild, his jaw stubbled. He sniffed his T-shirt; at least it smelled okay. He didn't want to take too much time—he had a feeling he was going to get on Abby's bad side if he kept her waiting and worrying too long. Maybe she liked the unkempt bad-boy look.

He started toward the stairs. *Keys,* he remembered, and hurried back to his room. There they were, right where he'd left them on the nightstand. He glanced at the clock and shook his head in disbelief. *Again?* The digital clock was blinking *12:00.* Obviously something was wrong with the thing—the power was still on. He swiped his keys and stuffed them in one jeans pocket, checking the other to make sure the mystical seashell was still there.

Descending the stairs, David heard his parents talking in hushed tones in the kitchen. As he entered, he noticed two things. First, their conversation abruptly came to a halt. His mother and father were standing slightly apart, smiling pleasantly at him. Second, the kitchen was an absolute mess. The countertops and cabinet doors were slathered with some kind of dark goo. It was thick, oily, and dripping off the surfaces of the kitchen—the doors of the refrigerator and oven, the dishes that were waiting to be put in the dishwasher, and even the window over the sink. And it *smelled*. Sulfur maybe, or rotten meat. As it oozed onto the kitchen floor, the oil seemed to gather in the center of the room, its darkness gaining density.

"David, darling," his mother said. "You're finally awake. I hope you enjoyed yourself last evening." She smiled sweetly.

David made no reply. He felt the hairs on the back of his neck prickle—something was wrong here. Her eyes...they were just a little too dark, almost as if they too were filled with that toxic oil.

"David," said his father, "it is rude not to answer your mother when she speaks to you." His eyes, too, were strange, otherworldly.

"That is *not* my mother," David said.

"Of *course* I am, Silly Billy," Margaret giggled. Her voice was childlike; sickeningly sweet. "Who *else* would I be? Someone had a *liiiiittle* too much wine last night, didn't he?"

Open armed, she stepped toward David, right through the oil on the floor, as if she didn't notice the mess. The oil sucked at her feet, bristling, sprouting glistening black spikes that looked like oily fur standing on end. She didn't notice that either. A grin stretched across her face, a little too wide, like it was carved into her flesh.

She pulled him into a hug, her hot breath in his face that same sour meat smell, the smell of something dead and rotting. It filled his nostrils, turning his stomach. He couldn't breathe. Panicked, he plunged his hand into his pocket, retrieving the sigil of the Solas Beir on pure instinct. It pulsed rapidly now, in synch with his frightened heartbeat. Not thinking, only acting, he plunged the Sign of the Throne into her face. As the silver shell made contact with her cheek, the skin began to smoke, turning black with heat, sinking inward like a rotting melon. She wrenched away, grabbing her face with both hands, screaming like an angry hellcat.

David's horror at this was short-lived. The thing pretending to be his father growled. It was a low, menacing snarl that made David's intestines feel like they were squirming around in his gut—a primal response to unadulterated fear. He turned and fled, shoving the sigil back into his pocket, not daring to look back. There was no need anyway—he could clearly hear the squishing, sucking sound of the oil on the kitchen floor as the creature plowed through it in hot pursuit of its prey.

David clawed open the wood door to the garage, flew through it, and pushed it shut. Beside the door was a heavy steel tool case; he shoved it over on its side, blocking the door to buy time, just a little time. He reached up and palmed the button for the automatic garage door opener as he raced to his motorcycle. As he shoved on his helmet, a deafening bang shook the garage. A wrench lying on his workbench fell to the floor with a metallic clang. David looked behind him to see the blocked door dent and splinter, the tool case threatening to go scooting across the garage floor as it was violently rammed.

He turned anxiously back to the paneled garage door, straining to hear the small motor of the opener whir to life. All he could hear was the relentless thrashing of the creature against the blocked door and the roar of the bike's engine. There was nothing else.

Come on, COME ON! David thought, as if by mere force of will he could open the door. To his surprise, the door did open, a little, but not enough to allow his escape.

David put down the bike's kickstand, and the engine sputtered to a stop. Running to the garage door, he forcibly shoved it upward and rolled it back on its metal tracks. He leapt back to the motorcycle and kick-started it again.

For a second, he held his breath, worried that the bike too would fail him, but he heard its familiar roar. Then the toolbox clattered across the floor as the door exploded and showered the garage in a ticker-tape jettison of wood fragments. David didn't wait to see what emerged—he held down the throttle and was gone.

೮೦೮೮೦೮೮೦೮

Abby was worried to the point of panic. By the time she was done debriefing her mother, showering, and getting ready, it was after five-thirty—and still no call from David. The sun was setting fast, and pretty soon, the Darkness would gather and grow strong. The Shadows would be on the prowl. After trying David's cell and his parents' landline twice each and getting no answer, not even voicemail, she knew for certain that something was wrong.

Where was he? He had promised to call, and after last night, she was certain he would keep his word. *If* he could. But that was just it, wasn't it? She thought about the Shadows and feared the worst. She had to find him and get him to Eulalia so they could fix the portal. Her resolve outweighed her fear. She grabbed her hoodie, keys, and phone, and walked out the door. Looking at the phone, she noticed that Jon had called yet again. She didn't want to talk to him, but at least she knew her phone was working and she hadn't somehow missed David's call.

As she stepped off her front porch, lightning streaked across the clouds and the sky opened up, pouring down rain. *Great.* She looked back at the house, annoyed at herself for forgetting her umbrella, and then decided she didn't care if she got wet. She yanked up her hood and started walking down the driveway, aggravated for the ten-billionth time that all the money she had saved from working had to go toward college and not a car. Behind her, she heard a door slam. *Jon.* She ignored him and kept walking.

"So, what, you're not talking to me at all now?" he asked, jogging up to her.

"No," Abby said, walking faster. "I'm still mad at you."

He kept pace with her. "Where are you going?"

"None of *your* business," she said. "Leave me alone."

Jon grabbed her arm. "Abby, stop. Please."

She stopped and glared at him. He was getting drenched, and she couldn't help but feel a little smug about it, even though she was getting wet too.

"Look," Jon said. "I'm sorry, okay? I really *was* trying to be cool about you being with David, but then I saw him kissing you, and I just flipped out. It wasn't fair of me to accuse you of doing something wrong or tell you that you had to be with me instead."

"No," Abby replied. "It *wasn't* fair. Especially since I've been really supportive about you and Marisol."

"I know," Jon said. "I was being overprotective. I love you. But I get that you want to be with him and I respect that. And you're right—I do like Marisol. A lot. I do want to be with her. I've been trying to move on from you and me, but I had a little relapse."

Abby raised her eyebrows. "A relapse?"

Jon nodded. "Yes. I screwed up and I'm sorry. I was an idiot. Can you forgive me?"

Abby smiled. "I forgive you, you idiot." She started to pull him into a hug and then pushed him away. "Ugh! You're sopping wet!"

He grinned and grabbed her, pulling her against his wet T-shirt. "So we're good? You still love me?"

She tried to wriggle from his grasp and realized it was a futile effort. "If I say yes, will you stop trying to soak me?"

Nodding, he gave her a lopsided smile that made him look like an adoring but simple-minded puppy. She had to admit it was endearing, even though she was irritated that he wouldn't let her go. Between him and the rain, her jacket was dripping, and the water was seeping through to her T-shirt.

"*Fine*," Abby said. "We're good."

"Aaaand?" The stupid puppy grin widened.

She gave him a dirty look. "And I still love you. Idiot."

"And all is well," Jon laughed, kissing her forehead and releasing her. "So where *are* you going?"

"You're not going to like it," she said.

Jon frowned. "Oh. To see *him*."

Abby gave him a look of warning.

"No," Jon said, holding up his hands in surrender. "It's fine. I'm not objecting."

"Really?" she asked.

Jon nodded. "I'm a changed man. I'll play nice from here on out. Scout's honor." He held up three fingers as if that proved he meant it.

Abby laughed. "You weren't a Boy Scout. *You* were a juvenile delinquent."

"Delinquent? I prefer the term *lovable rogue*," Jon countered. His eyes smoldered, and he took a step toward her.

Abby held up her hands to keep him at bay. "Nice try, Jonathon. If only we could bottle that formidable charm of yours and use it for good instead of evil."

Jon put his hands on his hips and grinned. "Kidding. But admit it—you *do* still find me charming."

"Yeah, you're a veritable prince. But seriously, Jon, I really do hope you and David can get along, for my sake," Abby said. "Anyway, I really need to go find him. He was supposed to call me, and he hasn't. I have a bad feeling that something is wrong. That he's in danger."

The cocky grin vanished from Jon's face. "From those shadow things, you mean?"

"Yeah. I told him about Cai Terenmare. *That's* what we were doing all last night, by the way—talking," Abby assured him. "He believes me and we're going to repair the portal tonight. I'm headed to his house to make sure he's okay."

"Well, you can't walk there in this storm," Jon said. "And if those creatures are out there waiting for you, there's no way I'm letting you go alone. I'll drive."

Jon jogged back into his house and grabbed his car keys from the side table by the front door. As he backed his car out of the garage, he saw that Abby had taken refuge on his front porch. He felt guilty for forcing her to stand in the rain while they talked, so he made up for it by pulling up as close to the porch as he could so she wouldn't get any wetter.

He was sorry for acting so jealous about her and David. That she hadn't objected to him driving her to David's house was a sign he hadn't done irreparable damage to their friendship. If it would make Abby happy, he would try to make amends when he saw David. That didn't mean Jon trusted him, though. He still thought the guy was going to rip out Abby's heart sooner or later. It was only a matter of time before she got hurt. But at least Jon and Abby were still talking—he'd be there for her no matter what happened with David.

Abby got in and buckled up. "Thanks for coming with me. I'm glad I don't have to do this alone." She took his hand and squeezed it.

Jon nodded and put the old Mustang in drive, exiting the muddy driveway. "What do you think we'll find when we get to his house?"

"I'm not sure, but—Jon, I swear I saw one of the Shadows at the inn last night." Abby filled him in, starting with when she fled the ballroom after the confrontation with Moira, and ending with when she told David the truth about his origins.

Jon listened, trying to keep an open mind, insane as it sounded. They had been friends far too long for him not to

225

believe her. Still, it was hard to wrap his mind around the idea that these things she kept seeing might actually exist outside those strange dreams of hers. He had never seen anything even remotely close to that—not even El Cucuy, the spooky Mexican closet monster his mom told him about once. The mere idea of the Shadows gave him the creeps. Once they got to David's house and saw he was okay, they could take him to the queen and all this craziness would be over. He hoped.

Suddenly, through the blurred glass of the windshield, Jon could see a single headlight bobbing toward them in the rain, speeding fast in the wrong lane. He hit the brakes. Out of the corner of his eye, he saw Abby brace herself against the dashboard, her seatbelt cinching her in tight. The Mustang's brakes locked, sending the car skidding along on the wet road. Jon wasn't going to be able to stop in time. The motorcycle accelerated and cut to the right at the last second, tipping wildly.

The car kept skidding and then stopped abruptly as it slammed into something solid. Jon hit his head on the steering wheel. As he slumped forward, he felt Abby reaching for him. "No, no, *no*..." she said, repeating the word like it was a prayer.

Groaning, Jon lifted his head from the steering wheel and with shaking hands rubbed the bulging goose egg he felt forming. "Owwww..."

"Are you okay?" Abby asked, taking his face in her hands, inspecting his injury.

"More or less. Ow—don't *touch* it," Jon whined when her fingers brushed the bump on his forehead. He started to squirm away from her, but he twisted his neck too much and the pounding pain in his head increased. He submitted to being mothered. "You?"

"Shaken up, but yeah, I'm fine," she said, looking him over. She released him, apparently satisfied that he would live. "What did we hit?"

"No idea. I remember seeing the bike skid by and then, bam! We got hit out of nowhere."

"You didn't see anything?" Abby asked.

"No...maybe. Some kind of large, black animal—a bear?" Jon craned his neck over the steering wheel, trying to peer through the streaks of water pouring down the windshield. The rain was relentless. Jon realized that during the collision he must have accidently hit the off switch for the windshield wipers. He turned them back on. They scraped halfway across the glass and died.

Suddenly, something banged against Abby's window. She jumped and let out a small scream. The banging continued, the frantic beating of a hand against the glass. The motorcycle rider wrenched off his helmet and tugged at the handle of the passenger door, trying to get in.

"It's David." She tried without success to yank open her door—the lock was jammed and she couldn't get it to release. "Help me unlock the door—he wants us to unlock the door!" she yelled.

"Oh! Sorry—stupid tricky locks." Jon reached over and released the lock.

David opened the door and slid in, sharing the seat with Abby. He slammed the door closed and punched the button for the lock. His eyes were wild and frightened. He didn't say a thing, but stared out the windshield, looking for something.

I almost killed him, Jon thought. *If he hadn't turned the bike in time...* "Are you okay, man? I almost ran into you."

David turned to look at Jon. "I know. It's what I was betting on."

Jon was incredulous. "What? Are you *crazy*? You were driving on the wrong side of the road *on purpose*?"

"Yes. Sorry about your car. But you hit the thing dead on target."

"The thing?" Abby asked.

David nodded. "Yeah. Remember my nightmare monster? Well, guess what—it's back. And it's trying to kill me."

As if on cue, the whole vehicle shook as something massive peeled itself from the crushed grill of the car. A muscled, hairless cat beast emerged and placed its front paws on the hood of the car, its wicked talons screeching against the metal. Its eyes glowed dull red in the black abyss of its sockets. Spotting its intended prey in the vehicle, the creature flattened its small ears and growled, a low, reverberating sound. Jon could feel the vibrations of that sound as it passed through the floorboards, echoing through the car's battered frame, shaking the vinyl bucket seats. The beast's ragged muzzle was pulled back, revealing a mouth full of needle-sharp teeth.

"Holy crap," breathed Jon, in the understatement of the year. He knew what the thing was going to do next. It was going to climb the hood slowly, toying with them before crushing in the windshield and eating them all alive.

David unbuckled Abby's seatbelt and then strapped himself in with her. He said something to Jon, who was transfixed by the creature. Jon turned to David. "What?"

"Put the car in reverse," David repeated. "Back up quickly. Then hit the gas and ram that thing."

Jon nodded. Effective methods for slaying psychopathic cat beasts had not been covered in school, but they should have been. *Note to self,* he thought, *if we survive this, Dr. Buchan should add, "monsters with personality disorders" to her syllabus. It's really important to be prepared for this kind of thing.* The screeching of the cat's claws on the hood underscored that point.

"Hey, you heinous hell-fiend—now you're messing with my car." Jon revved the engine and threw the Mustang into reverse, putting some distance between them and the creature. The beast seemed undeterred as its front paws slid off the car to the ground. It sat back on its haunches, confident, its scrubby tail twitching. Was it laughing—*actually laughing*—at them?

"I'll give you something to laugh about, Chuckles." Jon smiled grimly to himself. He patted the Mustang's steering wheel affectionately. *Sorry, baby,* he thought.

Then he slammed his foot down on the gas pedal. The car peeled out and sped forward.

The creature was not amused. It stood its ground, growling, bracing itself for impact. The car hit it all right—hit it and plowed over the top of it, settling onto two tires at an angle, with the beast underneath.

"Is it dead?" Jon asked.

"I doubt it," replied Abby and David at the same time.

Jon looked at them. "Seriously?"

"Unfortunately, yes. We need silver to kill it," Abby explained.

"What, like a werewolf?" Jon asked.

229

This time David answered. "More than you know. Quick—everybody out before it turns us over and crushes us. Aunt Moira's place is just over there, and I know she's got silver in that house."

☙CȜ☙CȜ☙CȜ

Abby and David followed Jon out the driver's side door and ran toward the Buchans' Victorian home in the rain, which had slowed to a drizzle. As they were passing through the front gate, the Mustang began to rock violently back and forth while the beast tried to crawl free.

By the time they had reached the front door, a loud crash reverberated behind them as the car tipped all the way over and the creature wrenched loose. The beast leapt on top of the overturned vehicle, causing the windows to shatter and the roof to cave in.

"My car!" Jon cried. He looked distraught. Abby felt bad for him—she knew how much he loved his car.

"Sorry, Jon," she said, "but we *really* have to go. It's coming."

And it was—the beast fixed its eyes on Abby and grinned. It was a mischievous, satisfied grin that would have appeared playful had it not been on the ugly mug of a bloodthirsty monster that wanted to rip her throat out. Abby pulled on Jon's arm while David opened the front door.

"Fine. It can have the car."

"Make you a deal," David said, slamming the door behind them. "If we kill that thing, I'll get you a new Mustang. Seeing how you saved my life and all."

"You better."

"I will," David promised.

Abby looked around the living room—where was everyone? The Buchans' car was outside, so they had to be home. "Cassandra? Riordan?" Abby called.

"Up here in the office!" Riordan shouted from his study upstairs. Abby could hear an edge to his voice—something was wrong. The lights in the house began to flicker.

"Okay David, you and Jon get the silver, and I'll grab the salt," Abby said.

David beckoned Jon to follow him into the dining room and Abby ran to the kitchen. Through the kitchen door, Abby could see that there was an uneaten meal on the table—she was even more worried now. She heard a clatter as David and Jon scooped up silverware from the sideboard. They met Abby in the hall near the stairs. She had commandeered several containers of salt.

"The salt won't hold the beast for long," she explained, "but maybe it will buy us time to figure out how to kill it." She turned and charged up the stairs with David and Jon close behind.

Abby led the way to Riordan's office. As she stepped into the room, a large black shadow cat emerged from behind a stack of books piled on the floor; it hissed and jumped at her. Screaming, she poured salt on it, reducing it to a smoking ruin of black sludge. David and Jon hurried into the room, looking alarmed. "I'm okay," she said, waving them off. "It tried to bite me, but I annihilated its butt."

David let out a low whistle and grinned. "I'll say. Nicely done."

Abby started to smile, but then the lights began to flicker again and Riordan called out, "I'm sorry, Abby—we should have left when you warned us. I believed you—I just didn't know what they were like—I didn't *know*..." He sounded scared. Abby looked across the room to see him and Cassandra pressed up against the bay windows, holding their children. There was no sign of Moira.

"We were eating dinner," Cassandra said, her eyes wide with horror. "They just appeared out of thin air. Suddenly they were *everywhere*." She nodded her head toward the ceiling.

Abby looked up. The ceiling was covered with black shadow cats—they started to slink down the walls, bristling and dripping toxic oil, surrounding the humans. Quickly, Abby, David, and Jon crossed the room to the Buchans. Abby poured a circle of salt around everyone, and David handed silver eating utensils to Riordan and Cassandra. Abby also swiped Riordan's silver-plated, dagger-shaped letter opener from his desk, studying her choice as she held it out threateningly. It wasn't very sharp, but it was better than a fork or a butter knife.

ഇൽ൞ഇൽ൞ഇൽ

David watched with horror as the Kruorumbrae advanced to the circle's edge—but they were not crossing. Maybe the salt boundary would hold them back. There was a larger, lemur-like cat in their midst, about the size of a German shepherd. It walked right up to the line of salt and sat down on its haunches. Its rotting smell was all too familiar to David. A Cheshire cat grin was carved into one side of its face, and the other was ruined, dripping. David thought he could make out the spiraled shape of a nautilus in that mushy flesh. There was something disturbingly human about the feline face, like it

232

belonged to a child. It clicked its tongue knowingly at him, chiding him like a scolding parent. Then it turned its red eyes on Abby.

"Well hello, girlie. Remember me?" it asked. "Why did you run away last night? Didn't you want to play?"

David could see the terror in Abby's eyes as she stepped back. He stepped in front of Abby, shielding her. "Leave her alone."

Undeterred, the creature turned to David, continuing its singsong mocking. "I *love* to play. Your parents did too."

"Leave my parents out of this."

The thing laughed, clearly amused. "Too late."

It's lying, David thought. *It has to be. My parents are not dead.* He understood the creature was baiting him, trying to pick a fight so he would leave the safety of the circle. But in his heart, David knew the creature might be telling the truth. The thought terrified him.

Riordan reached out and swiped at the creature with a silver knife. He had a clear shot while it was distracted, but he was holding Rowan, and the added weight threw him off balance. He missed and stumbled, almost dropping the chubby toddler.

Instantly, the Shadow turned its attention to Riordan, crossing the line with one long-fingered paw as its jaws snapped at the air where Riordan's hand had been a split second before. The flesh around the claws smoked and fizzed, and the creature pulled its paw back. It settled on its haunches nonchalantly and inspected the wound. Then it casually licked the burn, delicately stretching out its fingers to get between the talons.

When it spoke again, its tone of voice was dryly mocking, the lilt of playfulness gone. "Careful, Daddo. That circle will only help you if you stay *in* it. But you know, sooner or later you're all going to have to come out."

"Get away from us," Abby said, her voice low.

David looked at her. The fear in her eyes had been replaced by a look of determination. He took her hand and squeezed it.

The creature simply smiled and put a claw-tipped finger to its lips. "Shhhhh...hush now." It began to pace back and forth, dangerously close to the salt boundary, its voice loud and animated like the ringmaster at a very disturbed circus. "Laaaaadies and gentlemen! Your attention please! Please keep your hands, feet, arms aaaaand legs inside the circle at all times! Any fleshy bits crossing the line will promptly be removed! And hold on tight to those little kiddies—there's nothing we enjoy more than fresh-faced baby! Mmmm-MMMM!"

The other shadow cats tittered in response and crept closer to the circle. They seemed to be vibrating collectively with some kind of energy. They looked ravenous.

Suddenly the whole house shook. There was a loud crash from somewhere downstairs and then the old, wooden stairs strained and creaked as something huge ascended.

The creature taunting the humans smiled broadly and giggled, its long, furry tail twitching manically in anticipation. The other Shadows pressed together, close to the salt boundary, waiting and hungry.

Large as a bull, the cat thing that had smashed Jon's car entered the room, its bulky shoulders knocking the doorframe loose. The creature's hairless skin was taut, stretched across thickly muscled limbs. The beast's barreled rib cage and brawny abdomen were big enough that a large man could easily fit inside. David glanced down at Abby, and couldn't help thinking how she could fit in there with room to spare if the creature devoured her. He would die before he let that foul thing touch her.

The beast's eyes burned red-hot and its nostrils flared with rage. Its voice was a low growl, deliberate, deadly, as it addressed the lemur-like creature. "Malden. Stop toying with the meat-bags. You will be feasting on them soon enough."

At this, the smaller creature grinned wickedly, its tongue running over what was left of its lips. The other Shadows grew frenzied, pressing even closer to the line. Those on the edge of the salt boundary got singed and didn't seem to notice. The humans were tantalizingly close and the Shadows had but one collective desire: to feed. The tiny band of humans squeezed as closely together as they could, pressed up against the glass of the second-story windows, clutching the three children tightly out of reach.

David could feel Abby's heart beating wildly as she leaned up against him. He held her tight, trying to calm the panicked beat of his own heart.

"Stop." A voice rang out, strong, clear, and authoritative.

To David's astonishment, the smaller Shadows immediately stepped back from the line; a path cleft between them as they broke into two groups that settled quietly on either side of the room. Malden's mad grin vanished. He tucked his tail between his legs, backing away submissively to stand on the right side of the room. The beast, however, stood its ground, turning to face the speaker.

"I said stop, Calder." Moira Buchan stood in the battered doorway. Although she was tiny in comparison to the monster, she held her head up and her body straight and tall, not hunched over with age. Her face was still lined and weathered, but her eyes burned—dark, piercing, and ageless.

The creature met her gaze and growled defiantly, as if it meant to strike her down.

"Aunt Moira!" David cried. He was no longer angry about their argument the night before—he only feared for her. He couldn't stand there and let the beast slaughter her. He started to cross the line so he could reach her and pull her to safety. Jon and Abby grabbed his arms to prevent him from leaving the circle. "No!" He struggled against them. "It's going to kill her!"

"You *can't*, man," Jon said. His grip was like iron. "There's no way you can reach her without it getting you."

"Please, David," Abby pleaded. "If anything happens to you, everything falls apart."

David conceded and took a step back. They were right. The beast wouldn't hesitate to kill him if it got the chance. As he studied Moira, a thought troubled him. *Calder. She called it Calder. How could she know about Calder?*

As if in answer, the beast growled and lunged toward Moira. She calmly raised one hand, and the creature crumpled to the floor, writhing in pain.

"How dare you?" she asked. "How dare you defy *me*?" Thick black smoke swirled around her, starting at her feet, then rising upward. Her dark eyes burned red through the haze, and there was an audible ripping sound. When the smoke cleared, Moira was gone. Almost.

In her place stood a tall, proud woman with silvery blonde hair, wearing a thin, flowing sheath of the same color. Her face was young, fiercely beautiful. The shell that had been Moira Buchan's body lay at her feet, a tattered, semitransparent husk, not unlike an outgrown exoskeleton cast from the body of a shedding cicada.

"Lucia?" Abby whispered.

"No," insisted David. "*No.*"

Calder looked at David. He struggled to his feet, chuckling. "Yes. *Yes.*"

Lucia said nothing. She met David's unbelieving gaze, her dark eyes ancient and knowing. Then she turned back to Calder.

The monster was fully on his feet again, and looked no less defiant than before. "I dare," he replied coldly, "because you are weak."

"Weak?" Lucia scoffed.

"*Weak.*" Calder spat the word. "Too weak to follow through on the one thing Tierney wanted of you. You should have killed the boy long ago. But have no worry. I will finish the job for you."

"Fool!" Lucia cried. "You stupid, hulking fool!"

Calder roared, advancing toward her. She held up her hand and he kept his distance.

"You know nothing of the old magic," Lucia said. "The boy was an innocent. Shedding his blood would have undone our efforts—the balance of fate would have tipped in their favor, and he would have become a martyr, inspiring them to victory."

"Lies. Nothing but lies," Calder said. "Citing the old magic is nothing more than an empty excuse for your weakness. But it doesn't matter, because he's not so innocent now, is he? He has been with the humans too long—he smells of them. The boy who would be Solas Beir must die."

Lucia faltered. "Fool. There's no need. We need only keep him from returning." Around her, David could see the Kruorumbrae shifting restlessly. She was losing her control over them.

"All these years of useless obedience to *her* will, and she has kept the truth from us all," Calder scoffed, addressing the Kruorumbrae. He looked at her and laughed. "Poor Lucia. All this time in exile, and for what? Do you really think the Kruor um Beir ever loved you? That he will actually want *you* when he takes the throne?"

She didn't answer.

"The only reason Tierney gave you so much power is so he could use you to destroy the Solas Beir," Calder spat. "Nothing more."

David could see that the beast hit a nerve—Lucia was *furious*. "And the reason you have *no* power is because you never learned to respect your master." With that, she raised both hands, unleashing the full force of her power in a burst of electric blue energy.

Calder writhed in agony. Malden and the other Shadows stood still, mesmerized and excited by his pain. There was no loyalty here—the Kruorumbrae were feeding off his pain and fear as they would anyone else's.

Riordan leaned over and whispered in David's ear. "I think that now is our chance for escape."

David looked at him and nodded. Riordan moved in front of David, blocking him from view. Quietly, David turned and opened the window behind him. He squeezed through the opening and let himself drop quietly to the lawn.

ঙ৫৪ঙ৫৪ঙ৫৪

"You next, Abby," Jon whispered.

Cassandra slipped Abby the keys to her car. "We'll hand the children down to you," she whispered. "If anything happens to Riordan and me ..."

"Don't say that. *Everyone* gets out," Abby whispered back, tucking the letter opener into her belt loop.

"Okay." Cassandra looked as though she didn't believe it, but there was no time to argue.

Abby eased out the window and Jon helped her down, lowering her into David's waiting arms. She looked back up at him, and Jon nodded at her, trying to hide his growing sense of despair. He might not survive this, but at least Abby would. Then Riordan tapped him on the shoulder and he moved away from the window to keep watch so Riordan and Cassandra could lower the children down to David and Abby. He could see that Lucia hadn't noticed anything yet—she was too focused on punishing Calder. And the Shadows were too busy enjoying the show.

After the children, Jon insisted that Cassandra go. He and Riordan slipped out last. The moment they were on the ground, they ran for the Buchans' SUV. David was already at the wheel and Abby and Cassandra had just finished buckling in the children.

As they slid into the vehicle and shut the doors, Jon looked back. "I can't believe we made it out alive. We got lucky."

The Shadows weren't coming for them yet. Through the second-story windows, he could still see the electric blue glow illuminating the room, could still hear the crackle of energy.

"We didn't get lucky," Cassandra replied. "Lucia let us go."

"Why? Why would she do that?" Jon asked in disbelief.

Cassandra nodded toward David. "She didn't want him to die."

ಬುುಗುಬುುಗುಬುುಗು

David drove the Buchans' SUV past the gate of the ruined mansion, parking it close to the front door. Everyone scrambled out of the car and sloshed through the mud, running for the relative safety of the old building.

There seemed to be an unspoken understanding between all of them that they needed to work together to survive. David thought the fear of being caught outdoors by the Blood Shadows was on everyone's minds, but no one wanted to be the first to express that fear. He knew it would only be a matter of time before the Shadows arrived and attacked. If he and Abby could restore the portal in time, they might have a chance. He hoped so.

Riordan carried Rowan, the terrified child clinging to him like a baby monkey. Cassandra cradled Siobhan—the little girl's face was securely buried in the warmth of her mother's neck—and Jon carried Ciaran, piggyback. David held Abby's hand, and she led the way through the mansion, into its dark, cave-like depths. Eulalia and Nysa were waiting for them in the hall with the shattered mirrors.

"Hello, my son." Eulalia greeted David formally, as if she were unsure how he would react. "I am so happy you have returned."

In spite of her appearance, David immediately recognized her, now that he was freed from the Shadows' influence. He could feel the connection to his true mother from the core of his soul, and wondered how he could have forgotten her.

David took her good hand and withered hand in his strong ones. He looked into her seeing eye, surprised that it was the same as his own two. "Hello, Mother," he said. He pulled her into an embrace, and Eulalia began to weep.

David looked over at Abby and could see that she too was moved; tears were welling up in her eyes. He saw her look down as Nysa slipped a tiny hand into hers and tugged on it. The little nixie beamed up at Abby, a sweet smile on her face, her crazy, flaming hair aglow in the darkness of the room. Abby laughed and wiped her face with the back of her hand. Then she scooped up Nysa and spun her around. The water sprite's giggles were musical, magical. David couldn't help but smile.

"Do you have the sigil of the Solas Beir?" Eulalia asked, pulling away from David's arms.

Nodding, he retrieved his half of the Sign of the Throne from his pocket. Abby put Nysa down and unhooked the clasp on her necklace, sliding the pendant off the chain.

"Good. Quickly then." Eulalia gestured toward the mirror at the end of the hall, and they all hurried over.

Once at the mirror, Eulalia instructed David and Abby to stand face to face. Abby held her half of the silver nautilus cradled in her open palms. David placed his half on top and then covered her hands with his. Basking in the connection and warmth of Abby's touch, he felt strong and whole, like the fog clouding his mind had truly lifted. He finally understood who he was and who he was meant to be.

The Sign of the Throne grew warm between Abby's and David's hands. There was a low thrumming and a brief flash of blue light, and then everything went dark and silent as the halves slid apart.

David studied the sigil, confused. "What happened?" he asked. "Did we do something wrong?" It had seemed like the magic of the sigil was working, but then—nothing.

"No, it is not you and Abby. The connection is weak. The Sign of the Throne has been halved for a long time now, and the portal has been broken even longer," Eulalia explained. "It may take some time to rebuild the connection,"

"We don't have much time, Eulalia," Abby urged. "Lucia is back. The Shadows will come for us soon."

Eulalia nodded. "Yes, I know. Just as I knew you were coming. But do not think about the Kruorumbrae right now—clear your minds of them. Try again."

David and Abby turned back to each other, concentrating hard. This time, there was a brief episode of thrumming but no light at all. David was frustrated, and he could tell by the strained look on Abby's face that she was worried.

ЮСЗЮСЗЮСЗ

Nysa shared Abby's concern. The Kruorumbrae scared her too. With her keen senses, she could hear them coming, feel the almost undetectable tremble of the ground that heralded their arrival. There were so many of them. More than ever before, and bigger and stronger in their hunger. Abby needed help.

The nixie slipped away, through the doors that led to the conservatory. She would find Cael. He would know what to do. Transforming mid leap, she dove into the pool and swam for the drainage pipe that would lead her to the reflecting pool outside. She was faster when she was all fish; tiny, but like a streak of golden-orange lightning. In seconds, she slipped through the portal and jumped out of the sparkling pool in Cai Terenmare, transforming once again to hit the ground running on strong, chubby little legs.

She hurried through the castle of Caislucis to the corridor housing the mirrored portal. Guards were stationed outside the open door, but Nysa was so small and fast, she was all but invisible.

Ahead, Cael was talking with Phelan, his second in command, chief of the guard entrusted with the security of the stone fortress in which they stood. Their voices were low, tense. Several soldiers stood in a semicircle in front of the mirror, swords drawn, ready for whoever might come through—hopefully friends, but more likely foes.

Unsuccessfully, Nysa tried to get Cael's attention. She called his name and pulled on his tall boots, but he and Phelan were focused on the portal, drawing their swords as well. Cael wore a leather satchel at his side, and as she tugged at his pant leg, Nysa caught a glint of something curiously shiny, something that reflected light into her eyes. Something strangely familiar. It called to her.

Unnoticed, she flipped open the top flap of the leather bag, and retrieved the shiny. It was a silver hand mirror, overly big in her undersized hands. It reminded her of something

Eulalia had described once in one of her stories. Something that might open a portal. Something that could help Abby. She hoisted it up to balance it against her little chest so she could carry it. It felt heavy in her small arms. Still unnoticed, she slipped away from the guards and hurried back to the shimmering pool of the portal.

ℬℭℬℭℬℭ

Abby sensed David's growing frustration and she thought maybe Eulalia could too.

"Once more, only this time, look into each other's eyes," Eulalia said patiently. "Feel the power of the Sign of the Throne drawing you to each other, feel the strength of your connection—focus only on that."

Abby moved closer to David and searched his eyes. There was a tension in the air between them, and the more she focused on her fear, the harder it was to connect with him. She had to get a handle on her emotions.

"Okay," David said, staring into Abby's eyes. "Once more, with feeling." Then, in what she knew to be an over-the-top attempt to distract her from her fear, he grinned at her flirtatiously and winked. Considering the situation, it was completely inappropriate.

It worked. "Dork," Abby laughed. He looked good even when he was being an idiot.

"Yes, ma'am. Ready?" He smiled, looking at her with determination.

David's confidence was contagious—Abby started to feel sure it would work. "Yes. Let's do this."

David placed his hands over hers, and the thrumming began again. The soft, pale blue glow of the sigil's light escaped through the gaps between their fingers and grew stronger, pouring like silver-blue water onto the floor. Their faces were lit by the building glow; a strong, electric blue light reflected in their eyes, which were locked on one another and nothing else.

Abby could feel the energy swirling around her, pulling her closer to him. She had no doubt David felt it too, a connection that bound them more steadfastly than any spoken vow.

As the light coursed over the floor, the broken shards from the mirror rose in its wake, captured in a tide of blue. The bits of glass were drawn to each other, their edges melting to bond with other fragments, rising to fit neatly in the empty frame.

When the last shard rose and fell into place, a strong flash of light lit the portal, and a shockwave of energy emanated from the mirror to the outer edges of the room, washing over its inhabitants with a feeling of warmth. Above them, rays of moonlight peeked through the glass dome as the storm stopped and the clouds parted, bathing the room in a clean, silver glow.

"Wow," breathed Abby, her eyes still locked on David's. She didn't want to break the spell, to have any distance between them, no matter how small.

"*Wow* sums it up pretty well, I think," David said, his eyes burning into hers. The silver nautilus was whole now, beating with the combined rhythm of their hearts, in concert with the universe.

A loud banging came from outside the doors of the hall—something was trying to get in. The Kruorumbrae had arrived.

Abby pressed the Sign of the Throne into David's hands, still not wanting to look away. He pushed the sigil out of sight into the safety of his jacket pocket, and then pulled her into his arms protectively. "We're going to be okay," he said.

ഔങ്ഔങ്ഔങ

Eulalia couldn't help but flinch when the one of the heavy doors at the hall's entrance splintered and burst, leaving a ragged hole in bottom half of the wooden door. As one, the shadow cats spilled through the opening in a tidal wave of black syrup, appearing to consume the rays of moonlight as they came.

"Quickly now, everyone through the portal," Eulalia cried, ushering them forward. She stretched out her good hand and, releasing blue energy from her fingers, burned a curved line in the wood floor, arching from one side of repaired portal to the other, bounding herself, David, and the humans within. "It is not a complete circle," she explained, "but it will provide some protection."

The Kruorumbrae were so hungry that they couldn't stay in one form; they transformed from their usual feline shape to their true state—foul-faced goblins covered in stiff black hair, with mouths full of gnashing teeth, hot breath reeking with the smell of rotted meat—then back to cats again.

Eulalia felt faint from the force of their desire. It was a steady, primal buzzing, strikingly similar to the vibration of the buttons in a rattlesnake's tail. The sensation reverberated throughout her body, more a feeling than a sound, and it was overpowering. It made her ill—she was starting to lose her ability to think clearly.

She looked at Abby, surprised that the girl seemed less overwhelmed by the Kruorumbrae—she was sure that, as a c'aislingaer, Abby could feel their desire, too. Maybe Abby's focus on David was helping her.

शकशकशक

Mesmerized, Cassandra surveyed the writhing mass of black and clutched her daughter to her. There were so many of the creatures now. She had been frightened before, trapped in Riordan's office, but watching the Shadows roll into the room as one from many, her terror threatened to cripple her sanity. She wrenched her gaze away—she had to think of her family. If she couldn't pull it together, they would all die. She looked at her husband—Riordan looked exhausted, his arms heavy with Rowan. He needed her.

Cassandra gestured for Jon to hurry over with Ciaran. Jon joined her, but put Ciaran down and helped him take his mother's hand. Cassandra looked at Jon, puzzled.

"You and Riordan take the kids through first," Jon insisted. "I'll stay with the queen to make sure Abby and David get through. We'll be right behind you."

Cassandra understood. "Thank you, Jon."

With Ciaran between them and their twins in their arms, Cassandra and Riordan passed through the viscous surface of the mirror to the promised safety of the other side. Cassandra gasped at the sight of the strong, stony-faced guards who greeted them with drawn swords. She relaxed, however, when the guards parted to let them through unharmed.

"The Solas Beir?" a man questioned. He seemed to be in charge. His dark brown eyes burned into Cassandra's, demanding an answer.

"Yes," Cassandra nodded. "He's coming through next."

ℬℭℬℭℬℭ

The second the Buchans slipped through the glass, David heard a loud roar and a crash. He whipped around to watch as Calder tore the remains of the two doors from their hinges and violently hurled them across the room toward the portal. Grabbing Abby, David pushed her flat on the ground, shielding her with his body. He felt the movement of air as one of the wooden doors soared over him, ruffling his hair.

The projectiles whizzed toward the mirror and would have destroyed the gateway to safety if not for Jon, who was in their path and took the blow, knocking then off course. Jon managed to twist his body to the side and protect his head with his arms as he ducked. Had the doors hit him head on, the wooden missiles might have clipped his throat, crushing his windpipe—or worse, decapitated him. Instead, the corner of a door collided with his upper arm. After impact, the doors clattered to the floor just outside the semicircle, and Jon crumpled to the ground.

"Jon!" Abby screamed, reaching for him.

David let her go and she crawled over to Jon. He felt a deep sense of guilt watching her futile efforts to help her friend. He was Calder's target, not Jon. There was nothing they could do to help Jon here—they needed to cross into Cai

248

Terenmare to heal him, and quickly, before something worse happened.

Jon groaned, his knees drawn to his chest in a fetal position. "I think it's broken," he said to Abby through clenched teeth. "The pain is shooting up and down my arm like fire."

"Mother, I thought we would be protected!" David had to shout to be heard over Calder's roaring.

The deadly beast had somehow escaped Lucia's wrath, and was clearly hell-bent on revenge as it stalked into the room. Spying Jon curled up in pain, a smug grin spread across the monster's muzzle, as though he were congratulating himself on the success of his aim.

"Yes, David, I know. I meant protection from *them*," Eulalia said, pointing toward the Kruorumbrae, "*not* from flying debris. I am sorry, Jon. Can you stand?"

Jon nodded, cradling his arm. "Yes. It just hurts."

"We'll go through now," David said, helping Jon to his feet.

ಬಂಜಬಂಜಬಂಜ

Abby was horrified by the way the Kruorumbrae moved as one organism, rolling together in a fluid black wave. They had reached the edge of the circle, and still more of them were spilling into the room, piling into drifts around Calder, leaving a moat of space around his body so they did not become victims of his rage. It was a miracle they had not yet crossed the line—piled up as they were, it would not be long before they pushed forward, incinerating those unlucky enough to be first to cross.

Abby could sense that Jon's physical pain was almost irrelevant now, overtaken by his terror of the Shadows pressed against the circular boundary, and of Calder stalking forward. She was terrified too, but her need to protect Jon and David dissipated the fear, transforming it into righteous anger.

As David helped Jon stand, Abby stared Calder down defiantly, ready for a fight, her fists clenched at her sides, her feet planted. The beast kept his blood red eyes on her and smiled wickedly, as if the two of them were privy to a joke no one else understood. Suddenly she got the punch line—the monster was coming for the Solas Beir, never mind the consequences of crossing the boundary. The imperfect circle would not protect David.

With that epiphany, time seemed to slow down. Abby saw Calder coming. Her eyes focused on the detail of his muscled legs as they folded into a crouch, then sprang upward as the beast launched himself over the Kruorumbrae, across the line burned into the floor, straight for David's throat. Almost as if she were watching from a distance, Abby saw herself moving in response, spinning to place her palms flat against David's chest, stiff-arming him as she pushed him through the portal, noting his look of complete shock as he fell backward through the mirror, then turning back and drawing the silver letter opener from her side like a sword. And then time sped forward, and the beast was on top of her.

ಬಂದ ಬಂದ ಬಂದ

David was falling. He felt a brief sucking sensation around his body as he passed through the portal, and then a sharp pain when he landed on his tailbone and skipped across a cold, hard floor like a stone over the surface of a lake. He was momentarily dazed as he took in his new surroundings—a dark, stone room lit with torches, soldiers standing around him with swords, and the Buchans huddled behind them, waiting anxiously.

The leader of the group held out his hand to help David up. The dark-haired man's face was ruggedly handsome, and it was clear by the dignified way he carried himself that he had been proven in battle. His neck boasted a deep scar where it looked like something had taken a bite out of him. David guessed that whatever creature had attacked this man had not fared well.

"Welcome, Solas Beir." The man pulled David to his feet. "I am Cael, and I am charged with the defense of your kingdom. Have no fear; you are safe now."

David nodded solemnly. "Thank you, Cael. But I can't stay—I have to go back for the others."

Cael stepped in front of the portal and the guards surrounded David. "I am sorry," Cael said, "but I must prevent you from doing that. Your safety is of utmost importance, Your Majesty."

"You don't understand. Something terrible has happened. If I don't go back, they will die." David was insistent, an edge of panic to his voice.

"The queen knows what she is doing," Cael said. "She would willingly sacrifice her life for yours."

"And Abby?" David asked.

"She knew the risks," Cael said.

"No—I *can't* lose her." David pushed toward the portal, but the guards held him back.

"I am sorry, but what you ask is impossible," Cael said.

Resigned, David stopped struggling; he could see the guards would not disobey their commander and let him go. He understood they were trying to protect him, but he couldn't care less about his own safety. He was distraught—he simply could not lose Abby and his parents on the same day. If she died, he would lose his mind, and what use would he be as the Solas Beir then?

ಔಚಔಚಔಚ

Eulalia could not see Abby anymore. The c'aislingaer's body was eclipsed by the massive form of the beast, hidden and buried under his weight.

Although the creature lay limp and still, he seemed in remarkably good condition for having crossed the boundary, his body only singed and smoking, not aflame. But that could change. The longer he lay within the circle, the more likely it was that he would burn, combusting from within before the flames exploded outward. Anything in contact with his body was at risk to catch fire.

The Kruorumbrae seemed to understand this, and had voluntarily moved away from the circle, giving the fallen monster a wide berth. They were still hungry, however, and the sight of their comrade lying on the floor did nothing to silence their constant buzzing. They sounded like an angry hive of wasps.

Above the feverish din of the Kruorumbrae, Eulalia heard Jon shouting at her. "He's crushing her! Help me!" He struggled in vain to lift the beast off Abby's body, his face pinched with pain.

"Yes—stand back," Eulalia instructed. She let the power flow from her hand, and Calder rose from the floor. She levitated his body back across the boundary. Turning him over, Eulalia set him down, lying on his back.

The silver letter opener was lodged deep in his gut. The beast coughed, and thick, black liquid bubbled to his lips and oozed from the wound in his abdomen, loosening the silver weapon.

Moving her hand in a swift downward motion, Eulalia used her power to shove the letter opener deeper, pinning the monster in place. Then she turned back to Abby.

Jon was cradling her in his arms. Abby's body looked frail and broken, with deep, bleeding gashes raked across her stomach, sides, and back. This was where the beast's claws had caused the most damage, first from enveloping her in a deadly hug, and then in trying to get away when her silver weapon was plunged in his belly. Her face was ashen.

"Oh, Abby," Jon cried. "What have you done to yourself?"

Abby opened her eyes and searched Jon's face. Eulalia was shocked at how the girl's beautiful ocean eyes were a glazed, dirty grey. Abby closed her eyes and shuddered, struggling to breathe.

"No—don't you dare. Abby!" Jon shouted, pulling her close to him. "Open your eyes—you have to stay with me. Abby!"

Abby's eyes fluttered back open. What worried Eulalia most was the stain of black liquid around the wounds on the c'aislingaer's stomach—no good could come from Abby being exposed to the creature's blood. They had to hurry and immerse her in the pool of healing.

"Quickly, Jon," Eulalia said. "We will lift her together and carry her through the portal. There is a chance we can still save her."

Nodding, Jon carefully scooped Abby up in his arms, trying not to cause more damage. Eulalia saw him wince with pain, but he held Abby steady in spite of his own injury.

Eulalia tried to use her power to ease the load for him, but she was so exhausted. She used to be so powerful; however, being away from her world for so long in her weakened state had drained her. Eulalia needed the pool of healing as well. She hadn't even been strong enough to help Abby and David fix the portal—she had only been able to lend instruction and watch. It was their connection that was strong.

As Eulalia moved toward the portal, she caught a flash of silver out of the corner of her eye, a contrast to the writhing field of black goblins outside the circle's edge. Lucia stood in the doorway, wearing a light silver gown. She nodded solemnly to Eulalia, making no move to prevent her escape. Eulalia returned the nod in acknowledgement of her sister's presence, and then she and Jon took Abby through the portal.

ଧଠ୫ଧଠ୫ଧଠ୫

David was waiting anxiously. As Jon and Eulalia carried Abby through, he feared the worst: she was gone. Then he heard the rough rattle of her breathing as she fought to stay alive. Jon seemed to be in great pain and Eulalia looked weary. How did things go so wrong?

"Jon," David said, "give her to me. I'll carry her."

Jon shook his head angrily.

254

David suspected that some of Jon's anger was directed his way, that Jon blamed him for what had happened to Abby. David blamed himself. If Abby had never gotten involved with him, if she hadn't tried to save him, she wouldn't be here in this mess, dying. It *was* his fault. And how was he supposed to live without her?

"Jon," David repeated gently. "You're injured. Please. Let me."

Jon finally surrendered and placed Abby in David's arms. He tenderly pulled her close.

"David," Abby croaked, her lips dry. Calder's black blood was smeared on her cheek in a long, ugly streak.

"Oh, Abby, why?" David cried. "*Why* did you do that?"

"Because," she managed, "it was *you*. I couldn't let him hurt you."

"Come," Cael said. "We must get her to the pool of healing."

₦₧₦₧₦₧

The writhing sea of black parted in front of Lucia as she and Malden approached what was left of Calder. Black ichor continued to seep from his mouth and gaping wound. Eyes squeezed into slits in a mask of pain, he rasped, "You lied. All this time—you hid the boy right in front of our faces—you made us help you. Tierney will know of your treachery."

Lucia knelt down near Calder's ear, making certain he could hear her. "On the contrary, my friend. He will know of *your* insolence. *You* are the fool who cost us the throne. This is the last time you disobey me." She retrieved the letter opener and turned to Malden. "Finish him," she commanded coldly, turning her back on the beast.

ഒരു ഒരു ഒരു

Malden was overjoyed to receive such a gift. Feeding on Calder would be the ultimate power surge. Well, almost. He had a feeling feeding on Lucia would be even more powerful. Maybe someday he would find out—but not today. Happily, he leapt onto Calder's chest and began feeding noisily, intent on draining the beast of what little life remained.

"Wait," Lucia ordered.

What now? I'm eating here, thought Malden. He looked up at his mistress.

Lucia pointed to a set of doors on the side of the room. A tiny nixie stood frozen in the doorway, petrified at the scene before her. In her hands was a silver hand mirror. "Take care of that first and bring the mirror to me," Lucia said. "*Then* you may finish feeding. The others may have the scraps." The buzzing from the Kruorumbrae intensified in anticipation.

Annoyed, Malden jumped down from his prize and streaked across the floor to the nixie, grinning widely.

Nysa looked down at her legs as if she had forgotten they were there and then retreated as quickly as those little legs could carry her, back the way she had come, dropping the mirror in her hurry to escape.

Malden caught her by the back of the neck with his sharp teeth and shook her violently. The tiny water faery let out an unearthly shriek as she struggled against the iron vise of his jaw. Malden tossed her down to the floor like a rag doll. The nixie managed to crawl away toward the edge of the pool, but

Malden grabbed her by the ankle with his teeth, tearing at the flesh, biting her all over. Nysa shrieked again, and Malden shook her viciously and slammed her against the lip of the pool.

As Malden bit the nixie again, she pulled on her necklace, and thrust her small fingers into the mushy hole of Malden's cheek, pushing something shiny deep into the flesh. He let go of the nixie and howled in agony as his face began to smoke once again, dripping blackened, melted tissue. The nixie slipped out of his reach and rolled into the water, sinking to the bottom of the pool.

Malden plucked the silver cross pendant from the hole in his face, wincing as his fingers began to blister from contact with the precious metal. He tossed the charm on the floor. "Oh, you people have *really* got to stop doing that."

He stared at the nixie lying on the bottom of the pool. The water around her small body had a pink tinge; blood was seeping from all the places he had bitten. For a moment, Malden considered going in after her, and then abandoned the idea in favor of his waiting meal. The nixie would die soon enough. He bounded nonchalantly back to the entrance of the conservatory, retrieving the mirror. Though it too was made of silver, he barely felt its sting. He could feel it pulsing with power; there was dark, corruptive magic in this looking glass. Perhaps that was why the metal did not burn his flesh.

Like a dog, Malden obediently delivered the mirror to Lucia, dropping it at her feet before turning back to Calder. Then he drank deep, feeding until his hairy belly bulged. Satisfied, he left Calder, barely clinging to life, for the rest of the Kruorumbrae.

En masse, they swept over the beast like maggots, consuming everything. When they were finished, there was nothing left but the hardwood floor, which had a strange sheen—almost as though it had been freshly polished.

RESTORATION

Abby opened her eyes to find David and Jon sitting on either side of her bed, watchful and concerned, each of them holding one of her hands. She smiled—she felt refreshed and comfortable.

"Hey, sleepyhead, how do you feel?" Jon asked.

Abby sat up to look around the room. Panels of silk in red, orange, yellow, and purple hung from the ceiling and walls, almost covering them. Through an arched doorway, sunlight glinted off the white marble of a balcony, reflecting the rays into Abby's room, intensifying the colors of the fabric. Everything seemed so vibrant. Even the simple shift she wore was a deep emerald with swirls of cerulean.

"I feel good—really good," she answered. "How long have I been asleep?"

"Not long," David said, brushing a stray curl from her forehead. "You were badly hurt, so we took you to the pool of healing. You slept for a few hours, and now your injuries are almost completely healed."

"Wow, that's quick," Abby said, running her hands over her stomach. "Amazing—no pain at all. I kind of thought I was going to die."

"So did I," agreed Jon. "You almost did, you dork. Don't do that again. Deal?" He took back her hand and squeezed it.

She returned the squeeze. "Deal. How's your arm? The bones must have been shattered."

"Good as new," Jon replied, flexing his arm to show her.

"Good! What about Eulalia? Was she healed?" Abby asked.

David smiled. "So well, you won't even recognize her."

"I'm so glad. I can't imagine how much she has suffered," Abby said. She looked at David, suddenly alarmed. "And *you*—oh no!"

"What's wrong?" David asked.

"Did I sleep through your coronation?" Abby asked.

David shook his head. "Nope. But you have to get ready—it's almost time."

"And I'd better do the same," Jon said, excusing himself. "This is going to be a party like no other. See you soon." He kissed Abby's forehead and left for the adjoining room, closing the door behind him.

Abby studied David's face to see what he thought of the kiss, but David didn't seem threatened by Jon's display of affection. She couldn't help but notice that Jon and David seemed to have bonded while she was asleep. That was good. It seemed like Jon was keeping his promise to curb his jealousy, and David was behaving himself by not rubbing his relationship with Abby in Jon's face. She didn't want to be in the middle of a fight—it would have been impossible to choose between the best friend she adored and the man who could be the love of her life. Maybe almost losing her had forced Jon and David to make peace.

David took both of Abby's hands in his. "Hey there, pretty girl."

She smiled. "Hello, handsome boy. Happy birthday."

"You remembered."

"Yes," Abby nodded. Then she frowned. "But I failed to get you a gift—sorry."

"You just gave me a gift by finally opening those gorgeous eyes of yours," David said.

Looking up at his handsome face, Abby found herself at a loss for words, so she smiled again.

"Thank you for bringing me to Cai Terenmare," David continued, returning her smile. He kissed the palms of her hands and gazed at her intently. "And thanks for saving my life."

"You are very welcome," she managed, lost in his pale blue eyes.

He frowned. "You do realize, however, that seeing you like that was seriously horrific. I'm going to need therapy now, thank you very much."

Abby grimaced, scrunching up her nose. "Yeah—sorry about that. It *was* pretty gruesome. Next time, I'll try to keep the gore to a minimum."

"Thank you. That's very considerate," David laughed. Then he eyed her seriously and cupped her face in his hands. "But Abby, what I mean is, I hope there's *never* a next time. Please don't ever do anything like that again, okay? I couldn't stand losing you, especially not like that."

Abby felt her skin tingling in response to his words. "Okay. But in my defense, I couldn't stand losing you either."

"Touché." He leaned forward and kissed her. She wrapped her arms around his neck and he scooped her out of the bed and onto his lap. He kissed her again passionately, and then stopped himself. "Sorry—I forgot that you still have to get ready."

She smiled, a little goofy, her arms still locked around him. "No apologies necessary. So…what do I wear to this thing?"

David nodded toward the dressing area of her room. "That."

Draped over a chair was a beautiful white dress encrusted in sparkling white diamonds and delicate pearls that looked fit for a princess—or a bride.

Abby's eyes grew wide. She suddenly felt awkward. It wasn't like she hadn't daydreamed about a future with him, but this seemed a bit sudden. "Um—"

"You don't like it?" he asked.

"No, I do. It's gorgeous," Abby said. "But…it's very…*white*."

David's face suddenly flushed red. "Oh! No—no, it's not *that* kind of dress. White means something different here than in the human world. In the tradition of the People of the Light, weddings are more colorful affairs. My people reserve white for royal banquets and ceremonies."

Now *there* was a crucial detail Eulalia had neglected to mention. Well, too late now—perhaps it was best to just move past her moment of weirdness. Maybe he would forget about it.

"Awww, look at you. You're adorable—*my people*," Abby teased.

David shrugged. "Yeah, well, I'm trying to embrace my long-lost heritage. I kind of got a crash course in the culture while you were sleeping."

"Good use of the time then," Abby said.

"Well, *yeah*, especially considering this whole coronation thing. *Congratulations, you're king.* Yeah, no pressure there. I'm a little freaked out—I have *no* idea what I'm doing, Abby."

Abby placed her palm against David's cheek and looked into his eyes. "You'll be a great king."

He looked at her, doubtful. "Will I? The Solas Beir is supposed to be this fearless leader. I'm not so sure I'm that guy, not that I'll go around admitting that to anyone but you. Somehow I don't think that would instill a great deal of confidence in my abilities."

"Well, I don't see a little humility as a *bad* thing," Abby said, playing with the collar of his shirt. "You recognize that you still have a lot to learn, and that your people will teach you. I actually think that's a great start for a leader." She looked up at him and smiled. "You've got potential, kid."

David laughed. "Wow, thanks—kid. I think *you* have potential too." He kissed her on the tip of her nose and then moved on to kiss her neck, his hands buried in her hair.

Abby felt her pulse race at the warmth of his touch. She leaned into his kisses and he pulled her closer in response, hungry.

"So...back to that *other* thing," he ventured, whispering in her ear. "Do you have some objection to the idea of marrying me?"

Abby smiled, surprised. *So he's going back there, is he? Interesting.* "Not necessarily," she answered, trying to be aloof and mask the wild beating of her heart. "It's a little too early to tell, but I don't have too many objections just yet."

David stopped kissing her, and pulled back to stare at her in astonishment. "So you *do* have objections?"

She tried to hide a smug smile. Well now, *that* was not the response he had been expecting, was it? "Yeah—you're kind of needy, and it's been nothing but drama since I met you," she teased.

"Needy?" There it was again—that thing where he raised just one eyebrow and grinned. It was a mischievous, flirtatious look that begged for trouble, trouble she wouldn't mind getting into. Not at all.

She forced herself to resist. "No, I'm just messing with you. Now, go away so I can get ready." Abby kissed his cheek lightly and jumped off his lap, teasingly out of reach.

"Fine. I'm leaving." David laughed and started to go toward the door, and then turned around and caught her waist, pulling her back to him, kissing her once more.

ဆဝငဿဆဝငဿဆဝငဿ

When Abby emerged from her room, David and Jon were waiting for her in the stone corridor outside her chamber. They were wearing long-sleeved tunics and matching pants of pure white silk, in a style that seemed to be inspired by both India and medieval Europe, although Abby guessed that Cai Terenmare fashion didn't originate in either of those places. Swords in elaborately carved silver sheaths hung from black leather belts at their waists, and they wore matching boots, polished a shiny black. David's suit was a little more elaborate, with embroidery and interwoven strands of gold and silver, but Jon looked just as handsome in his. She grinned—they both cleaned up pretty well.

She floated over to them, stepping lightly in silken slippers, her white gown flowing gracefully around her body. Her shoulders were bare, and the jewel-covered, form-fitting bodice of her dress contrasted with its airy, billowing sleeves.

"Wow, Abby," said Jon, offering his arm.

"You look beautiful," David said, offering his as well.

Abby smiled and stepped between them, taking both of their arms. "Why, thank you. And how lucky am I, to be escorted by the two hottest guys in the kingdom?" She kissed David's cheek, and then pulled Jon closer to peck him on the cheek as well.

"*Very* lucky," agreed Jon. "I am *pretty* hot."

"I was just thinking that *exact* same thing, Reyes," David teased. "You *are* pretty."

"Oh, not nearly as pretty as you are," Jon said, reaching across Abby to take a good-natured swipe at David, who leapt deftly away, laughing.

"Play nice, Corbin," Abby said, grabbing David's arm and pulling him back to her side. Jon smirked at David and Abby shot Jon a warning look. "You too, Reyes." She smiled. "Come on, boys. You can argue about who's prettier later."

David led Abby and Jon to the grand hall, a room with a towering cathedral ceiling supported by gothic-like arches and ribbed vaults. Abby was astounded by the abundance of white—not only was the stonework milky white, almost as if it were ivory, but long, flowing banners of white silk accented in silver and gold hung below tall, arched windows, which were opened wide. The banners rustled in a breeze that smelled of jasmine blossoms and the sea. Brilliant rays of light streamed in from the windows, giving everything a soft glow.

Every being in the room wore some kind of garment in the purest white. David pointed out a few of the people he had met while Abby was healing. Some, like the stony-faced Councilwoman Erela, with her soft feather wings and draping Grecian-like gown, were familiar to Abby from Eulalia's tales of Cai Terenmare. Abby was delighted to finally meet the tiny but legendary Fergal, who looked dignified in a prim waistcoat. Nerine, her fins temporarily transformed to legs, stood with a small cohort of other merfolk, who were shy but happy to be present. A small band of faeries in varying shapes, sizes, and colors sang together, filling the room with enchanting music.

Abby looked for Eulalia and found her close to Cael and Obelia, the head of the court council. They were standing at the front of the hall, on a raised dais in front of two thrones and a ceremonial table. Abby was shocked at how beautiful the queen looked—Eulalia was strong and healthy again. Her withered arm was restored, her skin glowed with the vigor of youth, and both of her brilliant blue eyes were cleared of blindness. Her gown was in complete contrast to the torn grey rag she had worn for so many years; it was so clean and white that it seemed unnatural to imagine the queen in anything else. Eulalia's raven-colored hair seemed even darker against the purity of her gown, and the long, shiny waves culminated in a delicate tiara of diamonds and silver leaves. Seeing Abby, Eulalia's face lit up with a beautiful smile. Abby returned the smile, elated to see the queen as she should be.

Abby searched the crowd for the Buchans and found them standing proudly near the dais. Riordan seemed stunned and amazed, like he was trying to wrap his mind around the strange diversity of mythical creatures populating the room, creatures who seemed just as welcome in Caislucis as any of the beings who looked human.

Cassandra looked ecstatic when she caught sight of Abby, healed. She reached down and tapped Ciaran's shoulder, pointing to Abby. The little boy looked up and waved at Abby, jumping up and down with excitement. Abby shot him a grin and a wink, and Ciaran grinned back. Siobhan waved too, standing between her parents, holding her father's hand. Rowan ignored Abby completely. He was busy, reaching for a plump, toga-clad faery. The violet-colored sprite looked up just in time to see a chubby toddler hand coming his way, and took that as a cue to find another location from which to watch the coronation.

Abby searched for other faces she knew. "Where's Nysa?" she whispered to David as they approached the dais.

"She hasn't arrived yet, but don't worry. I'm sure she'll be here soon," David whispered back.

David led Abby and Jon up the steps of the dais, to stand beside the ceremonial table next to Eulalia, who took Abby's hand in hers.

"Hello, Abby," Eulalia said, smiling. "Thank you for returning my son to me—for returning the Solas Beir to all of us."

Abby nodded. She couldn't speak—she was so happy that tears were coming to her eyes, so she just smiled.

Jon distracted her. "I think we're dead," he whispered. "With all the white and that pretty angel lady, this *has* to be heaven." He smiled flirtatiously at Erela, who ignored him and turned away to speak with a fellow council member. "Or not. Ouch."

Abby giggled and wiped her eyes. Jon never changed, and she loved that about him.

ഃ൨ᑕ൫ᑕ൨ᑕ൨ᑕ

David stood before the dais and Obelia began the coronation ceremony, her voice ringing clear and strong in the towering hall. "The Solas Beir has returned!"

With this proclamation, cheers erupted from the audience. It took several moments before everyone quieted down enough for her to continue.

"Yes, my friends—today we rejoice as one, celebrating this victory," Obelia said. "With our voices, we give our thanks for the Solas Beir's safe return, and we ask for him to be a blessed and wise leader for our people. May he grow in knowledge and power. We do not fail to acknowledge those who were lost in this world and beyond, in the effort to bring the first son of our people home—they will always be remembered and honored. Nor do we forget those with us today who delivered him to us." The councilwoman bowed to Abby and Jon and then bowed to the Buchan family. The audience began cheering again. Obelia smiled, then raised her hands to quiet the crowd. She beckoned to David. "David Corbin—step forward and kneel."

David walked up the steps to kneel in front of Obelia on the dais. She took his hands in hers. "David Corbin, so named in the human world, born to Cai Terenmare as Artan, son of Ardal, the Great Bear King: do you promise to represent the Light, to protect your people against the Darkness, and to use your throne and your power for the benefit of your people as long as you shall rule?"

David nodded. "I promise."

Obelia turned to Eulalia. "The diadem and the Sign of the Throne, please." The queen approached the ceremonial table and handed the diadem to Obelia, who placed it on David's head. "Then, as head of the council, I crown you Solas Beir, with this diadem as representation of your authority. Her Majesty, Queen Eulalia, entrusts you with the Sign of the Throne as a symbol of the Light."

Eulalia smiled and placed the silver nautilus in David's hands. He nodded, smiling back at his mother.

Obelia smiled as well. "Now, rise, Solas Beir. May your rule be wise and long, and may there ever be peace in your kingdom."

As David rose, he felt warmth emanate from the sigil of the Solas Beir, which glowed bright blue. He could feel the warmth transferring to his body, which was powerful and strong. He turned to his people, holding the Sign of the Throne out to them. He bowed, and the room again erupted in cheers and applause. Tiny faeries flitted above, setting off bursts of golden light that looked like sparkling fireworks.

David turned back to Obelia to grasp her hands in thanks, and then did the same to Cael, giving him the Sign of the Throne to return to the safety of the vault. He held his mother and kissed her cheek. Then, putting his arms around Abby and Jon, he led them down to greet the Buchans and to begin the festivities.

A magnificent feast was held in the banquet room next to the great hall, and there was music and dancing. Jon looked pleased to find that he was seated next to a pretty mermaid, and Riordan entered into a deep conversation on the properties of portals and parallel worlds with Gorman, the Caislucis historian. Cassandra and the children were treated to animated stories from Fergal, who danced on top of the table.

David, holding his mother's and Abby's hands, walked around the room, greeting each person in attendance. Eventually, all the introductions were made, and David and Abby were able to sit down and enjoy the meal.

"I think the Autumn Ball pales a bit in comparison to this," Abby whispered, blotting the corners of her mouth with a cloth napkin.

"Just a bit," David replied, placing his napkin on top of his empty plate. He took her hand. "Come with me—there's something I want to show you."

Abby looked around the room. "Won't we be missed?"

"We won't be too long." David rose, pulling her after him, and walked discreetly toward a doorway leading to the courtyard.

ಬಂಬಂಬ

The courtyard was built in a shape that was familiar to both David and Abby. Among the ivory pavers were silver tiles marking the curve of a logarithmic spiral.

David noticed Abby's interest in the layout of the tiles. "It's a giant nautilus shell, a larger rendition of the Sign of the Throne," he said. "You have an amazing view of it from your balcony."

"Oh, it's beautiful," Abby said. She was smiling but she didn't sound impressed. "Is that what you wanted to show me?"

He grinned and pulled her into his arms. "Not at all. Do you trust me?"

She nodded. "Of course."

"Then wrap your arms around my neck and hold on tight."

"Okaaay." Abby did as he asked.

David held her close and they began to rise into the sky. Abby's grasp on him tightened as the courtyard below grew smaller. "Oh my…"

"Are you scared?" he asked. They hovered, twenty feet off the ground.

"No—are you kidding? This is incredible!" Abby gasped. "Eulalia mentioned this might be one of your powers, but…how did you know you could do this? Did this happen while I was asleep?"

"No," David replied. "It was during the ceremony, when the Sign of the Throne started glowing—suddenly I just knew I could fly."

"Wow," she breathed.

He nodded. "Yeah. Pretty cool."

"I wonder what other powers you'll have," Abby said. "Anything else you've noticed since the ceremony?"

"Well you're just a tad impatient, aren't you? I *was* pretty impressed with myself," David said, "until you said that."

"Sorry," Abby apologized. "I'm very excited."

He laughed. "I'm rather thrilled myself. Okay, hold on tight. I'm going higher, over the turrets. I don't want to drop you."

"I don't want you to drop me either," Abby said, tightening her grip.

He kissed her nose. "Then don't let go." He pulled her closer as he flew higher, gaining speed.

They rocketed up and over the spiraling towers of Caislucis, past the edge of the cliff on which the castle was perched, soaring over the water toward a small island just off the shore. The island was mostly rock, but there was a flat space at the top that was home to lush grass and a lone shade tree covered in tiny white flowers that smelled like honeysuckle. David slowed himself, drifting downward to land softly on the grass.

Once on solid ground, he loosened his grasp on Abby and kissed her. They sat down and admired the castle from a distance. They were surrounded by the rhythmic sound of waves.

ঙোৰ্গেঙোৰ্গেঙোৰ্গে

"That was amazing." Abby snuggled close to David, sitting with her back against his chest.

David wrapped his arms around her. "Thanks. I aim to please."

"Yes, you do," she replied, tilting her head back to kiss his jaw. She looked up into the craggy branches of the tree. "It's so beautiful here."

"It's unbelievable, isn't it? Had I known how wonderful this place is, I never would have doubted that I should come."

"You doubted?" Abby twisted around to look at his face.

"Well, yes," he admitted. "Knowing that those things killed my parents, that they almost killed you...I just couldn't fathom living in a world that spawned creatures like that." He looked down at the grass, as if he were avoiding her probing gaze.

"What changed your mind?"

"I...I'm still in shock about my parents, to be honest," David replied. "I can't believe they're gone. I can't even grieve yet—it's that unreal. Moira too, I suppose. Or at least, the Moira I thought I knew. After all that happened, I wasn't sure if I even wanted to be Solas Beir. But then I realized if I were, I might be able to prevent something like that from happening again, be able to protect people I love. It helped that you recovered so quickly—you really can't imagine how worried I was. So I guess in spite of everything that is so messed up, there are good things in this world, and you being alive is proof of that." He paused, looking up and staring into her eyes. "Abby, I want to ask you something."

"Sure. Anything."

"Will you stay here with me?" He played with a strand of her hair and she felt his fingers brush against the bare skin of her shoulder. She leaned into his touch. "I know it's a lot to ask—you have your family back there."

Abby's eyes widened in realization. "My family! They must be so worried—Jon's mom, too." With all that had happened, she hadn't even thought about her parents and what they must be thinking. She tried to remember how long she had been gone. Far too long for them not to be worried sick.

"I'm sorry—you don't have to stay if you don't want to." He let the strand slip through his fingers and he looked away. "I shouldn't have asked you that—it's not fair to ask you to abandon your life to stay here with me."

Abby took his face in her hands. "No, don't apologize. I *want* to stay with you." She looked into his eyes. "Don't you know that I'm madly in love with you?"

"Really?" he asked, staring back at her.

She nodded. "Yes, really."

He grinned. "I love you too, Abby."

She threw her arms around his neck and kissed him. He crushed her to him, his hands in her hair, and kissed her back. When he let her go, he gave her a sweet smile. Then, he pulled her into the crook of his arm and they lay back on the grass with her head on his chest.

"I'm glad you said yes about staying with me." He ran his fingers through her hair. "I really need you in my life."

"I need you too." She looked up at him. "But I do need to go back, just for a while, so my mom and dad know what happened. Do you think my family would be able to come here, if they wanted?"

"Of course. And you're right—we do need to get you home soon so they know you're okay. Riordan and Cassandra are going back too. Riordan will be inheriting the old mansion, and he and Cassandra have agreed to be the guardians of the portal."

"Really? After everything that's happened? I would think they would be running far, far away to keep their kids safe from the Shadows," Abby said.

"I don't know that there is anywhere they *could* go to hide from the Shadows. I think that's why they're being proactive about this."

Abby shivered, remembering how close they had come to being dinner for a writhing mass of Kruorumbrae. "I guess I can understand that. Do you think my family is vulnerable? Will the Shadows come for them?"

David looked down at her and pulled her tightly against him. His warmth stopped the cold fear seeping into her blood. "I don't know, Abby. But we should definitely warn them.

They would be welcome to stay in the safety of the castle. Jon and his mother too."

"You've become friends with him."

"More or less. We're trying to be," David stated. "We've come to an understanding at least. I guess we bonded watching you recover from your injuries—neither of us wanted to lose you. I get the feeling he might still be a little bit in love with you, but he's been pretty cool about you and me so far."

"That's good. He's my oldest and best friend," Abby shared. "I need him in my life as much as I need you, even if it's in a different way. I can't imagine having to choose one of you over the other."

"I would never ask you to do that. Besides, he was there to protect you when I couldn't. Granted, that was entirely *your* fault, but—"

Abby sat up. "Oh! Don't even!"

He laughed. "Well, it was." David casually tucked his hands behind his head and gave her a cocky smile. It was an arrogant gesture that begged to be challenged.

Abby was happy to take him down a notch. She rolled onto her knees and threw a leg over his chest, straddling him. "Yeah, well, don't think I won't toss you on your scrawny butt again if I need to."

He looked at her, raising that eyebrow. "Oh, you think so, do you?"

She grabbed his wrists and yanked his hands out from under his head, pinning his arms to the ground. "Yes—I do."

He grinned. "Hmm, I'd *really* like to see that."

"Tempt me and you might."

He stared at her as if considering it, and then narrowed his eyes. "I would, but I'd get grass stains all over that pretty white dress of yours. Plus, you've insulted my butt. It is *not* scrawny."

She laughed, releasing his arms. "It's a little scrawny. I kind of like it though."

"Oh, good. I was worried." The cocky smile returned as he pulled her back down into his arms.

"Hey," she said, laying her head on his chest. "I have a serious question."

"What's that?"

"Your parents—won't people wonder what happened?" she asked. "Especially since Calder trashed your house and Jon's car? And what will happen to your bike?"

"Ah yes, the great cover-up," David said. "Apparently there's some kind of magical pixie-dust cleanup crew for that kind of thing. The bike and car will vanish and the authorities will find my parents' boat missing, presumably lost at sea."

Abby stared at him, trying to figure out if he were joking or not. He kept a straight face, so it was impossible to tell. There was something in his eyes though, a deep sadness. She wondered if he were trying to cover his grief about his parents with humor. Maybe he didn't feel comfortable being that vulnerable in front of her yet, but she hoped he knew she would be there if he needed her. Still, she didn't want to pressure him, so she pressed on. "And you were on the boat, too, supposedly?"

David shook his head. "No. It will be like I never existed. I will be able to come and go and no one will recognize me unless I want them to. Another perk of being the Solas Beir."

"Is that how it will be with me?"

"It could be. It depends on what you want. I'm not going to force you to cut ties with the world you've always known.

You're saying yes now, but you might change your mind about being here with me."

"I won't," she insisted.

"You might," David countered, "especially now that you've bathed in the pool of healing. I don't know if you realize this, but both of us are near-immortal now. It's a side effect of the pool—even if you return to your world, you won't age like everyone else. It will be slow, and you'll live a long time. And if you're here, you won't age at all."

"Like Adelae?"

"Yep. Sans insanity."

"I should hope so," Abby said. "So if I stay here with you, I'll really live forever?"

David nodded. "Yes. But I don't want you to make the decision lightly. When you live forever, it's a *long* time to be with someone."

"Well, what if you get tired of being with me?"

"Not going to happen." He kissed her again. "Now they really are going to miss us, you know. We should get back to the celebration."

"You're right," she said. "Let's go."

David stood up and pulled Abby to her feet. She locked her arms around his neck and they rose into the air again. Abby looked back at the island happily. Then she saw movement and she froze in horror.

Something large was perched just below the grassy area where she and David had been standing not a minute before. Against the rocks at the base of the island, its dark, grey-dappled skin acted as camouflage, making it impossible to see until it moved. The thing splashed into the sea, moving too fast for Abby to identify it, aside from one distinguishing feature that contrasted with the rest of the creature's body: a blur of black-and-white stripes twisting around a serpentine tail. She tightened her grip around David's neck. "David...?"

David's attention had been on flying, his brow furrowed in concentration as he steered them back toward Caislucis. "Yes?" he asked. He glanced at her quickly and then returned his gaze to their destination.

"Not to sound paranoid, but I think we were being watched," Abby said, trying to inject calm into her voice. She didn't want to distract him from his task, not now that they were soaring hundreds of feet above the sea. "I just saw something leap from the rocks into the water." What would have happened if they had stayed on the island a moment longer? *Stop it*, she thought. *You don't even know what it was. Don't jump to conclusions.* But the tail, that black-and-white striped tail...

David looked back. "I don't see anything—but maybe next time we sneak off together, we should find a less vulnerable location." He turned back to look at the castle, adjusting his flight slightly as he moved past an ivory turret.

"Good idea," Abby agreed.

They were almost to the courtyard. A few couples had come outside to dance. "Looks like the party is still going," David observed. "See, no one even noticed we were gone. I'll land on your balcony and then we'll go down and join them."

ಬಂಗಿಬಂಗಿಬಂಗಿ

David touched down perfectly on the white marble balcony leading to Abby's room. He took her hand and they went inside, passing under the columned arch. Temperate coastal air wafted in from the sea.

"I have to say, I'm *very* impressed with your landing skills," Abby said, smiling at him. "I mean, it's amazing that you can fly and all, but I really think landing is the crucial part."

"Thank you. I think," David laughed. "*Was* that a compliment?"

"Yes, it was..." Abby stopped, her thought interrupted. The easy smile vanished from her face.

"What's wrong?" David asked, pulling her close to him. Abby's face had drained of color.

"Is that blood?" She pointed to a red streak on the pale stone surface of the floor. It began at the door and disappeared around the corner of the bed. She broke from David's embrace, and hurried to the other side of the bed. He followed close behind.

Nysa was lying prone on the floor, silent, still, and bleeding from a number of places on her body.

"Oh no! Nysa!" Abby dropped to her knees beside the tiny nixie. She caressed Nysa's cheek. "Her skin is hot, feverish." At Abby's touch, the little water sprite stirred and opened her eyes. The nixie's eyes were a pale, sickly yellow—the warm, amber glow was gone.

"Abby," Nysa whispered.

David knelt down beside Abby. "Nysa—what happened?"

"Got hurt bad. Malden..." Nysa's eyes fluttered closed.

There was a knock on the door, and Eulalia called out, concerned. "Abby? David? Is everything all right?"

David jumped up to open the door. Eulalia and Cael entered, looking alarmed at the look on his face.

"David—why did you and Abby leave the banquet? I noticed you were missing and I had this horrible feeling something was wrong," Eulalia started.

David cut her short. "Mother, Nysa's hurt—Malden attacked her. We have to get her to the pool to heal."

Eulalia hurried over to the nixie, inspecting her many wounds. "There is no time—she has been like this for too long—he poisoned her with his bite."

"No, it can't be too late!" Abby insisted.

"David—you have to heal her. It is time to try to use the first of your powers," Eulalia said.

A wave of guilt washed over David. "Yes, okay. What do I do?"

"Hold your hands over her wounds," Eulalia instructed. "Focus your mind on healing them—visualize the poison disappearing and the wounds closing, healing. Then let go and feel the power course through your body."

David knelt down again and placed his hands over Nysa's body. Then he closed his eyes, cleared his mind, and concentrated. In his mind, he could see black particles of poison floating within the nixie's blood; they started shrinking and finally disappearing. He could see the blood flowing from the bites coagulate, and new skin form over the wounds. He felt his hands grow warm, almost hot. He opened his eyes and just as he had imagined, the wounds were healing.

Beads of sweat formed on Nysa's forehead as her fever broke. She opened her eyes. The sick yellow color in her eyes was fading, and there was a peaceful smile on her Kewpie-doll face.

David smiled back, relieved, and then grabbed his stomach as his guts wrenched inside him.

Abby noticed first. "David—what's wrong?"

"I think I'm going to be sick." He leapt up and ran for the bathing area in Abby's room.

"I have him," said Cael, following.

David grabbed a washbasin and vomited violently, emptying the contents of his stomach. Black particles of poison, exactly as he had imagined, floated in the mess.

"Oh, so much for the feast," he groaned. "That was horrible."

Cael poured David a glass of water to wash out the nasty taste. David gargled the water and spit into the basin. Cael took the basin and placed it out of the way to be cleaned, and then poured David a fresh glass of water. "Feeling better?"

David took a long drink and then nodded, handing back the glass. "Yes, thanks. That has never happened to me before."

"Why is he sick? He's never been sick before. Never," Abby said. "Isn't he supposed to be invulnerable to things like that? Especially now that he's Solas Beir?"

"The power of the Solas Beir always comes with a price," explained Cael. "The poison had to be purged by someone."

"Could have warned me," David grumbled.

"There was little time," Cael apologized. "And would that have prevented you from healing the nixie?"

"No, of course not. But will that happen every time I heal someone?"

"Not necessarily. With poison, yes, but there will likely be other consequences to using your power. The debt comes due eventually. It is a system of checks and balances to prevent the Solas Beir from abusing power."

Cael's words sounded harsh, but looking into the man's gentle brown eyes, David could see that he wasn't being unkind. He was taking advantage of a teachable moment. David understood intuitively that this man knew a great deal about paying the price, about putting others before himself, about making sacrifices. David also sensed that many of those sacrifices had been made for him.

"Good to know," David replied. It occurred to him that being Solas Beir might be a blessing and a curse, perhaps more of a curse than he had realized. He ventured further. "Are there, uh, similar consequences for flying?"

Eulalia seemed to understand what he hadn't said. "You have already been using power."

"Yes, I'm sorry," David admitted. "It was during the feast, and I didn't realize there would be a consequence."

Eulalia shook her head. "No, you need not apologize. It is wonderful news that you have already discovered that ability. Experimentation is part of learning. Now you just need to know when it is appropriate to use the power."

David was relieved. "I'm glad you're not angry with me."

"I am curious, not angry," Eulalia said. "It seems unusual that you would be able to levitate so quickly. That seems to be one of the more challenging abilities for most Solas Beirs. To defy gravity is to defy reason."

"Well, I'm not sure about levitation, but I was able to fly all the way over the castle wall and out to that little island offshore. I carried Abby with me."

Eulalia and Cael were silent. A look passed between them.

"What?" David asked.

"I am both impressed and concerned," Eulalia explained. "Impressed because of the height and distance of your first flight, and that you were able to carry someone with you. That is very unusual. You did not have any trouble with this?"

David shook his head. "None at all—it felt very easy."

"Extraordinary," Eulalia mused.

"Why did you say you were concerned?" David asked.

"You left the castle grounds—that could have been very dangerous. There are many dangers in this world that you do not yet know about, especially when it comes to the sea. It is best if you do not leave the grounds without protection, at least until your powers are fully developed," Eulalia explained.

"And we do not yet know how Tierney's followers will react to your presence. Even now, his spies could be watching, gathering information to help the Kruorumbrae," added Cael.

"I think you're right," Abby agreed. "When we were on the island, I think something *was* watching us—something big, with a black-and-white striped tail, like a sea serpent—"

"A siren? Impossible. They are all dead," insisted Cael.

"I'm not sure *what* I saw—I didn't see the face. Only the tail as it splashed back into the ocean. It seemed like the rest of the body must be huge though." Abby shuddered, repulsed.

"It cannot be a good omen. You see, there *was* a consequence for using power," Cael said.

"I don't understand. How is that a consequence for flying? They seem unrelated," David queried.

"Some consequences are indirect, a ripple resulting from action, seemingly removed but nevertheless connected," Cael explained.

"Sorry, I still don't follow," David admitted.

"I do." Abby chimed in. "It's the same as a synchronicity—something that seems coincidental but is actually related."

"So then, it's my *fault* we may have been spied on?" David asked.

"It's not really a matter of fault," Abby clarified. "It's more of a chain reaction—a series of events set into motion. It would be like dropping a pebble in a pond—I don't have to hit the banks of the pond with the stone for them to be wet—I only need to cause a big enough wave. But I'm only in control of the stone, not what happens next."

"So what, like karma?"

Abby nodded. "Like karma on caffeine."

"Caffeine?" asked Eulalia.

David laughed and shook his head. "Uh, never mind." He walked back over to the bed where Nysa was resting, and sat down next to her. "How are you feeling now, Nysa?"

"All better, thanks. Sorry you got sick, too." Nysa said. The bright amber glow had returned to her large eyes.

"It's okay. I'm just glad you're all right." David put his arm around the nixie's tiny frame. She clasped her little arms around his bicep, nuzzling it affectionately with her cheek.

"You said Malden bit you—how did that happen?" asked Abby, sitting down next to David. "You disappeared when we were in the room with the portal—didn't you return to the safety of the reflecting pool?"

"Abby needed help. I only took the mirror to help Abby," Nysa insisted. She looked to Abby, her eyes wide, pleading for understanding.

Cael stiffened. "*Which* mirror?"

The nixie ducked under David's arm, hiding behind him. "I went through the portal," she said, "to tell Cael Abby needed help. Cael did not see me. Too busy with soldiers. I *only* took the hand mirror to help Abby."

"The *silver* hand mirror?" Cael's tone was stern, but he seemed angry with himself for some reason. He dropped his hand to his side, reaching for something that wasn't there.

"What is it?" David asked. "What are you looking for?"

"My leather satchel," Cael answered. "I thought I had it with me, but now I remember. It is in my chamber—I left it there when I dressed for the coronation. But I should have noticed that the mirror was missing. No—what I *should* have done was kept it locked away. I am so sorry, Solas Beir. I was careless."

Eulalia put her hand on Cael's arm. "Cael, this is not your fault."

He looked at her, shaking his head. "It *is* my fault, Eulalia. I should have known the mirror was too dangerous—it seduced the nixie."

"But what if we had needed it to open the portal?" Eulalia asked. "You cannot blame yourself. You acted with the best of intentions, in an effort to protect our kingdom."

"And now my good intentions may mean the ruin of the kingdom," Cael said, looking pained. "No, my queen, I was a fool to think the mirror could have been used for good, even as a last resort."

Nysa peeked out from behind David.

"Nysa, did you take the mirror from Cael's satchel?" David asked. The nixie nodded.

"Nysa, where is it now?" Eulalia asked gently.

"Malden was eating Calder, but then Lucia told Malden to hurt me. He bit me and I dropped it. I hid in the water a long time. When I peeked out, the mirror was gone. Everyone was gone. I was alone and very sick," Nysa said.

"So you came to my room for help," Abby finished.

"Yes," Nysa nodded. "I help Abby, Abby helps me."

"If Lucia has the mirror, the next thing she will do is free Tierney from the Wasteland," Cael concluded.

"And *then* what will happen?" David asked. He took Abby's hand. Her skin felt cold; he drew her closer, enveloping her with his warmth.

Eulalia grew pale and stepped into Cael's arms. Cael pulled her close, protective.

When she spoke, they were all afraid. "Everything will change."

EPILOGUE: THE WASTELAND

Under the sapphire sky of his prison, Tynan Tierney sat on a desert floor, head bowed. His hands cupped the scarlet sand as he mumbled the numbers to himself, counting, counting, counting.

Far behind him, on the crest of a rust-colored dune, a lone figure in a hooded cloak was watching him. Silently the figure approached, coming to a stop a few feet behind the prisoner.

Tierney raised his head, staring out into the vast expanse of red before him. "Lucia," he said.

"Yes, my lord." She pushed back her hood, revealing her face.

Tierney let the last grains of sand fall from between his fingers and stood up. Lucia followed his gaze as he studied the barren landscape, the line where the cobalt sky bled and became sand. "You have failed me," he said.

"No, my lord." Her voice was steady.

He turned to face her, his dark eyes blazing with anger. "The boy is still alive. He has been crowned Solas Beir. How is it then, that you have *not* failed me?"

"Not me, my lord," Lucia said. "Calder."

Tierney raised his eyebrows in surprise. "Oh?"

"Calder disobeyed. He betrayed us," she said. "But he has been punished."

In an instant, Tierney crossed the distance between them, suddenly stopping short. Lucia braced herself to receive his rage. Instead, he smiled and stroked her cheek, from temple to jaw, his touch firm, hungry. His face had grown gaunt from his imprisonment in the Wasteland, but he was still handsome.

She felt her pulse quicken, her skin tingling at his touch. She willed herself to stay in control, to remain guarded.

"Ah, Lucia, my love. You are well versed in matters of disobedience and betrayal. How *does* your young nephew feel, knowing it was you who killed his father?"

Lucia remained silent. There was an accusation hidden in those mad eyes, eyes that were so frighteningly dark and angry, and she knew well to hide her fear. Tierney would equate fear with guilt, and where there was guilt, punishment was sure to follow.

He seemed unsurprised by her silence. "And now, you have come to free me?"

"Yes, my lord," Lucia replied.

"Yes, my *love*," he corrected. His strong fingers caressed the bare skin of her neck, tracing the line of her clavicle.

"Yes, my love."

He looked into her eyes. "And together we will set things right? We will finish what should be finished?" he asked.

"Yes, my love," she said.

With her confirmation, he pulled her into his embrace, kissing her hard—passionately. She let herself fall into him, giving herself over completely.

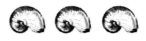

CHARACTERS
(in alphabetical order)

Abigail "Abby" Brown: an ordinary girl with an extraordinary destiny. Daughter of Frank and Bethany Brown, sister of Matthew Brown.

Adelae Buchan: (AD-eh-lay BYOO-can) sister of Samuel and Thaddeus Buchan, founders of Newcastle Beach. Legend says that Adelae went mad when her brother Samuel was bewitched by a magical mirror and vanished. She is rumored to be the "lady in white" who haunts the mansion ruins across from the Newcastle Beach Inn.

Amelia Gannon: David Corbin's long-time girlfriend. Daughter of Philip Corbin's English business partner, James Gannon.

Ardal of Caislucis: (AR-dahl of KASS-loo-sis) the last Solas Beir, also called the Great Bear King. Father of Artan. (In general, people in Cai Terenmare use their city or region of origin as a surname.)

Artan: (AR-tan) son of the Solas Beir Ardal and his queen Eulalia. The lost heir to the throne.

Brarn: (rhymes with barn) the raven who guides Abby and is a friend to Queen Eulalia. His mate is the raven, Eithne.

Cael: (kayl) Queen Eulalia's champion and first knight of the castle, Caislucis, charged with ensuring the safety of the Solas Beir and the royal family.

Cai Aislingstraid: (KIGH AY-sling-stride) a soul who sees, a person with the ability to see the future and communicate with others through dreams.

C'aislingaer: (KIGH-sling-ahr) the slang term for Cai Aislingstraid.

Calder: (KAHL-der) a vicious monster loyal to Tynan Tierney.

Cassandra Buchan: Professor of Psychology and Statistics at the University of Santa Linda. Married to Riordan Buchan. Their children are Ciaran (KEER-ahn), Siobhan (sh'-VAWN), and Rowan (ROH-un).

David Corbin: Adopted son of wealthy couple Philip and Margaret Corbin, who live in Newcastle Beach.

Erela: (eh-REL-lah) A winged woman who serves on the Solas Beir's court council.

Eulalia: (YOO-lahl-ee-ah) Queen of Cai Terenmare, widow of the last Solas Beir, Ardal, and mother of Artan, heir to the throne.

Fergal the Valorous: (FER-gahl) a shape-shifting faery, loyal to the queen. His spirit animal is a frog.

Gorman: A small indigo man who serves on the Solas Beir's court council and is the historian and librarian for Caislucis.

Jonathon "Jon" Reyes: Abby's best friend and neighbor, son of Blanca Reyes.

Kruor um Beir: (KROO-or um BAIR) the King of Blood and Shadows, and the one who rules those who serve the Darkness.

Kruorumbrae: (KROO-or-um-bray) evil shape-shifting creatures who feed on others, often referred to as Blood Shadows or simply Shadows.

Lucia: (loo-SEE-ah) Queen Eulalia's sister, accused of assassinating the Solas Beir and kidnapping his heir, betraying her family to Tynan Tierney.

Malden: (MAHL-den) a sadistic shape-shifter loyal to Tynan Tierney, with historic ties to Newcastle Beach.

Marisol Cassidy: (mah-REE-sol) daughter of Marcus Cassidy, a wealthy businessman, and Esperanza Garcia, a former supermodel. She is friends with David Corbin, Michal Sloane, and Monroe Banagher.

Michal Sloane: (MEYE-kahl) a wealthy girl who is best known for being a bully. She and her friends, Marisol Cassidy and Monroe Banagher, are referred to as "M Cubed" or M³. Michal and her parents are close friends with the Corbin family.

Moira Buchan: (MOY-rah) Riordan Buchan's aunt and heir to the ruined mansion next to the Newcastle Beach Inn. She is a close friend to the Corbin family.

Monroe Banagher: a wealthy girl who is friends with Marisol Cassidy, Michal Sloane, and David Corbin.

Nysa: (NEE-sah) a water sprite called a nixie, loyal to the queen. Her spirit animal is the golden koi.

Nerine: (NEER-ih-nee) a mermaid and daughter of the Sea King.

Northern Oracle: One of the four Oracles ruling the outer realms of Cai Terenmare who work in concert with the Solas Beir to keep balance between the Light and the Darkness. The Northern Oracle governs the Gauntlet and the Ice Mountain Territories. The other Oracles are the Eastern Oracle, the Southern Oracle, and the Western Oracle.

Obelia: (oh-BEEL-ya) head of the Solas Beir's court council.

Phelan: (FAY-lan) a knight, and Cael's second in command, charged with the security of Caislucis.

Riordan Buchan: (REER-den BYOO-can) a writer, mythology enthusiast, and admirer of all things Gaelic. Married to Cassandra Buchan, and father of Ciaran, Siobhan, and Rowan. Nephew to Moira Buchan.

Solas Beir: (SO-lass BAIR) Ruler of Cai Terenmare. In representing the Light, the Solas Beir is endowed with great power and is meant to be a servant to the people. Solas Beir can be translated literally as Lightbearer, but this less formal term is used to refer to a future ruler who has not yet ascended to the throne. The term Lightbearer can also be used as an insult, referring to a ruler who is weak.

Tynan Tierney: (TIGH-nan TEER-nee) the leader of the Kruorumbrae, creatures of the Darkness. He calls himself Kruor um Beir and seeks the throne of the Solas Beir. He is often referred to simply as Tierney.

Western Oracle: One of the four Oracles, she governs the seas and is mother to the murderous sirens who reside near her island temple.

PLACES AND TERMS
(in alphabetical order)

The Barren: the vast desert in the center of Cai Terenmare, spanning from the Great Plains to the Eye of the Needle.

Cai Terenmare: (KIGH TAIR-en-mahr) a parallel world to Earth filled with magic, shape-shifters, mythical creatures, and blood-thirsty monsters.

Caislucis: (KASS-loo-sis) castle and city of the Solas Beir, perched on the cliffs above the Western Sea.

Eye of the Needle: a rock spire near the City of the Eastern Oracle.

The Gauntlet: a narrow, icy canyon that serves as gateway to the House of the Northern Oracle in the Ice Mountain Territories.

Island of the Western Oracle: temple and home to the Western Oracle and her siren daughters.

Lone Tree Island: a small island in the Western Sea near Caislucis.

Newcastle Beach Inn: a mansion built by Thaddeus Buchan as his home, and later deeded to the Newcastle Beach community. It sits across the street from his brother Samuel's mansion, which was damaged in an earthquake and is in ruin.

Pool of Healing: a sacred pool within Caislucis that can heal almost any wound.

Sign of the Throne: the sigil of the Solas Beir and an object of great power belonging to the Light. It is used to open and close portals from Cai Terenmare to other worlds.

Sigil: a seal, signet, sign, or image with magical power.

Silver Hand Mirror: an object of power also used to open and close portals, but created and corrupted by Darkness.

The Wasteland: a parallel world to Cai Terenmare that serves as a prison. In this endless desert where time is frozen, prisoners are compelled to count grains of sand for all eternity.

THE RABBIT AND THE RAVEN

Book Two In The Solas Beir Trilogy

Melissa Eskue Ousley

ESCAPE FROM THE WASTELAND

The walls of the large, wood-paneled room were dominated by floor to ceiling mirrors in gilded frames, all shattered, save one. Piercing through the glass dome on the rooftop, the moonlight created a perfect circle of bright white light on the hardwood floor inside the otherwise darkened room. There was a stillness in the air, as if the entire world were holding its breath. It was an electric tension, the kind of silence that precedes a thunderstorm; a prickle of static anticipation. A single particle of dust hung frozen in the beam of moonlight, suspended motionless, as if it too were waiting.

The circle of light dimmed for a second—a brief flickering that could have been the wind pushing a wispy cloud across the face of the harvest moon. Then a low rumble emanated from the bowels of the mansion, followed by a sharp crack. The dome imploded in a shower of glittering glass shards, littering the circle of light with razor-edged droplets, ringing out like chimes against the floorboards.

Two lithe figures, dark as night, leapt nimbly through the rain of glass, materializing from nowhere. The larger figure took the lead, walking with long strides toward the empty doorframe with dangling hinges. The smaller figure hesitated, taking the time to tuck something into the folds of a gown, something round with a metallic glint that flashed in the light, and then, with quick, graceful steps, hurried to catch up.

ಬಿಲೋಡ್ಲೋಡ್ಲೋಡ್

"You know we're dead, don't you?" Jon asked Abby.

Abby gave him a look, but didn't answer. Instead, she finished pulling on her boots and then buckled a belt around her waist. Hanging from the belt was a sword, sheathed for now, which she hoped she wouldn't have to use anytime soon.

The last time she had faced the Kruorumbrae—in the not-so-distant past—things hadn't gone so well. Technically, the good guys had won that round, saving David Corbin and ensuring he became Solas Beir. But no victory comes without a price, and both Abby and Jon had paid dearly.

Abby glanced at Jon's arm, now healed. It had been shattered when the beast, Calder, ripped a heavy wooden door from its hinges and hurled it across the room like a discus. Abby had nearly died from the creature tearing her torso open with its claws. The attack was meant for David, but Abby pushed him out of the way and took the blow.

She had survived. Calder...not so much. Abby's silver blade had found purchase in the beast's belly, and Calder's nasty little friends had finished the job. So much for loyalty.

In spite of her near-fatal injuries, there was no question that Abby would do it all again if she had to. Truth was, she was madly in love with David. She would have walked through an inferno to save him, though thankfully it hadn't quite come to that. Still, given an alternative, she would rather not be tackled by a giant cat monster from hell again.

If she hadn't been mentally preparing for battle, Abby would have thought Jon's reaction to going home almost funny. Never mind legions of bloodthirsty cat goblins; he was worried about how his mom would react to his disappearing act.

It had been little more than twenty-four hours since they'd left home, but considering everything that had happened, it felt like they had been in the kingdom of Cai Terenmare for much longer. Their going missing for an entire night and into the next one would be killing their parents, even though Abby and Jon had some pretty compelling reasons for being gone.

Abby knew how her mother would react. She would be worried sick until Abby came home, and then she would be steaming mad.

She'd say, "Why didn't you at least call?"

Well, Mom, funny thing: cell phones don't really get signals in a parallel dimension.

"And what—you couldn't pick up the phone before you left?"

Yeah, we were kinda busy trying not to be eaten. Sorry.

Abby thought things might be worse for Jon though. For all his bravado about being this mischievous boy who could charm his way out of anything, he and his mother were really close, and he hated to disappoint her. His father had never been part of the picture, and even though Abby's dad had tried to fill the void, stepping up as a father figure to the son of his wife's best friend, it was Jonathon and Blanca Reyes against the world. Except, of course, when it was Jonathon Reyes and Abigail Brown against the world. When Jon was on your side, he was for you completely. Abby loved that about him.

ABOUT THE AUTHOR

Melissa Eskue Ousley lives in the Pacific Northwest with her family and their Kelpie, Gryphon. When she's not writing, Melissa can be found hiking, swimming, scuba diving, kayaking, or walking along the beach, poking dead things with a stick.

Before she became a writer, she had a number of educational jobs, ranging from a summer spent scraping road kill off a molten desert highway, to years spent conducting research with an amazing team of educators at the University of Arizona. Her interests in psychology, culture, and mythology have influenced her writing of *The Solas Beir Trilogy*.

www.MelissaEskueOusley.com

www.facebook.com/MelissaEskueOusley

Twitter: @MEskueOusley

PROOF

CPSIA information can be obtained at www.ICGtesting.com
Printed in the USA
LVOW101031170513

334289LV00011B/26/P

9 781938 281327